Rio Grande Rhapsody

By
Beverly Ann Allen

AcuteByDesign
the little book company that could
A Michael Marion Sharpe Company

Rio Grande Rhapsody by Beverly Ann Allen © 2020
AcuteByDesign Publishing
Michele Thomas, Executive Publisher
Michael Sharpe, Publishing Adviser
ISBN: 978-1-943515-33-2

AcuteByDesign
the little book company that could
A Michael Marion Sharpe Company

For Barbie Lou
and
Alexandria Rhea

Acknowledgments

Frida Kahlo said, "At the end of the day we can endure much more than we think we can." Rio Grande Rhapsody is in part dedicated to the strong, smart women who have filled my life, and have endured the dumpster fires that seem to combust in life just when you think you barely have it all together. Who knew that a little forgiveness and a whole lot of stubborn inclination could not only keep you from getting burned but light the path forward? I raise my toasted s'mores to you broads.

I would like to express my gratitude to Michele Thomas and Michael Sharpe at AcuteByDesign for taking a chance on my book. Thank you for embracing and celebrating diversity, and for the opportunity to showcase the culture of my beloved New Mexico.

To my momma: You have forever been my rock and my solid support. I appreciate your making time for my late-night phone calls over the last several years, asking the same question: "How does this sound?" Hopefully this book makes up for some of the times you were at your wits end with your impossibly willful child.

To my Beta readers: Barbara Allen, Lexy Custer, Katie Noble, Robyn Newsom, Aaron Newsom, Liz Grabber, Nathan McKenzie, Dawn McKenzie, Regina Santo, Laura Kohr, Starr Perkins, and RJ Mirabal: thank you for honest assessments of my manuscript.

Thank you, Jesus, for the encouragers in my life: Gwyn Del Toro, Pam Lesperance, Denise and Mica Comstock, Joy Lucero, Kerry Walker, our Chick Club, and more. Writing is such a solitary and, at times, lonely endeavor; your support kept me keeping on.

Muchas gracias to my friend (and singing partner!) Laura Ibarbo, for assistance with the Spanish translations in Rio Grande Rhapsody.

To our Sonny Boy Blue, my "Wolf," who passed while I was writing my book. You, precious soul, were my constant companion and presence, lying under the kitchen table when I was typing away. We will forever miss your pure, loyal heart.

Cole and Lexy, you are my hearts walking around outside of my body. Mom prays that you will continue to do whatever it takes in this life, because you've got what it takes. Never, ever forget that grace is all we have, and all we need.

And last but not least, to my daddy. You told me when I was a kid you hoped, one day, my stubbornness was used for good. There is no question from whom I inherited that personality trait: you fought cancer and leukemia, suffered a broken back and other health issues. My prayer was that God kept you around long enough to make an impact on my two little children, who needed the example of integrity and strength in their lives. I thank God, Mom, Dr. Barbara McAneny, Dr. Farzaneh Banki, and your unyielding determination to triumph over that which should've ended you, that you're here to see my first published novel. Thanks for sticking around, you adorable bastard.

Pilar stood at the bank of the great river, her pulse ragged, as the heels of her boots sank into the sand. She was no longer aware of the gnarled, naked branches of the silent cottonwoods lining the bosque, as the fleeting claret brushstrokes in the sky slipped behind the western horizon. She was oblivious to the fishy odor she had always detested.

Blood had managed somehow to get in her hair and smeared across her forehead. She contemplated the black, swirling water at her feet, dropped the hatchet she had been carrying, and began to walk.

The icy cold took her breath away as the gauzy skirt of her ball gown ballooned and pooled on top of the water. Soon her body was engulfed beneath the surface. The strong current wrapped its frigid arms around her body and beckoned her deeper, an old, familiar friend baptizing her in its ancient, dark waters.

Now she was numb and neck deep, the only sound a deafening throb beating in her ears. She kept walking, moving with aching purpose, exhaling with each step. On tiptoe now, her feet failing to scrape the river bed, unable to propel herself farther, she lay back into its embrace, submerged in her watery grave.

Ave Maria echoed in her mind one last time, and she closed her eyes.

9

ONE

Albuquerque Old Town
Autumn, present day

"So, show of hands here. Who has been on a ghost tour before?" asked our jubilant tour guide. She sported the shorts version of mom jeans, with a fanny pack hiked up high on her torso, and carried an open laptop.

In New Mexico even the locals look like tourists, I mused.

We *Burqueños*—citizens of Albuquerque—are about as laid-back and informal as you get. A/k/a the Duke City, it was so named after the Spanish Duke of *Alburquerque* and originally spelled with two *r*'s until the 1880s. It's believed that Anglo railroad employees and frontiersmen, who were unable to pronounce the name of the dusty, high desert town dropped the first *r*, and it stuck.

Here in the Land of Enchantment—home of Georgia O'Keeffe, Holly Holm, and *Breaking Bad*—one need only douse whatever it is they're eating in green chile, relax, and behold the splendor of our breathtaking sunset skies. Whatever you're doing, it can wait: this is the land of *mañana*.

It was about dusk. We were standing in a group of about a dozen on the south side of the San Felipe de Neri church in Albuquerque's Old Town Plaza. The church had been erected on its current site in 1793. It had been rebuilt here, I was later to discover on the tour—among other mysterious happenings from Old Town's colorful history.

It wasn't the first time the once-mighty Rio Grande had flooded the area, dissolving the original church's *adobe* walls.

Reaching toward the heavens above our heads loomed twin white-washed Gothic spires. They were adorned with shutters and intricately carved gingerbread detailing. Hovering over the heavy wooden turquoise doors above the rectory perched a widow's-walk, whose vantage point offered a unique perspective of her hamlet below: teardrop-shaped hedges lining red brick pathways, dotted with rose bushes. They led to the inner courtyard, and out onto the street surrounding the plaza. Its gazebo was shrouded in blue spruce and ancient cottonwood trees.

Standing here at street level, one could be certain that upon its resurrection, the church had arisen solidly from the valley's antiquated mud, now contained by five-foot thick walls of earthen brick.

The savory aroma of green chiles roasting outside the La Hacienda restaurant drifted through the warm evening air, a sure sign that autumn was on its way. To a local like me raised on the *bosque* next to the Rio Grande river, the scent was simply resplendent. In a few weeks, the plaza would be overrun with tourists in town for the Albuquerque International Balloon Fiesta.

Now was as good a time as any, Tricia had assured me, to take a ghost tour.

"It's a Groupon, for heaven's sake, Molly. It can't get any easier than that. You *are* doing this with me!"

I couldn't argue with her. It was kind of shameful; here we were, Old Town merchants, sharing a common breezeway separating her art gallery from my music store just off the Plaza. We had recommended the tour to countless shop visitors in town for the weekend but had never managed to take it ourselves.

The fuchsia sunset washed an otherworldly veil over the façades of shops and cafes surrounding the plaza. Magnificent, centuries-old cottonwoods stood casting long shadows over the west-facing stucco buildings where we waited. Tucked underneath the portals were Navajo jewelry-makers and other artisans, packing up their silver and turquoise wares for the evening.

Our friendly Old Town Ghost Tour guide repeated herself. "A show of hands?"

Three or four hands went up in response to her question.

"Ah, good! Whereabouts?" she inquired, pointing to an older couple across from us.

"Savannah, Georgia," said the man.

"Ooo, great! Some incredible ghost stories come from the deep South..." She nodded in approval with wide eyes, then turned to a family standing beside them. "How 'bout you guys?"

A woman with her husband and gangly teenaged sons responded: "Bath, England."

"Ah, *yes!*" said the guide enthusiastically. "I've taken that one. Fascinating, isn't it?"

The family agreed.

"Ok," she said, sizing up the rest of us, awaiting the promise of a mysterious evening to come. "How many of you are locals?"

Half a dozen of us raised our hands.

"Very good. I think there just may be some surprises in store for some of you tonight." Tricia looked at me

13

with raised eyebrows. I wiggled mine back at her, and we exchanged mischievous grins as the group headed down San Felipe Street.

"I'm Sandra," she said, looking back at us as we were walking, "and if at any time you have any questions, be sure and just holler. That's my husband, Rob, back there." Everyone turned to see a balding man wearing a matching *Old Town Ghost Tour* t-shirt like his wife and dark glasses like my father wore back in the '70s. Rob gave a wave with a neutral expression on his face.

"Apparently Rob's not nearly as enthused as Sandy is about the ghosts around here," whispered Tricia.

Earlier that day we had discussed the existence of the Dearly Departed. "We're not that far from Roswell, after all," Garrett, Tricia's husband and co-owner of the art gallery, had piped up. "You know, if you believe in one, you probably believe in the other—am I right?"

We shrugged.

"However, right now, I believe in lunchtime." He gave Tricia a peck on the cheek and headed off to Del Patio for his usual chile con carne burrito and Diet Coke.

"I'm excited about tonight," she said. "Don't you even have the slightest curiosity whether or not ghosts are for real?"

At that moment a customer had entered the breeze-way separating our shops, headed for the art gallery. Tricia walked away with a wave.

"See ya at 7:30!" Her petite frame barely moved as she hustled toward the gallery.

It always gave me a chuckle; she was a sassy little thing in her blue jeans, leather boots, and white Henley, with a silver concho belt cinching her middle so tight, it was a wonder she could breathe. But in spite of her petite size, you didn't mess with that little spitfire of a woman. I admired her can-do spirit and direct, calls-it-as-she-sees-it attitude.

The truth was, I wasn't sure *what* to think about ghosts.

I, personally, had never seen one. I did very much, however, believe that there was an unseen world that existed very close to our own, a world consisting of angels–both for good and evil. I attended a community church, unlike my mostly Catholic neighbors. As a woman of faith, I believe in life after death, heaven and hell, and that our souls continue existing in some form after our bodies in this life have broken down and failed us. Beyond that, I wasn't convinced that ghosts, or spirits–tormented souls that roamed the earth to fulfill some sort of unfinished business–were real.

Outside of the church on the corner of North Plaza and San Felipe, Sandra the Tour Guide continued: "Rob will be bringing up the tail of the group, you know, just in case we run into any...*supernatural visitors* on the tour." She intently eyeballed each of the tourgoers, then chortled and gestured us toward the northeast side of the church as she began walking in that direction. She hollered behind her. "Everyone, make sure your cellphones are off or set to vibrate! Be sure and stay together."

We gathered just outside of the rear courtyard of the San Felipe church.

"Now, before we meet any of our specter friends, let's see how many of our local Burqueños are aware of the significance of this tree," Sandra continued, pointing to a weathered but stately cottonwood tree nearby. The group scanned what appeared to be a typical, southwestern cottonwood, the likes of which propagate in thick groves along the seams of the Rio Grande. They leave clouds of cotton sloughed from their branches on the ground in drifts, like snow. It's illegal to dig one up there for transplanting, in spite of their prolific existence. To many, the regal cottonwoods of the Rio Grande are synonymous with the desert Southwest. It's one of the few indigenous tree species that thrive there, alongside the breezy desert willow and yellow chamisa.

To others, they mean complete misery during allergy season.

"In my experience, there is only about one percent of locals who know the story of this tree." Again she asked for a show of hands.

I raised mine.

"See!" she smiled as the group turned to face me, impressed at my apparent knowledge of the Secret of the Tree. "There is our one percent."

Tricia looked at me, surprised.

"You knew?" she whispered. I feigned modesty and shrugged.

Sandra guided the crowd's gaze to a niche in the tree about 6 feet up the trunk, hidden by folds of overgrown bark. "Look closely, and you'll see a carving of the Lady of Guadalupe."

The group quietly gasped at the discovery of a colorfully painted carving of a curved figure recessed into the trunk.

"Wow," said Tricia. "I never knew that was there."

Another lady, one of the locals, exclaimed, "Oh my, the Lady of Guadalupe! After all these years of living here in the valley, and I've never seen this. What a vivid blue... What's the story behind it?"

"Well," began Sandra. "After the Korean War, there were only twenty-six young men who returned home to New Mexico, one from this very parish. His name was Toby Avila. The story goes that Toby prayed to God to keep him from being killed in Korea like so many of his beloved comrades. If God saved his life, Toby promised he would return to the church here in Old Town and do whatever it was that God wanted him to do with his life and serve here at the San Felipe parish.

"Just one week after carving the Lady of Guadalupe statue in the tree, Toby Avila died—some say with specks of blue paint still on his hands."

Surprised murmurs could be heard from the crowd. "His son keeps up with the paint touch-ups from time to time to this day. All right, everyone, this way."

We crossed the street and headed south, stopping before a group of quaint shops, most of which were built in traditional pueblo-style architecture: log *vigas* jutting out just below flat rooftops, painted in desert sand tones, some with cracks in the stucco exposing the adobe brick underneath.

"'Su Casa de Chocolate,'" said Sandra, gesturing to a small store that stood out among the rest. It had a pitched roof whereas the others surrounding it were flat (a trademark of buildings in the desert where rain was sparse), a wrap-around Victorian-style porch, painted in purples, teals, and lemon yellow, with spindles and gingerbread accents.

"One of Rob's favorite haunts, if you will," winked Sandra, the group turning toward her husband. Rob was absentmindedly staring off into space, apparently accustomed to his wife's droning. The teenage boys snickered between themselves.

Undeterred, she giggled and continued: "Notice how different this precious little shop is compared to its neighbors."

She turned the laptop she'd been carrying around with her and showed us a black and white photograph. "This is what the candy store looked like 130 years ago." She walked past the semi-circle of tour goers, each inspecting the grainy, black-and-white photograph. "Notice anything?"

Tricia took a hesitant guess. "Uh...not really—it actually looks pretty much the same as it does now."

"Exactly!" enthused Sandra. "What most people don't know is that beginning in the 1850s, most of the new homes built by settlers in the river valley were exactly like this one, including all the shops in the plaza here. It wasn't until almost a hundred years later, in the 1940s, when Albuquerque Mayor Tingley and politicians from Santa Fe decided to update the façades of the shops—many of which were once private homes—for the purpose of luring tourists to the city. They wanted folks from back East who came out to Albuquerque to experience a bit of the Wild West— which, frankly, it still was. Remember that New Mexico wasn't granted statehood until 1912. So, anyway, that's when they had them changed to what you see now on most of the storefronts: Pueblo-style architecture."

My heart sank. All my life I'd visited this unique, enchanting village around the plaza in downtown Albuquerque. When I was growing up, we'd brought all of our visitors from out of town here. It was always a special occasion for our guests to see some of the "traditional" Hispanic and Native culture centered around the plaza church. *So much for authenticity.*

"Wow, that's disappointing," I said to Tricia. "I guess you learn something new every day..."

"Yeah, bummer," she sighed. "All in the name of progress, I suppose."

Nearby, Sandra smiled and shrugged. "Just a little Old Town history for you." Turning to the group she added, "Over here, we of course have the La Hacienda Mexican restaurant. Well," she paused, cueing up another photo on the laptop. "This is what it looked like back in the 1890s during New Mexico's territorial period, when it belonged to the Vega family."

From the grainy glow of the screen I was surprised to see a two-story, Victorian-style home, complete with a wrap-around porch, two chimneys, and pitched roof. It sat in the heart of a lush pasture, cottonwood trees towering high above, with manicured shrubbery flanking the porch, and horses grazing around the house.

"Onofre Vega, the patron of the *familia,* was a wealthy landowner who had four children," explained Sandra. "One of his children carried on his legacy as a shrewd and successful businessman, owning 2,800 acres of farmland with sheep and horses, and growing some of the region's finest green chile. Do you see any hint of that here when you look at the restaurant?"

My eyes scoured the familiar place, having dined here countless times over the years. There was a section of the restaurant that had two stories, but it had been closed off to restaurant patrons as far back as I could remember. Beneath the upper level was the restaurant and its adobe

19

hacienda-themed rooms, with its original red brick floors. There, I guessed, was where the wrap-around porch we had seen in the photograph had been.

The group was coaxed along by the complacent Rob, as his wife explained further: "We are going to stand across the street so we can get a good view of the restaurant."

Toward Tricia and me, Sandra whispered loudly, "This is the part the restaurant owners don't like us broadcasting..."

We each found space near the edge of the plaza, with the gazebo at its center—popular for weddings and other local celebrations—to the west of us. "Ladies and gentlemen, if you look right up there," she pointed to an upper window, "that is the window where six-year-old Nicolas Vega fell to his death in 1891."

A stunned hush fell over the crowd.

"Some say....that the ghost of little Nicolas comes out of that very room when the restaurant closes its doors at night."

An involuntary shiver ran down my spine.

I could also feel Tricia's gaze on me. When I turned, her eyes were enormous and her lips formed a circle. She was attempting to stifle a goofy grin.

A small laugh burst out before I could control myself. Sandra, frowning, gave me a distinct look of disapproval. I cleared my throat, shooting a glare at Tricia. *"Thanks a lot,* Tiney-Behiney," I whispered as Sandra turned to field questions from the intrigued crowd.

"If the apparitions don't get you," Trisha wailed in barely audible mock horror, *"then The Ghost Nazi will! Ooooooo...."*

"Shhh!" I giggled. "Sandy's gonna get her panties in a knot."

"Is there any significance to the blue doors and window frames in most of the other shops?" inquired one of the tourists.

"Ah, yes. *Turquoise,*" she corrected, "was long believed to ward off evil spirits in the traditional Native and Spanish cultures in the desert Southwest. You'll see it painted around doorways and windows throughout the state."

"It's also the color of our clear New Mexico skies," offered another proud local.

"Yes, that's right," nodded Sandra in approval. "And speaking of the sky, we're going to have to keep moving. It's getting dark! Let's head around the plaza, then on to the old saloon."

"Finally," mumbled one of the teenage boys.

"Don't worry, son," assured his mother. "We're bound to see the ghosts any time now."

TWO

Spring 1891

The young padre's burro brayed in protest as he pulled her from a gangly grove of asparagus among the feathery salt cedar lining the irrigation canal. Her neck twisted behind her body before reluctantly succumbing to the tugging of the wicked bridle in her mouth. "Time to go, Faya. It's going to be a long day's journey."

Father Julien Faustino had been awake long before the first light of dawn glowed in the eastern sky, silhouetting Tome Hill and its trio of crosses at the summit. The prior morning, he had made his ascension hundreds of feet above the Rio Grande floodplain for the Good Friday pilgrimage, alongside countless villagers reenacting the passion of the Christ. Making the homage with them were the *Hermanos Penitentes* serving the Tome parish, Our Lady of the Conception.

As he headed north in the direction of his home parish some 25 miles up the Rio Grande, he reflected on the graciousness with which he was received by the parishioners. They included the *genizaros,* whose indigenous people were still re-establishing ties with the Catholic church after a disastrous history stemming from the Pueblo Revolt centuries before. It appeared

that fences were being mended and old grudges forgiven by the current generation of farmers and ranchers working the land their forefathers fought to keep.
Father Faustino knew his mentor, the Most Reverend
Archbishop Jean Baptiste Lamy, would approve of how
his legacy of love and trust was continuing in his absence.

Still, he pondered as the beast plodded her way
through the bosque in the early morning light; in spite
of the warm reception and jovial celebration of the
Lenten season with this welcoming congregation, his
heart was on his own little church in Albuquerque, the
San Felipe de Neri. As the sun now began its blinding
work of illuminating the new day, the padre ducked under stray branches of cottonwoods swiping at his head.
He steered Faya away from the bosque and toward the
sandy hills bordering the flood plain on the East before
giving way to the Manzano mountains. When the day
began to warm, he would descend once again into the
shade of the ancient trees. But for now, the solitude that
miles of an uninterrupted panoramic view afforded him
was cathartic.

Padre Julien couldn't quite put his finger on
something he felt was brewing in his bustling little village. Perhaps it was his sense of obligation of his position in the still-unbridled frontier town, a debt he felt
he owed his friend and teacher, Archbishop Lamy. His
spirit felt a sense of unrest in spite of the Holy Week
24

celebrations he had been a part of over the past several days on the outer fringes of his diocese along the river valley. He wondered about the new family—members of the landed gentry—that had just moved to their pastoral town all the way across the Atlantic Ocean from England. Starting a new life in this strange new world seemed idyllic to the father, but his wife was wretchedly ill at ease.

Now, as the season of Lent was coming to a close, the good father's concern was appeased by the hope offered at the conclusion of the spring equinox, when the world was in a season of renewal and rebirth. Whatever it was nagging in his conscience, he felt sure it was nothing that the blood of the Holy Christ Jesus could not cleanse and make new.

He had guided Faya down to the bosque again by midday as they made the final approach of their journey. They had stopped briefly for a bowl of frijoles and horno bread at the Isleta pueblo parish. He could see the base and rise of the Sandia mountains in the East and estimated his arrival back at the San Felipe de Neri sometime late that afternoon. By then, Easter festivities would be underway. He'd be home in time for a good night's rest before the biggest celebration on the liturgical calendar took place the next day.

When Father Faustino finally made his way into town that evening, the sun was low in the western sky, giving credence to the name of the red mountain range to the east. The *Sandías,* the watermelon mountains, appeared to have a fiery glow in the approaching dusk, like a slice of the juicy fruit.

On the edge of town, he was greeted by the haphazard shacks that had sprung up seemingly overnight to accommodate the burgeoning industry accompanying the arrival of the railroad. Opportunists had seized the day, providing services such as rented rooms and brothels in the squalor of ramshackle lean-tos, whose windows, often missing panes of glass, were aglow in the cool of the desert night.

Now reaching the town plaza where the San Felipe church stood as beacon in the lush river valley, the padre was greeted by waves and shouts from villagers as the old burro never veered from her path or pace. As they passed the saloon, he could hear the tinny sounds of a player piano echoing through the square. Children, taking advantage of the warm spring evening, chased one another through the gazebo at the plaza's center to his left, and he waved back and smiled warmly at them.

Glancing to his right, he spotted Mariana Vega sweeping her front porch. She paused momentarily to wipe her brow and, catching sight of him, replaced the stray strands of hair that had fallen into her face behind her ear. She raised her hand in greeting, smiling as she watched him ride past, the image of her providing respite for his weary soul.

THREE

Albuquerque Old Town
Present day

It just happened that tonight was the appearance of a rare and serendipitous "super moon," an astronomical phenomenon lending itself to the mysterious atmosphere after the sun finally disappeared below the horizon. Ethereal clouds wafted across the expanse of its wide, porcelain face. It was still warm out, but I knew that soon the sultry summer evenings would be coming to an end, filling me with a sense of melancholy as it did this time every year in the fall.

The tour was winding down, as well. In spite of myself, I'd been fascinated with the historical information of Old Town I hadn't known before the ghost tour. Like the fact that the adobe walls of the Catholic church had eroded after flooding by the Rio Grande too many times so that it had to be rebuilt in a location farther east of the river. It had formerly stood on what was now the west side of the plaza. And that, beneath our feet where we'd been standing (and to the apparent horror of the modern-day shop owners on the other side of the wall against which we were leaning), there lay, in fact, the remains of early village settlers.

Sandra explained: "Everyone knows you're not supposed to bury the dearly departed on the south side of the church, right? Bad karma, and all that. So when developers who were unfamiliar with the history of the original church began building the shops in this portion of Old Town, they had no idea they were eternally sealing up the very graves of some of Albuquerque's earliest citizens." She added with a chuckle, "But by then, it was agreed that it wouldn't be very good for business to exhume the bodies to be properly reburied. Right? Things don't slow down here at Old Town. So when would you be able to do that, and get it all done, like in one night, so that the next day people can do their shopping?" Sandra eyeballed the crowd with her head cocked to one side. "Consequently, folks, here they lie."

Everyone stared at the earth beneath their shoes. Rob then proceeded to play us a sample of what was claimed to be recordings of one of the poltergeists six feet under. "These are the actual audio recordings taken right here at this spot by our EVP team."

Those of us not privy to ghost-hunter slang were informed that EVP stood for "electronic voice phenomena."

"Probably a frontiersman, we've deduced from the cursing. Listen again."

We all stepped closer for a better chance of deciphering the garbled content. I strained to listen but managed to make out only the muffled inflections of a deep male voice in slow-mo, apparently resonating from within its earthen tomb. A few eager heads around me nodded, in agreement that they, too, could understand the mysterious message. When it was over, Sandra apologized.

"Excuse his French!" she laughed.

Trish and I exchanged looks that said we weren't entirely convinced. I was relieved she hadn't vocalized her sentiments with one of her sarcastic gems.

Soon we were all off to the tiny chapel on the north-eastern side of Old Town. There we were regaled by tales of an elderly female ghost who inhabited it on occasion, dressed in a long, black gown with a veil covering her face, haunting unsuspecting visitors when she came to wail and grieve the loss of her child, primarily on religious holidays.

There was a small, dark *nicho* at the rear entrance of the chapel through which one of the tourgoers was encouraged to stick her arm. And so, naturally, like the air-headed damsel-in-distress of a low-budget horror flick (*No! Don't do it! Run!!*), she did. We all fully expected for someone to grab it on the other side, and in spite of being armed with this mental readiness everyone jumped when Rob, who'd mysteriously disappeared from the room only moments prior, half-heartedly yelled in a delayed response to grabbing the woman's arm. Why we were all thrilled by this was anyone's guess. But I suspect there was a camaraderie forming among members of the group in the midst of supernatural surroundings, each with high expectations of being collectively scared to death.

Sandra rested her knuckles on her waist and shook her head. "Oh, that *Rob*. What a goof!"

By now, everyone was slightly on edge, examining the dark side patios and alleyways we meandered past. Each of us was on the lookout for vaporous apparitions and wraithlike visions who might reach out and snatch us away into utter blackness, and unspeakable terrors. Inside the windows of cafes and restaurants—the only places still open this time of night—we glimpsed waiters rushing to and fro in ochre-colored interiors, and harried busboys clearing dishes of half-eaten food from the tables.

We stopped in front of what was now a tourist's trinket shop, inside of which visitors could purchase a set of maracas emblazoned with *Nuevo Mexico!* in hot pink and lime green, or a miniature Jackalope. The stuffed rabbits, many with real fur and glass eyes with tiny antlers glued between their ears, were a gold mine for merchants intent on promoting the urban legend.

"So," the father of the twin boys leaned into me with a smirk, averting his gaze so that at first I wasn't sure if he was indeed speaking to me.

"Seriously...are they *real?*" He shifted his weight, then looked me squarely in the face, brow furrowed.

"Oh, uh, you mean the jackalope?"

He nodded. His sons leaned in as well, their shiny faces intent on a response.

"Yes, they are," replied Trish, apparently now in the conversation as well.

The boys raised their eyebrows suspiciously.

"*No,*" I chided her with a gentle slap to the arm. The man gave her a breathless laugh that sounded like a balloon quickly losing air. His sons shook their heads at their father's obvious cluelessness.

"They're just part of the lore of the wild West," I explained, "but a lot of people ask that question."

He cleared his throat and nodded.

Back in 1890, we were told, the building before us served as the saloon on the town square.

Here we learned the story of Scarlet, the ginger-haired saloon girl, who was a favorite of the local gents willing to pay extra in exchange for her "services rendered"—Sandra had used air quotes—"in the cathouse upstairs. Because she was a rarity among the predominantly Hispanic *ladies of the evening* that shared the living quarters of the dwelling, a few of them, led by one particularly jealous woman of ill repute, plotted Scarlet's demise.

"You can imagine how popular she was with the gentlemen because of her unique auburn locks, which she wore down. Apparently she was a real stunner. Well, after her return to the cathouse, having been briefly chased off by the ill treatment of her 'coworkers'"—snickers erupted between the teenage brothers—"they managed to get her alone, dragged her up the staircase by her long, red hair, where she was murdered near the top landing. She had been stabbed twice, *here*-" Sandra indicated the space above the waistline of her high-slung denim shorts, "and directly through the heart. She bled out right there on the staircase.

"It's been said that the ghost of Scarlet roams the upstairs balcony to this very day in one of two forms," Sandra had informed the rapt crowd. "She either makes her appearance in her emerald green fringed flapper dress, *or*...completely in the *nude*."

Murmurs and grins were exchanged in the crowd. One of the teenage boys whispered "*Whoa*," to which his brother lifted a palm. He high-fived subtly in approval.

After a pause, the group was instructed to walk through the alleyway behind the tourist shop. The dim, almost artificial tin-blue light of the full moon shone silver tones across the potholes marring the narrow backstreet. One could make out the shapes of the dark graffiti covering the dumpsters, incoherent gang symbols left to mark the territory of the rival Mexican gangs in town.

"That's it, keep moving, right over here," instructed Sandra, beckoning the group with a wave. "Come on, you men back there...you'll have to come back later if you want to catch a glimpse of Scarlet!" The group erupted in laughter as a stout, balding gentleman who stood staring up into the second story balcony turned to rejoin the group, chagrined.

"That's it. Now," said Sandra, pausing for effect once everyone was gathered around, "you may have heard the legend of the Albuquerque Axe Lady."

Trish and I looked at each other. I shook my head. She shrugged.

"Well the story goes like this..." she began quietly.

It would be the final tale of the tour. We had been led down a red brick path that dead-ended at a darkened side street on the southeast corner of Old Town. We were invited to take our seats on nearby bancos and bar stools pushed up to a few tall patio tables beneath a portico. I'd been here plenty of times during the day—there used to be a card shop in one of the spaces close by, where I purchased all of the Christmas cards for the music store, mailed to my customers and the business contacts on my list. It had closed in the spring; I made a mental note while settling into my seat to find another company and place my order since the holiday season would soon be upon us.

There was an eerie quiet here now, the Ghost Tour presumably having made believers out of some of the skeptics among us, now all stoically devouring Sandra's every last word.

"Back before the turn of the 20th century here in Old Town, there was a grisly murder committed—some say by the daughter of a prominent community member. The truth is, we'll never know for sure who committed the heinous act because it was to become one of the greatest unsolved mysteries of the Rio Grande Valley.

"Legend has it that the perpetrator was the scorned

lover of a young man who had committed the unpardon-
able sin of falling in love with another girl. In an act of
blinding white rage, she allegedly took an axe to the two
after catching them during an evening tryst. It was to be an
ill-fated *rendezvous*, for they say the bodies were so completely dismembered, so ruthlessly and relentlessly *hacked
to bits*, that the victims were unrecognizable."

Sandra paused for dramatic effect.

It was silent.

I felt a rush of cool air at my back and turned in
haste to look behind me. My eyes searched the darkened
forms in the moonlight surrounding us: large flowerpots,
benches, public trash cans, a lone lamp post.

Nothing.

Everything was motionless except for a flag heralding the entrance of a tiny toy store around the corner, wag-
ging intermittently in the practically nonexistent breeze. I
shuddered and turned around.

Don't be ridiculous, Molly, I told myself, sighing.

The crowd was engrossed as Sandra continued:
"Some suspect that the murders were committed by one
of the children of the founding families who made their
casitas around the plaza. But alas," she sighed, "there are
no records of the culprit ever being apprehended."

I thought it odd, her word choice to describe such
a cold-blooded murderer: *culprit* seemed better suited to
cookie bandits, or handkerchief-wearing thieves from the
wild West, apprehended in the town bank with bags emblazoned with dollar signs in their clenched fists. I couldn't
formulate an appropriate adjective to describe such a
woman who was capable of chopping—*to pieces*—another human being, much less, *two*. To imagine the sheer

strength and force required, the adrenaline behind such rage...it was animalistic.

"To this day, couples who have strolled these streets at night have been chased by the figure of a woman wielding a hatchet high above her head, screeching like a banshee before bursting into a vapor and disappearing. And it's always couples, never lone individuals, and she's even said to be choosy concerning whom she'll chase, ignoring some but screaming at others. So, if you ever want to conjure the spirit of the Axe Lady, you could take your chances with your significant other here on a dark, lonely evening..."

Her dramatic words hung thickly in the stagnant night air as the older couple from the Savannah ghost tour shifted, moving closer together as the man put his arm around his wife's shoulders. *I guess that's one good thing about being single,* I mused, *I don't have to worry about being chased by a lady ghost wielding an axe....*

I was just about to lean into Tricia to warn her to never go out strolling after hours with Garrett, when a cellphone ringtone shattered the quiet.

It was the theme from "Ghostbusters."

All of us gave a collective jump, a few audibly gasped as a grade-B movie scream escaped the lips of the mother of the teenagers.

There was relief and nervous laughter. Rob, formerly presumed mute by the group, sheepishly held up his phone—an admission of guilt—as it glowed in his hand, bringing it up to his ear.

"Hullo?" he croaked, and walked a few feet away from the group.

In a verbal exchange straight out of *Jurassic Park*

during the tyrannical encounter with the T-Rex inside the Land Rovers, after the lawyer makes a run for it, one of the teenage boys—clearly shaken by the story of the Axe Lady—remarked in disbelief to the other: "He's *leaving* us?"

As if Rob offered any protection from the angry spirits.

The other responded incredulously with a snort, "He *answered* it?"

Tricia, whose fright was palpable on her face, although I couldn't see her expression very well in the darkness, shakily exhaled.

"Well that totally freaked me out!" she exclaimed to the humor of those around us.

Sandra, pleased that the stories of the evening had had their intended effect upon her listeners, wrapped everything up with an upbeat tone.

"Well, *whoever* the scorned woman was, she sure gave a whole new meaning to the term *femme fatale*! Some say she's simply an urban legend. Regardless, she ended up taking the secret with her to her grave, because, like I said, no records were ever found. So, we will never know who did it...will we?"

FOUR

Father Faustino stood at the entrance of the San Felipe de Neri church with the still-cool morning sun slicing through the branches of the cottonwoods, bowing with his shoulders, warmly smiling and speaking the name of each person as was his gentle way—*"Gracias, la paz esté con usted."* and again, "Peace be with you." As they filtered past him—the sons and daughters, grandsons and granddaughters, nieces, nephews, wives, and husbands of families who had long ago settled in this small village as sheep farmers, produce growers, mercantile owners—he took their hands and held them, enveloping them inside his own, rather than a formal handshake, releasing each after imparting heartfelt sentiment.

During the liturgy, the padre had introduced the newly sanctified Pilar Vega, and after his benediction extended the invitation to all parishioners to the home of Mariana and Onofre for continuation of the celebratory fiesta of their fifteen-year-old daughter the following evening.

Emerging from the heavy, wooden entrance doors burnished with ironwork soldered some 250

37

miles to the south near El Paso del Norte, stepped the
petite Señora Vega. She smiled when she saw him,
squinting into the blinding shafts of light, her eyes
seeking respite in shade where she could see the pleasant features of his face.

"*Querida* Mariana," he whispered into her ear
as they gently embraced, their cheeks briefly pressing
together.

He was young, in his early forties—barely nineteen years old when first commissioned—for a priest
to rector a parish of the size of the stoic San Felipe de
Neri. After having served as prelate in various missions
in the New Mexico territory, Father Julien Faustino
had the eternal fortune of being ordained and appointed by the Most Reverend Jean-Baptiste Lamy during
the final years of his life as Archbishop of Santa Fe, in
the Cathedral Basilica of Saint Francis of Assisi. Of
the countless blessings bestowed upon Father Faustino
during his magnificent though finite relationship with
the archbishop, one of the most personally cherished
was the gift of speaking the French language. He then,
in turn, taught it to the orphans in the care of the nuns
at the Sisters of Charity in the tiny schoolhouse that
had been erected behind the parsonage after his arrival
in 1870. It had been the native language of his beloved
friend and mentor. To Father Faustino, speaking the
language foreign to most of his parishioners but deci-
pherable to little children was a way of celebrating the

archbishop's most revered legacy.

Along with this was the deeply shared conviction of both men by the invocation of St. Francis, the patron saint of the Basilica in Santa Fe: "Preach the Gospel at all times, and when necessary, use words." Indeed, this was not mere flowery sentiment to the young priest, which was the way of many who had come before him: It was the way Father Faustino diligently and sincerely desired to live his life.

Shadowing Mariana in the doorway now was the imposing form of her husband, replacing his hat to shield his eyes from the morning sun. Never acknowledging the outstretched palm offered him by the priest, Onofre Vega gave a cursory grunt to its intended recipient.

"Padre."

"Señor Vega," the father responded as Onofre swept past them. He gathered her small hands again. "I am so looking forward to tomorrow night."

Her eyes followed her hastily retreating husband. His blustery ways were enough to intimidate the most confident of bystanders, yet she was resigned to it, her always lovely expression not one of apology or chagrin, but rather a familiar resoluteness. She returned her gaze to him and gave his gentle grip a squeeze before leaving. "Yes. We can discuss further the ceremony when you arrive. At six, then?"

"At six," he repeated.

"Tres bien, merci." She nodded, smiling. "*Au revoir.*"

FIVE

Christmastime, present day

Tricia and I were headed out into the crisp night air.

"Keep the music going over the sound system," I instructed Cedar, my only employee, a music major in his senior year at the University of New Mexico.

The activity of autumn in Old Town had given way to the bustling, hectic holiday season. Outside of *Old Town Music*, a group of Victorian carolers donned top hats, bonnets, with fluffy muffs warming their hands, regaling shoppers with beloved traditional songs such as "I Heard the Bells on Christmas Day" and "The Coventry Carol."

Tonight was the first Friday in December, the night of the annual Holiday Stroll and Christmas Tree Lighting.

All of the merchants in Old Town stayed open past their normal hours, beckoning shoppers inside to examine their fineries and wares along with traditional New Mexican treats. We were serving spiced cider, and blue corn tortilla chips with guacamole. Every time the shop door opened, a swell of muddled Christmas songs drifted in, interspersed with beloved local news personality Steve Stucker, counting down the lighting of the plaza tree over the PA system. All around Old Town there were local music groups performing: high school show-choirs, barbershop quartets, brass choirs, all tucked into patios and stairways. They were heralding the "good news of great joy," celebrating the birth of a baby king. It was 8:30pm, and there were only remnants of the chips and less than half a Crockpot of cider. The initial rush of holiday shoppers had already breezed through, but a few were still straggling in. Cedar was keeping busy at the register but found time to peer out of the shop window at the resplendent Christmas tree on the west side of the Plaza, bedazzled in multi-colored LED lights.

"And when I return," I glowered at him pointing to the ceiling, "I had better not hear "Sad, Beautiful, Tragic," either."

"But it's vintage Taylor Swift," he pouted.

"Cedar. You are a grown man. Try to remember that, okay?"

He sighed. "Fine. Cedar shall do as m'lady wishes." He grabbed a CD off the counter and read the sleeve. "'Essential Guitar' it is!"

"Proud o' you," I teasingly winked. Cedar gave a mock expression of glee and a thumbs-up at my approval. In spite of the fact that it was wintertime, he was wearing his usual Birkenstocks without socks, and trench coat. He had worked for me since starting college, and his long blond hair and free, poetic spirit had attracted more than one of his young admirers to the shop tonight already.

While it wasn't snowing at the moment, there were still patches on the ground from the last snowfall, and it was icy on the street where the sand and salt hadn't covered it completely. I wore my black turtleneck sweater and a purple eternity scarf, with a lightweight jacket, and black suede boots with traction on the soles. We'd be traipsing around the square tonight and wearing layers was a good bet, particularly for a forty-something woman prone to sudden bouts of heat. I felt festive in my Lycra-blend jeans and the silver and turquoise earrings and necklace set that Trish had given me as an early Christmas gift to wear tonight.

"You ready?" I asked Trish. She was wrapping a third scarf around her neck and buttoning up her down jacket. She looked like an Eskimo. She smiled.

Usually she wore her bordering-on-silver hair in a messy up-do to showcase the silver Santa Fe-statement dangle earrings she was never seen without. Today, she wore it *au naturel*, loose and curly.

Despite our differences, Trish and I were similar souls: I with my stick-straight blonde-with-a-sprinkling-of-white shoulder-length hair, and my preferred classic "dressy" attire; Tricia's casual southwestern wear. Trish's fit derriere, or "Tiny-Behiney," as I referred to her sometimes, was a far cry from my poochy stomach and flabby underarms. Both divorced, we'd met when I was still teaching and her daughters were my music students. She and Garrett married when her daughter, Lacey, was just two years old. They still lived up in the Sandía mountains bordering the east side of the city, a half-hour drive from Old Town. Formerly computer programmers, they had tired of the daily grind and purchased the gallery to showcase the artwork of their daughter, who was now nineteen and a burgeoning artist.

I had sold the house in Albuquerque's northeast heights I'd purchased after my divorce a decade ago, when my children graduated from high school, in favor of a townhouse in the downtown area. It was a small, territorial-style community about a block from Old Town, and in warm weather, when the days stretched out longer into the evenings, I loved the leisurely strolls to work and home.

Neither Tricia nor I was ever going to be a self-made millionaire, but we did make a comfortable living doing what we loved. We found great enjoyment in the arts, comfort in our mutual philosophies and shared experiences, and both of us cherished our easy friendship.

As we stepped out into the night air, we were met with the aroma of enchiladas and sopapillas emanating from the La Hacienda and La Placita restaurants, which surrounded our shops. This scent was intermingled with the tangy whiff of fir branches that encircled the walkway columns.

And there was something more, something *magical*, that made this special historical place so alluring to its guests, something wonderful and enchanting. Lining each and every path, portal, and rooftop were hundreds of *luminarias*, small brown paper bags filled with candles anchored in sand. They dotted *bancos* and lit the entryways of shops, enticing holiday shoppers to come inside from the cold. I inhaled deeply and couldn't help but smile. The festive feeling was electric in the air all around us. Luminarias are a tradition uniquely original to New Mexico that no other place on earth can boast. What began as a way to symbolically welcome the Christ child by burning small bonfires in Catholic rituals on Christmas Eve centuries ago—borrowed from pagan practices—continued as a whimsical tradition that warmed the hearts of passersby.

When I was a little girl, our neighborhood beside the Rio Grande was covered in luminarias on Christmas Eve, every fencepost and driveway dotted by the glow of these primitive little lights. Every year I found myself hovering above one of the little bags, staring down inside, entranced by the flickering, dancing candlelight casting shadows on the frosty ground below.

"What are you doing, silly?" Tricia shouted back at me. I didn't realize I had stopped and was peering down inside of one. "You look mesmerized." She laughed.

I caught up with her and smiled. "I guess I was."

We stepped inside still-lively galleries and boutiques, *ooo*-ing and *ahh*-ing over dyed silk scarves, blown glass votives, and the artwork of R. C. Gorman, all the while sampling the festive pastries, confections, and salsas provided by the shopkeepers. Many of the merchants we knew well; some had hired seasonal workers and were mingling with potential buyers. Some of them had been in Old Town for years, while others gave it a go but were not so lucky, having to close up shop after just a few months. There were several of those that were affected by the recession in the first decade of the 21st century, never able to recover.

We passed one such place after having enjoyed a cup of red chile hot cocoa from the Basket Shop. This one wasn't much bigger than a glorified broom closet, and one could pass right by it never knowing it even existed. In its former life it was The Rainbow Shop, owned by our friends Diego and Bobby, life partners who joked that every time they stepped foot outside the door, they felt like they were "coming out of the closet!" A new sign out front now read Book It.

"Shall we?" queried Trish.

"After you," I replied.

My mind had been captivated by the brass choir in the plaza gazebo, and I hummed along with "Good King Wenceslas" as I opened the door for Tricia. Not realizing the acoustics from inside the 'broom closet' would drown out most of the sound outside, I continued to belt out, *"Hmmm hmmm hmmm hmmm...looked out, on the feast of Stephen....hm..mmm...hmm......crisp and clear and even!"*

The "closet" door closed with a jingle. Inside, I suddenly became aware that some shoppers were staring at me.

Embarrassed, I grinned sheepishly in acknowledgment of their glances and grins.

"Please, don't stop on our behalf," laughed a gentleman with salt-and-pepper hair and a matching close-cropped goatee—the shop owner, I assumed. He was wearing a dark blue corduroy vest and chinos, with a festive, silk chile pepper tie. "That was enchanting!"

I felt a blush spread over my face in spite of his pleasant expression.

There was an impressive spread of traditional New Mexican foods laid out for the Holiday Stroll on a couple of card tables with red and green plastic tablecloths covering them. There was *posole* with warm flour tortillas, green chile stew, guacamole with bright red and green tortilla chips, and *biscochitos.*

He approached us, greeting Tricia first with a handshake. *"Feliz Navidad–* welcome."

There was something warm and genuine about this man. Tricia introduced herself as owner of the art gallery "...next to Old Town Music." She gestured toward me, grinning. "And this is Molly. You'll have to excuse her, she's way too musically inclined. It's a job hazard." She added something about my being the owner of the music store. Immediately I noticed that he smelled heavenly...and that his eyes crinkled almost closed when he smiled.

46

"Hi, Molly. Oscar Cardenas. We opened just before Thanksgiving."

He offered an outstretched hand, and I accepted it; there was something disarming about this man. And *that scent, musk, maybe?* With a hint of...*what is that—bergamot?* Wait, did I just visibly inhale? Yes, *definitely bergamot...*

Realizing it was my turn to speak, I shook my head to clear my thoughts.

"Oscar," I glibly responded, "like the Grouch?"

Oscar laughed heartily. "Hmm, I've never heard that before."

I realized I was still shaking his (smooth, gentle) hand, then quickly let it drop like a hot potato. Distracted by his warm caramel eyes, I eagerly searched the shop with my gaze, glossing over nearby counter tops of stacked books, my eyes landing on the small, silver-tinseled Christmas tree on a table in the shop window. It was covered in glowing, red chile-pepper lights.

He followed my gaze. "Terrible, isn't it?" he smiled. "I'm not much at decorating."

"No—oh, *no,* I like it. Very...retro. It's cool. Yeah..." I nodded and fondled a glass pickle ornament wearing a sombrero and brandishing maracas, examining it as if it were a matter of science, continuing to nod my head. *What the heck is your problem? Relax for heaven's sake.*

"Molly's great at decorating. She designed the space between our stores," remarked Trish, aware of my awkward response and coming to the rescue.

"Oh, is that right?" he asked, looking back at me.

Unsure whether I should nod in agreement with the fact that, *yes,* I had indeed designed the space, or risk

47

the appearance of conceit that I was 'great at decorating,' I smiled.

And tried to breathe normally.

Stalled in conversation, Oscar invited Tricia and me to have a bite to eat.

"Please, help yourselves," he said, gesturing to his aromatic feast of festive goodies. Then he excused himself to mingle with other shoppers a mere couple of feet away.

Tricia was staring at me as I turned to pour a Dixie cup of cider, feeling the look of disapproval on her face without having to see it.

"Sorry!" I whispered without looking at her. "Give me a break. It's kind of been a long time. I'm out of practice."

Tricia nodded fervently. "Apparently!" she hissed through a clenched jaw, watching Oscar walk away. "'Oscar the Grouch'? Wow, that's all kinds of flirting there, Moll, dial it down a notch...Did you *not* see him? That man is *beautiful*."

"Uh, yeah—clearly," I mumbled, embarrassed at my faux pas. "Like it matters anyway—did you hear him say, '*We* just opened'?"

Tricia shook her head and leafed through a coffee table book. "He could be talking in general...Like him, and the books."

I couldn't help but laugh.

"And, there's no *ri-ing*," she whispered in a sing-song voice, leaning in to me.

I tried to casually glance around the room, focusing half-heartedly on display shelves stocked with books, many encased in plastic—rare editions, I guessed. My eyes were drawn to Oscar Cardenas across the small, dimly lit shop, watching him interact with an attractive college-age woman. She was batting heavily mascaraed eyelashes at the distinguished older shop owner. He picked up a leather-bound edition and began animatedly discussing it. Tricia casually glanced around the room, then smiled knowingly. "That girl isn't even remotely checking out his *book*."

I furrowed my brows in disapproval. "*Really, Trish?*"

She gave me a coy shrug.

I had noticed the pretty girl too, but also noted that Oscar didn't seem to acknowledge her obvious adoration. Or was it that I *hoped* he hadn't noticed her?

The young woman ran her hands through her silky, sun-kissed hair, then threw her head back and gave a full-bodied laugh.

Tricia looked back at me. "Honey, I give you 'Exhibit A.'" She was posing like Vanna White presenting a correctly guessed phrase on *Wheel of Fortune.* "You have *got* to up your game."

"*Quit,*" I protested, pulling her arm down and feeling an unsettling twinge in my gut.

What is that? Jealousy, maybe? Jealous of *what, exactly?* I reminded myself I wasn't even interested in men and dating right now. Plenty on my plate with the music store, paying a mortgage and raising kids...*except that I didn't have any kids at home anymore*...I had used that excuse for so many years that it was hard adjusting to the fact that I was indeed an empty-nester; my son was in the Navy, stationed at a submarine base in Groton, Connecticut, and my daughter lived in the dorm on campus at the University of New Mexico.

The truth was, I really didn't have excuses anymore. So, what was it then that was holding me back? *Perhaps that's why I'd felt unsettled...*I was running out of excuses. Maybe it was time to consider getting back "out there," although I couldn't begin to imagine where "there" was supposed to be.

I glanced back across the room at this man, this seemingly kindhearted, very nice-looking gentleman.

Who was I kidding? I didn't have a chance, with my forty-five-year-old body, complete with assorted stretch marks, moles, and wrinkles.

"With my luck, he's probably gay," I retorted flippantly, picking up a yellow bound issue of *The Scarlet Letter* by Nathaniel Hawthorne, "Publish date: 1845" labeled on the clear plastic wrapper.

"Seriously? Did you see his window display? Please!" she responded with a *pssht*. "That man is 100 percent heterosexual."

We meandered through the small shop sipping our cider, eventually heading toward the door to leave.

Oscar interrupted the pretty girl with a touch to her sleeve. She looked down to his hand, then up to me, giving a terse smile.

"Thank you, ladies, for coming in tonight." He gave a slight bow of his head and grinned.

"Merry Christmas," Tricia responded. I smiled back at him.

He watched us walk out the door. I turned and looked back inside as the door closed behind me, the bell jingling. I felt an electric shock go through my system when I noticed Oscar Cardenas was still looking directly back at me. He nodded, smiling through those unassuming caramel eyes.

Pretending I hadn't noticed, I flipped my hair and adjusted the scarf around my neck as we stepped into the chilly night air.

Tricia grinned at me, her eyes wide and sparkling when I caught her gaze. She started to laugh out loud while I attempted to ignore her.

After walking a bit in silence amongst the celebratory crowd, I finally acknowledged her smugness. "What?"

"You just flipped your hair," she grinned, brows lifted.

"What! Stop. I didn't either..." I protested, looking purposefully toward the throngs of holiday shoppers milling about the plaza.

"Yes, you did! You *so* totally just flipped your hair!" she announced, pleased with herself.

I shook my head and grinned as we headed toward the church, enchantingly alight with a million golden luminarias, candles flickering deep within their small brown paper sanctuaries, as the brass choir joyously rang out the sixth stanza of "Good King Wenceslas."

Returning to an otherwise empty store, I chastised Cedar for jamming to "Red" at the top of his lungs.

"Re-eh-eh-ed, Re-eh-eh-ed," he screeched louder at my complaint. "We've had only a handful of folks stop in since you left. I've already closed up shop for the night, put the register bag in the safe, et cetera, et cetera," then accentuated, "*Boss.*"

Holding in my hand the bag of freebies that I had accumulated from the excursion, I good-humoredly gave the bag a swing in his direction. He immediately dashed out of arm's length, apologized profusely, then headed toward the door to go home.

"Yeah, whatever.... Goodnight then, *Taylor Swift*." Double checking that the front doors were locked, I cued up Kenny Loggins's "Celebrate Me Home" on the overhead sound system and turned the lights off inside the store, a nightly ritual including looking back out onto the darkened plaza. Tonight I gazed peacefully at the hypnotic prism of lights on the freshly lit Christmas tree in the distance, and reflected on the events of the evening. I sighed. We'd had a great turnout of holiday shoppers readying gifts for the assorted music lovers in their lives. This was always good news for a small local business at the start of the Christmas shopping season. I felt exhausted and yet oddly invigorated.

At the conclusion of Kenny's serenade, I stepped out back to my waiting Honda Civic. Safe inside, I breathed in the cleansing December air, inhaling the intoxicating scent of winter on the Bosque.

SIX

Rico Ruiz's back was aching. Stepping out of the barn door, he leaned sideways against a weathered corral post and expelled a deep sigh, his calloused fingers massaging the base of his spine after removing his stained leather work gloves. He inhaled the acrid, musky scent of the horses kicking up the dry dust with their hooves as they meandered lazily about their containment. It was an all-too-familiar scent, but along with it he could also smell the faint, intoxicating aroma of pork tamales being carried in the all but absent summer breeze as it wafted across the pasture. It was coming from the house beneath the cottonwoods on the other side of the orchards.

He wondered if she was sitting under the shade of its wrap-around veranda.

Rico straightened and put his hand to his brow to shield his eyes from the brilliance of the mid-June sun in the afternoon sky. It was clear and turquoise; not a single cloud had ventured across it for days on end. He squinted to see if he could catch a glimpse of her there, his eyes scanning the horizon under the canopy of cottonwood branches.

It was one of the finest houses he had ever known. All his life he wondered what it would be like to actually live in such a palace as the Vega home, a two-story structure nestled into the lush Rio Grande valley, with the river a neighbor, horses and cattle roaming about, grazing in the irrigated fields. The fine home boasted two chimneys, gables from which soft, warm light poured out of windows at night, Victorian gingerbread spindles, and scarlet roses climbing up the steps and columns at the entry. It was complete with a cavernous barn and carriage house. He had never been inside, only as far as the back entrance around the other side, and only when running errands for Mr. or Mrs. Shannon.

And there had been that time when one of Onofre Vega's horses escaped its confinement. Rico had chased the animal down with a bridle as it loped around the Shannons' alfalfa fields, wildly skittish in its newfound freedom, reluctant to be corralled again. But he patiently and carefully circled, hiding the reins behind his back, holding out a handful of clover so the horse could see. He slowly cornered the beast, stroking its silky, muscled shanks, belly, and neck before slipping the bit into its mouth, the bridle over its flattened ears. "*Que bonita*," Rico softly soothed. "*Bueno*. That's a girl...that's a *good* girl...." Once he had the animal's trust, he hopped on bareback with the fearlessness and agility only a seasoned seventeen-year-old farm hand could possess, and guided her back home, under the cottonwoods, toward the carriage house.

It was Onofre Vega himself who met Rico coming up the path on his horse. For a Hispanic man, he was uncharacteristically large. He stood just over six feet tall with an impressive girth, a frown permanently stitched on his firmly set jaw. His brow was eternally furrowed with deep lines carved into his dark, weathered skin. He cursed as the horse approached with no regard for its rider. Rico proceeded to describe the tactics by which he captured the rogue beauty but only managed, "Señor Vega—" when Onofre grabbed the reins with a jerk, causing the horse to lurch. Rico jumped off, barely landing on his feet and followed them to the corral. There the heavy metal gate was wrenched open and the bridle abruptly torn from the animal's mouth, the metal bit clanging against its teeth. Onofre Vega reared back and dealt the horse a violent blow with the ends of the leather bridle, using enormous force, cutting deeply into the horse's backside. He then slammed the enclosure gate, turning on his heel to march toward the house, as the horse whinnied gutturally and galloped away. Instinctively, Rico leapt in the opposite direction and, unable to keep his balance this time, fell to the ground on his rear. Momentarily he sat there, trying to regain his composure before attempting to be vertical once again.

And then he saw her.

Pilar Vega, her black hair lustrous in the sun as she shielded her eyes from the morning glare, her father blowing past her on the veranda, the porch door slamming in his wake. She stayed staring at him sitting there for a moment—an eternity, to Rico Ruiz—then turned and followed her father into the house.

Since then, he had only had the opportunity to be in such close proximity to her during Mass, or at special holiday fiestas and parish festivities. But today... today he would get another chance.

His yellowed shirt clung to his body drenched in sweat. Rico knew in just mere hours he would see Pilar Vega in all her splendor at her *quinceañera*. The thought made his pulse race! He looked down at his filthy hands, lined in grime, turning them over to inspect the countless minuscule cuts and scars. He balled them into fists and ducked beneath the corral railing, heading toward the river.

There could be no dirty hands tonight, no manure under his fingernails. Onofre Vega would not dismiss him again tonight.

SEVEN

Present day

The holidays were officially in full swing. I barely had a chance to breathe between packaging and mailing gifts from Old Town Music and making sure inventory lasted throughout the remainder of the month. Christmas was less than a week away.

I'd just come around the corner of the storeroom with a stack of holiday guitar CDs to replenish a dwindling supply at the register, when I saw Oscar Cardenas in profile standing in front of a display case of songbooks. He was wearing a coffee-colored leather jacket and jeans. When he glanced at me emerging from the storeroom, he picked up a songbook; then thinking better of it, put it back.

Looking relieved at my appearance onto the floor he turned to face me. A nervous jolt went through my stomach, recalling our first meeting. *Just another customer,* I reassured myself. I took a quick breath and smiled.

"Oscar," I said extending my hand. This time being on my own familiar turf, I wasn't as distracted by the soft skin and lovely eyes.

Now he was the one who seemed a bit flustered. He shook my hand politely and a lengthy pause ensued.

I raised my brows in expectation.

"Is there anything I can help you with?"

"Do you teach piano lessons? I was...well, not me, but *we* were looking for someone to teach my granddaughter. Well, it's my daughter who's interested in getting her lessons—which I'm interested in, too, of course...." He stopped abruptly. "That is, if you give lessons?"

"I don't anymore, personally, but we do have students who come down from the university to teach," I explained, gesturing at Cedar who was at the front of the store helping a woman sort through sheet music for guitar. "We have a couple of studios in the back with keyboards, an upright, and a baby grand."

"Oh, that's great. I'll just make an appointment then."

I nodded. "That works."

I couldn't help but notice the color of his leather jacket matched his eyes, which were now glassy as he smiled at me through an extended silence. A bit unnerved at my boldness, I didn't take my eyes off him. He stuffed his hands inside his pockets and nodded.

"Okay." He paused as if turning to leave, then changed his mind. "Hey, say, I was wondering if you'd like to get a cup of coffee with me later, you know, after you get off work?"

My stomach lurched. The slightly clumsy nature of his request was disarming: the sarcastic smart-aleck in me wanted to respond with, '*Hey, say, sure.*'

But I thought better of it. "Uh, yeah. Okay," I mustered. "Aren't you working today?"

"My daughter's got it covered. And if a second shopper comes in, my granddaughter's there, too." He laughed.

And there were those sparkling caramel eyes, crinkling almost closed. Behind him I caught a glimpse of Trish in the gallery across the way, "adjusting a painting." She stole a quick glance in our direction and just as quickly was back to the serious business of frame adjustment.

We agreed to meet in an hour at La Placitas.

"SPILL!" Tricia whispered loudly after making sure there were no customers close by.

"*Well...*" I dragged out a long pause. "He wants piano lessons for his granddaughter."

She was still ecstatically expectant, with the now-familiar knowing expression on her face. "...*and??*"

I couldn't help but grin. "*And*, Tiny-Behiney—yeah, I saw you over there spying on us!—he asked me out after work."

Tricia squealed with delight, clapping her hands like a trained circus seal.

I couldn't even believe the words came out of my mouth: *He asked me out.*

"My baby girl's got a date!" Tricia gushed. "Seriously, this is *big*, Moll. Have you even dated once in the past nine years?"

I took a deep breath and exhaled slowly, shaking my head.

"I know, you 'haven't had the desire.' And you 'wouldn't go out with any man unless God brought him to you on a silver platter.'"

"Oh, I dunno..." I strung her along. "Maybe he's too...*mature* for me."

"Nonsense!" she snapped. "You want them from that generation. Younger, single men these days have no need for a good woman. They only need some version of a Harley Davidson and pornography to survive."

I looked at her with disgust, but then was reminded of the plethora of single male friends from high school I'd reconnected with on Facebook, and their hordes of seemingly desperate-for-a-man female followers hanging on to their every word. Their fans eagerly commented on their mindless status updates and stroked their seemingly shallow egos. Practically every last one of these guys who had been divorced for any length of time had countless selfies posing on their motorcycles.

"Holy cow...you're exactly right!"

Trish shrugged. "Aren't I always, honey?"

We were seated in the "tree room," with its ceiling built around a cottonwood in the middle of it over a hundred years ago.

We sipped our piñon coffees and made small talk for a while regarding the ambiance of the restaurant, the red brick floors, territorial-style windows overlooking the plaza.

I asked Oscar how business was going. *Suave,* I thought. *You might as well have asked him about the weather, for goodness' sake.*

"It's going. But I'm kind of old school," he said, admitting to his philosophy on new technology such as e-readers and smartphones.

"What, you mean you don't own a motorcycle?" I asked in a snarky tone, leaving off the part that Tricia and I had talked about earlier in the day.

I knew my remark was more of a defense mechanism; I was going to weed out any potential losers from the git-go. I refused to be invested for any length of time—even in the short time it would take to chat over coffee—with anyone unworthy of my attention. Because along with my precious energy and time could possibly come my affection, and eventually, the remote possibility of *my heart*; along with all the scars I'd accumulated over the years. I wasn't going to allow anyone in hastily, that was for sure.

Oscar squinted his eyes, cocking his head to the side in confusion.

Oh, mercy, those glorious, soft brown eyes...

I forced a small laugh in response to his confused expression. "Never mind."

He continued. "Well, like I say, I don't even own a Kindle or a Nook. Even my phone is stupid—just makes *phone calls*. Weird, right?" He pulled out his cellphone and flipped it open to show me.

"Seriously?" I implored, purposefully not responding to his attempt at humor. "I take my e-reader with me everywhere I go, practically. Of course, nothing compares with a new book."

"Or an old book," agreed Oscar. "You know, scientists discovered there's actually something to the smell of an old—and even a new—book. I did manage to read an article about it—on my daughter's laptop, ironically. There's just something about that smell people love."

"I agree," I nodded tearing open the lid on the small container of creamer and pouring it into my decaf. "Does your store have wifi?"

"Absolutely not," he laughed. "I am diametrically opposed to having internet in a bookstore. I want my customers to have the experience of holding a real, old-fashioned book in their hands. The kind with pages you turn, not tap on glass to get to the next one. It's a matter of principle."

I nodded. "Huh...I guess I can appreciate that." As

the evening progressed, my frostiness slowly began to melt away, and the conversation flowed more naturally. Oscar was the perfect gentleman and a keen listener. I was impressed by the fact that he gave me his rapt attention and could ask interesting questions, prodding information out of me about things that interested *me*. It had been a long while since I'd had a man not dominate the conversation but focus on what I was saying. It was as if he truly cared about what I had to say.

I confessed to my secret fantasy of owning a restaurant. "Primarily with the intention of decorating it with a cool-vibe atmosphere. And, of course, hiring a world-renowned chef," I laughed.

"I loved the entrance into your place, by the way, with the tumbleweeds hanging from the ceiling." He was referring to the breezeway between *Old Town Music* and *Lacey's*, Trish and Garrett's art gallery. I'd painted the space turquoise as the southwestern sky, and it was laden with clear Christmas lights year-round. Large, round tumbleweeds, which we jokingly referred to as "New Mexico state flowers," were suspended from the ceiling, giving it a dusty, western feel. "You creative types—I don't get how you come up with your unique ideas. I wouldn't have had a clue to do that, but it's a really cool look."

"Well, thanks," I smiled. "Decorating is one of my therapies."

He nodded. "Hey, are you getting hungry? You wanna order dinner?"

"Yes, actually, I am," I smiled. "That'd be great."

Oscar flagged down a passing waiter. He ordered *carne asada*, and I ordered chicken enchiladas.

"Red or green?" inquired the waiter.

"Green, please."

"Rolled or flat?"

"I'll take rolled."

He nodded and took our menus, heading for the kitchen.

"So, you're a green girl, huh?" remarked Oscar.

"Yeah...always have been."

"Ah. I'm more of a red kinda guy," he noted. "You say you 'always have been.' So, does that mean you're from Albuquerque?"

"Yes. Actually, Bosque Farms. I went to high school in Los Lunas."

"Oh, really?" he nodded.

Locals were familiar with the small towns along the bosque of the Rio Grande—Corrales, Los Ranchos, Peralta, and the other towns spread out around the greater Rio Grande Valley: Placitas, Bernalillo, Isleta Pueblo. They had largely Hispanic and Native American populations, making me, a blonde-haired, blue-eyed, freckle-faced kid somewhat of an anomaly growing up there.

"What about you, where did you grow up?"

"In Española. Back in the Dark Ages," he laughed. Española was a town outside of Santa Fe steeped in its traditional Mexican culture and influences. "You know, in Driver's Ed we rode a burro."

I laughed out loud. His eyes sparkled back at me, barely visible through warm, dark lashes.

"You're sure it wasn't a lowrider, *Vato*?"

"Don't laugh! I actually had one. It was the pride of the *barrio!* Complete with hydraulics, *esa*."

Before I could catch myself, I snorted.

No *way...Did that* really *just happen??*

In my nervous efforts to play it cool, I wasn't sure how to recover. Too late, I attempted to conceal my embarrassing outburst by covering my mouth. When I was bold enough to make eye contact, Oscar was doubled over in a silent belly-laugh. Which, of course, made me laugh harder...It took a while for both of us to catch our breath.

"For a *weta,* you know a lot about the ways of the 'hood," he noted.

"Well, *gracias.*" I was sure my face was still red.

When our food arrived, I folded my napkin in my lap and reached for my silverware. Oscar held up his coffee cup.

"To growing up on the Rio Grande!"

I grabbed mine.

"Hear, hear!" We clinked our cups together. Before long, we were discussing our respective children, and his grandchildren. His expression lit up talking about little Evangelyn, who was clearly the apple of his eye. He told animated stories about when she came to visit the store with her mom, and the time she got an "ice cream headache" when she was four.

"She wasn't sure what it was, but she knew it hurt real bad. So she squeezes her eyes closed and starts tapping her forehead, and saying, 'Our Father! Our Father!'" He pressed his fingers to his brow in illustration as he talked. I knew that most of the Hispanic people in this area were born into highly religious Catholic families, where they were taught to conjure the "sign of the cross"—*the Father, Son and Holy Ghost*—represented by a smooth maneuvering of the fingers lightly touching the forehead, chest and shoulders.

The image of this little girl never having experienced "brain freeze" had me in hysterics. I squeezed my nostrils so as not to snort while laughing again, wrapping my free arm around my sides. *"Stop!"* I implored, but we were both in stitches.

The discourse had been flowing easily and I lost track of time. It had been a long time since I'd allowed myself to think of a man in this way, so long since I'd boldly stared into a man's eyes. But I just couldn't stop myself— those searing, caramel-colored eyes of Oscar's...

Be in the present, Moll!! Being in this man's presence was going to be very distracting...*very* distracting, indeed.

Neither of us brought up our former marriages or ex-spouses. Yet I couldn't help being curious as to what his story was. Frankly, I had chosen very purposefully to never get involved with anyone who had been unfaithful in their marriage, which had so deeply scarred me in mine. It was a sorry state of things, but that tended to narrow the prospective pool considerably. On a certain level, this had offered me some measure of protection from having to make a commitment to the dating world. It hadn't taken long for me to get comfortable with the notion that it might, in fact, never happen for me, that I'd never find the right man, much less consider getting remarried. Looking now at Oscar, enjoying this easy, light-hearted conversation, I wondered: *Could he have cheated on his wife*, as my ex had me? Surely this seemingly sweet, unguarded gentleman had a "clean" history. He wasn't the kind to betray his wife, whoever she was; *surely* that wasn't possible. But then again, that's what I thought–*no, I knew* about Paul... until he left. Even with my reservations about dating, and knowing I didn't have the energy or desire to invest in a relationship I knew couldn't "go" anywhere with anyone who had committed such an egregious error, I felt myself letting down my guard. I was growing more confident and comfortable as the night wore on.

Eventually, patrons at other tables gathered their jackets and scarves and left the restaurant, and the wait staff began clearing tables, having brought our ticket to our table earlier. *How long ago* was *that?*

We were completely alone in the tree room now. Our waiter, dressed entirely in black, approached. "I apologize, but would you mind if I collect payment now? We're closing up the register."

"Of course. Here you are," said Oscar, reaching into his pocket to retrieve his wallet and handing him a credit card. "Thank you."

As the waiter walked away we both smiled at the mutual realization that, now looking around, we were probably the last ones in the entire restaurant.

"This has been nice," he said, stretching his hand across the table and covering mine. He left it there momentarily, then with a gentle pat pulled away. It was such a simple, innocuous gesture, but adrenaline rushed through my system, and I was at a sudden loss for words.

He rose to pull out my chair, and then helped me put my coat on, pulling on his leather jacket as well. I noticed the rich smell of it, the warm color, while Oscar pulled some cash out of his pocket for the tip. The waiter returned with the receipt and after exchanging a few niceties, we walked through the restaurant, past the kitchen, where pots and pans were being clanged around. A supervisor hollered instructions to his staff in Spanish as we passed the impressive staircase that led to the upper rooms.

Oscar was holding the door open for me, and I shivered as together we stepped back into the chilly night air.

But I realized it wasn't that it was really cold outside. Yes, the air was brisk and biting on my face, once warm a few moments ago in the restaurant. My heart was full, and my mind raced thinking about the evening which was about to come to a close.

Oh my word, what do I do now??

Is there some first date protocol? Was this even a *date??* I mean, do I shake his hand, or hug him? Or...*Oh Lord, what if he tries to* kiss *me!* I felt like I was back in high school again.

The regret at the memory of the garlic and onion laden meal I'd just consumed made my stomach churn...*I haven't done this in a century—*

"Thanks, again," said Oscar. We were standing in front of the music store.

And there were those beautiful warm eyes as he was smiling at me.

Good grief, that had been a short walk!

"No, thank *you*," I managed. "The coffee was great. Oh and the meal! The meal was great, too." I held out my gloved hand, thankful I didn't have to touch his warm, soft skin. (If Tricia had witnessed this, I would have never lived it down. I nervously stifled a giggle at the thought of seeing her shaking her head at me in disgust that this was the best I could muster.) "Hey, can I drop you at your car? Mine's just around back."

He accepted my hand, shaking it with a slow, firm grip. "No, I like to walk. I'm just around the corner, the other side of The Candy Lady."

"Great," I said. "Well, good night." I hastily turned and unlocked the front door of the store and stepped inside.

"Goodnight," he said, and gave me a slight nod—the same nod he'd given me the first night I met him. He waited until I was safely inside before leaving, walking away with a wave into the night, under the glow of a full yellow moon, his hands stuffed deep into his pockets.

I held on to the bar on the front door and watched as Oscar quickened his step, eventually settling into a jog, his body in silhouette now, heading in the direction of the brilliantly lit Christmas tree across the plaza; then he turned the corner and was out of sight.

Mercy, I thought as I steadied myself against the cold of the metal, recalling the innocence of his hand touching mine after dinner. The thought of it made me swoon.

What on earth are you doing to me, Oscar Cardenas?

EIGHT

June 1891

Mariana had been up since before dawn in the big, quiet house, busily preparing for her daughter's fifteenth birthday party. The night before, she and Papacio stayed up through the wee hours of the morning soaking corn husks, grinding *masa,* and tending to the pig roasting in an underground coffin alight in glowing coals.

Today, it was tender and juicy. Mariana shredded the pork and added red chile flakes to make the *carnitas* center for the tamales. With one of Mariana's aprons donned, Papacio slathered the inside of the corn husks with the pasty masa mixture, readying it for the inner pork delicacy. Mariana scooped up a wooden spoonful of carnitas, and once it was spread inside, carefully closed the ends of the husks and tied them together for steaming. She wiped her brow with a cotton cloth as sweat dripped from her head, piled high with damp, dark hair, and sighed.

"*Mija,* let me finish this," said the slight, wrinkled man with a wink. "You go ahead and finish the cakes."

Mariana sighed again and smiled. "Thank you,

Papa," she said, patting his shoulder.

The kitchen was a whirlwind of flour, spices, and clouds of steam. Chopped vegetables and limes lined the countertops next to colorful Talavera pottery bowls in various shapes and sizes, full of salsa and *mole*. Cloves of garlic sat ready to be crushed and ground in a mortar and pestle, with onions, tomatoes and *tomatillos* on cutting boards awaiting chopping. Dry red chile *ristras* hung on the walls; it would be a few more months before the green pods that grew in the chile fields on the other side of the barn would be ready for harvesting.

Mariana went over her to-do list in her head: the massive pot of *posole* was simmering over the fire next to the *frijoles,* she had prepared the *tres leches* cake chilling in the icebox, and now needed to mix the icing for the lime pound cakes. In the hectic rush, Mariana took a moment to savor the pride she would take in serving her guests her specialty dessert. She was known throughout the valley for her lime pound cake; more importantly to Mariana, it was her husband's favorite. Although Onofre never told her so, she knew from a request in the early years of their marriage that he savored the delectable, tangy cake. Simple men, she smiled to herself. Like her mama used to tell her: *"El camino al corazón de un hombre es a través de su estómago. "* ("The way to a man's heart is through his belly.") The confection was always expected of

72

her on special occasions such as this, her daughter's
quinceañera. She hoped she had made enough for all
of the guests they were expecting in just a few short
hours...

Suddenly she was reminded—

"Tortillas!" she screeched at the realization.

"Santa ma gania!" yelled her father, throwing
masa toward the ceiling.

They could hear footsteps practically skipping
down the staircase, and Pilar's laughter. "What does
that even *mean*, Papacio?" she giggled as she swung
around the corner of the kitchen, surprising him with
kiss on the cheek.

Her thick hair was pulled up on the sides and
clipped with a silver and turquoise barrette, secured
among her long ebony ringlets, so black they had a cobalt sheen to them. She was strikingly beautiful, taller
than her petite mother, but sharing her olive complexion, small mouth, and enormous brown eyes shrouded
in dark lashes. Her carefully perfected hairstyle was in
stark contrast to the lightweight cotton bloomers and
modest corset she had donned in preparation for her
big night, having draped a shawl around her bosom in
an attempt at modesty. She gave a scathing look at her
mother, whose hair was an upswept mess, with hand-
prints of white powder and what appeared to be batter
wiped on her apron and skirt. The sleeves of her blouse
were rolled up, and Mariana noticed her daughter's

disapproving look as she reached for a rolling pin and mound of dough.

"It means *la madre tuya es loca en la cabeza!*" the old man chortled to his granddaughter.

Just then, Onofre Vega appeared in the doorway, his form dwarfing that of his wife and father-in-law. The screen door slammed behind him.

His daughter rushed into his arms. "Oh, Papa! Isn't this so *exciting!*" she exclaimed. The hint of a smile appeared on his lips as he absent-mindedly stroked her hair.

Tonight, Pilar thought with a thrill, *tonight I will be able to dance!* She had practiced for months, her father her unwilling partner. The thought of her growing up—his beautiful baby girl—frankly made Onofre nauseated.

"Except that Mama won't help me get dressed!" she sharply spat, glaring at the laboring Mariana, whose brow was saturated in perspiration from the heat of the *cocina,* exacerbated by the looming afternoon New Mexico sun.

"Pilar," her mother spoke patiently as she began flattening the corn dough into small tortillas, then tossing them onto a sizzling griddle. "If you expect me to feed a hundred people tonight, *Jita*, I must get my work done first."

Exasperated, Pilar pouted and stomped her foot. "But I've *been* waiting!" she wailed. "Patiently," she

74

added in a more subdued tone, gazing up at her father.

When Onofre Vega spoke, it was almost exclusively in Spanish, *if* he spoke at all. He couldn't resist the imploring gaze of his sweet, innocent baby girl. His little *mija*. He glanced at his father-in-law wearing a woman's frock, his permanent disapproving frown growing deeper.

"*Andale,* Mariana," he grunted, swiping a warm tortilla from the stack on a platter as he exited the room.

Gentle old Florencio—*Papacio* to his grandchildren—his back to his family and wrist deep in *masa*, rolled his eyes. He didn't have to witness Onofre's judgmental look. He heard it in his voice, the same as he'd heard for the past twenty years that he'd lived with *la familia*.

Calmly, Mariana replied to her daughter. "*Mija,* I will be upstairs to help you with your *vesta de quinceañera en un momento, por favor.*"

Pilar gave her a heavy sigh and reached for the growing stack of tortillas. Papacio turned and intercepted her attempt by taking a swat to her bottom with the kitchen towel previously hanging over his bony shoulder. "Uh-uh! These are for your *guests*."

"*Ow!*" She pouted and raced upstairs.

"*Santa ma gania,*" he mumbled, shaking his head. "Such a spoiled brat…"

NINE

Present day

"Old Town Music, this is Cedar, how might I be of assistance to you this fine afternoon?"

Garrett shook his head, and we smiled at the exchange. Just the three of us were in the store.

"You'd think he was in front of an audience every time he answers that thing," Garrett leaned in to me using a stage whisper, referring to the dramatic pose and tone Cedar had always taken when the phone rang: he straightened himself into what appeared to be an almost stiff posture, dropping his shoulders and placing a palm on the glass countertop. He raised an eyebrow while dropping his voice into a resonant baritone, his eyelids lazily assuming a bedroom gaze.

"Why, thanks," Cedar purred, emphasizing the "*th*" in *thanks* as one would use it in the word *the*. We heard the high-pitched laughter of a female caller on the other end of the line. "And you have a lovely voice, too, m' lady."

We snickered, witnessing the exchange. "He doesn't require an audience. It's in his blood."

Garrett shook his head again. "I gotta give it to him, he's taken the art of answering the telephone and raised it to a whole new level."

"If you'd be so kind and allow me to check on that for you?" said Cedar, smiling then with an obliging laugh. "All right, then. Do be so kind as to hold, won't you?"

By now, our heads were down on the countertop, attempting to stifle an outburst.

"Ahem, m'lady," Cedar interrupted our now uncontained amusement. "This nice lady would like to know if we sell sheet music for autoharp."

I stopped and looked at him quizzically. "Cedar, you know we don't carry *anything* for autoharp. Including sheet music."

"Yes, I do know, m'lady," he explained with a sad frown. "But *she* doesn't know that. She just sounds so... *hopeful* if you will, and I do so despise the thought of letting her down."

I raised my hands questioningly. "Well, just *explain* it to her?"

Cedar nodded reflectively, then resumed the position, palm on the glass. He picked up the receiver. "Madam, it is with great trepidation that I must inform you of the misfortune that we indeed do *not* carry said sheet music." Once again we heard a tremolo of notes in cascading laughter emanating from the receiver.

I nodded my head and raised my eyebrows at Garrett in a *See what I mean?* gesture.

"We *do* however carry a plethora of sheet music for a wide variety of instruments, including flute, trumpet, guitar, piano, oboe, and the harmonica." After a pause, Cedar gave a full-bellied laugh. "Yes, Ma'am, that's right. We close at 6pm," still smiling. "Ah, very good, m'lady. I shall await your arrival, then!"

Together we beheld the wonder that was Cedar. I squeezed one of Garrett's shaking shoulders, and he leaned in toward me. "I'm telling you, this is how I drum up half of my business!"

"So glad the *music* store is able to *drum* up business," he snorted.

By the time Cedar hung up with a "Namaste," Garrett had tears running down his reddened face, which caused me to guffaw. I dropped my head into the crook of my elbow on the countertop.

"Mr. Cardenas!" greeted a buoyant Cedar in a less formal tone than he had taken with his lady caller.

Garrett and I looked up to see Oscar standing in the middle of the floor room with his arm over the shoulder of his granddaughter. My heart jumped at seeing him again.

"Oh, Oscar!" I blurted, walking around from behind the counter, my hand trailing off the arm of Garrett, who was attempting to stand upright and contain his giggling.

Cedar had already come around and was kneeling in front of the little girl. She was wearing a sheepskin jacket and striped, multi-color tights with pink western boots, her curly dark hair in pigtails high on her head. "Are you ready, m'lady?"

She smiled coyly and hugged her grandfather's waist.

"I'm Cedar," he said, holding a hand out to her.

She slowly took his hand and shook it. "I'm Evangelyn."

"I know," he responded brightly with a wink. He rose to his feet. "I see you've got your music book. Let's go put it to good use, shall we?" He held his hand out to her and she took it, looking back up at her grandfather.

"I'll be back in thirty minutes," Oscar assured her.

"I can bring her over to your shop when we're done. That would be no problem," offered Cedar. Evangelyn smiled up at him.

"You sure?" Oscar narrowed his eyes, glancing at his granddaughter. She didn't take her gaze off Cedar.

"It would be my privilege," he replied.

"Well, okay then."

We watched as Cedar escorted her to one of the practice rooms in the back. "I love your jacket," he gushed.

"I love *yours*," she replied, eyeballing the tattered duster he was never seen without.

Oscar looked back at Garrett and me.

"She's beautiful," I commented.

"Yes, well she's her mother's girl," he smiled. I noticed his expression was arbitrary, minus the usual bright, sparkling eyes; today it was all business.

"I didn't realize you'd already made an appointment to bring her in," I said apologetically.

"Yes," he responded curtly.

I realized I hadn't introduced Garrett, who still had the grin of a mischievous seventh grade boy on his face.

"Oh—this is Garrett," I said gesturing behind the counter. Garrett reached across the counter, and Oscar took his hand, giving it a hearty shake.

"*Oscar?*" Garrett inquired of me.

"Yes, sorry," I responded.

Oscar's face remained neutral. He restated Garrett's name, and we stood for a while in an awkward pause, listening to the upbeat tempo of a Sousa march on the overhead speakers.

"Well, I gotta get back." He pointed with his thumb and started for the door.

"You're welcome to hang out with us while she's having her lesson," I shrugged, trying to appear casual.

Oscar gave us an absent-minded smile. "No, I

wouldn't want to...interrupt anything." He nodded his head and kept walking. "You know, duty calls."

I watched him leave, pondering his stoic behavior. *Huh. Maybe he likes to keep things professional, separating business from pleasure...*

Garrett was in the process of dialing his cell phone, heading through the breezeway to the art gallery.

"Gonna see if Tricia needs anything at home for her sinus infection."

"Tell Tiny-Behiney I hope she feels better soon."

"I will," he waved with the phone up to his ear. "Hey, babe..." he trailed off out of sight.

Off in the distance I heard the haunting wail of a siren. Immediately I was struck with dread; something dire and disastrous was happening.

I found myself standing at the mouth of our cul-de-sac facing inward, a familiar perspective once again. Before me was our dream home, where we'd labored in the backyard, designed and created a retreat on behalf of our children, family, and friends—a haven—illuminated by a sky on fire. Smoke was coming from the windows, the glow of brilliant orange surrounded it. Choked, panicking, I searched the street for my husband. I couldn't breathe, my lungs unable to fill with air, eyes darting over the surreal landscape.

But then, there he was! Standing on the sidewalk. Oh, thank God...finally!

And yet, and yet...Paul had clearly not been searching for me. I didn't understand...couldn't he see the

81

flames?

Our children! Where were our children?! They were in jeopardy! Do something, Paul! HELP THEM!!

Incapable, he never rallied.

He stood unmoved, merely a bystander. Unaffected, unable to console, distant, unalarmed.

Apathetic.

All I could do was stand by and watch helplessly as everything around us was consumed by the flames...

I awoke sucking in air. I looked at the clock: 2:49 a.m.

I felt sorrowful, disoriented. I hadn't had this once-recurring dream in years—not since the early days after Paul left. Each time, the dream had taken on different scenarios: the terrifying wailing of a tornado, a drive-by shooting, or other disastrous scenes of impending doom, all taking place before my eyes from the vantage point of the mouth of the cul-de-sac.

And every time, I awoke feeling unfathomable disappointment, grievous that Paul could never see the disaster we were on the verge of succumbing to.

Why on earth, after all these years, would this nightmare rear its ugly head, again?

TEN

June 1891

Dozens of bundled bouquets of sunflowers inter-twined with Russian Olive branches laced the staircase down which Pilar Vega would be descending in just a matter of moments. The banister spindles were fes-tooned with velvet periwinkle ribbons at her insistence and with her father's blessing, from a shopping trip to Santa Fe.

Nicolas Vega, Pilar's copper-haired and freckle-faced six-year-old brother, was being shooed out of the front entry through which he'd previously come mere moments prior, bearing two blue-tailed lizards. He ran down the front steps and directly into a freshly shaven Rico Ruiz.

"*Rico!*" he exclaimed. With the throngs of peo-ple milling about he was pleased to find a friendly, familiar face. The thrilled Nicolas held up his newly captured treasures for his friend to behold.

"*¿Como estás, mi amigo pequeño?*" Rico smiled. "Ah, blue tails," he commented, nodding his approval as he stroked the head of one. Upon further inspec-tion, he noticed the tail of one of the lizards had been snapped off. "Uh-oh, this little guy's missing his tail.

You know it'll grow back, don't you?"

"Uh-huh, I know," replied a wide-eyed, grinning Nicolas. "*I* chopped it off!" With that, the boy ran off to scare some of the girls from the parish he'd seen earlier.

Rico, dressed in a pair of clean trousers and button-up canvas shirt with the sleeves rolled up, was honored that the boy—*Pilar's* brother—looked up to him.

The afternoon dip in the Rio Grande, while refreshing, did little to ease the heat of the waning day, even with his long, wavy hair gathered and wrapped at the nape of his neck instead of hanging loose around his shoulders. He looked forward to the sun setting and the promise of a cool Albuquerque summer evening.

"Frederico," called a voice behind him. He spun around to see Daniella Shannon.

"Señora Shannon," he replied.

The cultured lady standing there appeared uncomfortable. She was carrying a parasol and wore pristine white gloves with pearl embellishments. Her dark navy dress was buttoned tightly around her upper neck, and she waved a fan close to her face, her eyes darting around the crowd.

"Is there something I can do for you?"

"No," she blurted. Then blinking her eyes and pursing her lips, "I mean...*yes*. I can't seem to locate my husband." Clearly frustrated, she took a deep breath

84

and gave a tight smile. "Would you be so kind as to fetch him for me?"

"*Sí, Señora.*" Rico gave her a nod and turned back toward the house.

He knew at any minute, Pilar would be presented to the crowd, that she would now be accepted as a "proper lady" in upstanding society, just like Daniella Shannon. He briefly looked down at his hands, inspected them again. He was brutally aware of their differences.

If he could just make her see...He was a very hard worker, and he would be willing to do anything for her. He would never do anything to offend her upper class sensitivities, to embarrass her. She would see that he could rise up and ascend the transparent wall separating their worlds. She would understand and appreciate that he was willing to make any sacrifice for her.

Realizing he'd been tasked with finding Theophilus Shannon and not wanting to miss Pilar's entrance, Rico made his way through the crowd assembled under the ancient cottonwood trees. They were at the height of their blooming, with fluffy white poufs lazily drifting through the evening air and pooling at the base of tree trunks like drifts of snow beneath the Russian olives and lilac bushes. The scent was almost sickeningly sweet. Partygoers sipped cups of lemonade and sangría, covering their beverages from the swirling cotton

85

with their free hands.

Rico saw the hulking figure of Onofre Vega in a group of men heartily laughing, including Señor Shannon, his son Oliver, and Pilar's older brother, Joaquin. The two young men, both Rico's age, were inseparable since the Shannon family had moved to the valley late that spring.

A cattle baron from Great Britain, Theophilus Shannon had uprooted his family from the upper echelon lifestyle to which they were accustomed and herded them across the ocean along with the Durham shorthorn cows and bulls he bred. Having been lured by land grants of the Homestead Act of 1870, which enticed Europeans to the rugged western territories of the United States in the hopes of enterprising the abundant and largely uncultivated land, Theophilus had packed up his entire family and moved. It was there in the rich and fertile soil of the Rio Grande valley, he was sure, that together—*as the Pioneers!*—they would forge their way to prosperity and happiness.

His wife, to say the very least, was unconvinced.

"Excuse me, Señor Shannon."

The men turned to look at Rico.

"Freddie!" exclaimed Oliver, slapping Rico on the back.

His sandy-colored hair was parted and combed in attempt to tame its natural curliness, greased with the gentleman's pomade his father always wore, his easygoing, jovial personality inherited from him as well.

"Joaquin, you know our equine caretaker, Frederico?"

Joaquin Vega had not inherited his father's stature. He had the same midnight black hair that his father and sister possessed, but his build was lean, and he was shorter than the other men standing in the group. He gave a warm, wide smile to Rico as he extended his hand.

"Of course. Rico."

As Rico accepted his hand, he was pleased for the correction of his name. He knew the light -haired Oliver meant no harm, but no one with the exception of his late father called him Freddie. It made him feel... small.

"Frederico, did you need something?" Theophilus smiled. Rico thought how odd it was to him that when these Europeans asked a question, it sounded more like a statement instead.

In spite of the niceties, Rico was aware these men knew he hadn't interrupted their conversation to socialize. He understood his place.

"*Sí*, señor. Señora Shannon was wondering where you were, Sir." He gestured toward the festooned veranda.

"Ah," he nodded and turned to the other men. "Gentlemen, it's been a pleasure, but the 'old ball and chain' calls, as it were...."

The men chuckled as Theophilus turned to leave but was startled by the appearance of Mariana Vega.

"Ma'am," Theophilus bowed toward her and smiled. "If I do say so, you look stunning, Mrs. Vega."

She smiled and nodded at her neighbor. "Very glad your family was able to join us tonight, Mr. Shannon."

She was indeed breathtaking in a satin yellow gown and matching gloves that extended past her elbows. Her hair was a deep brunette, upswept with auburn tendrils framing the delicate features of her face. She wore pearls around her neck, and matching drop earrings. The setting sun made her bronze skin glow and her warm, chocolate eyes glitter; at thirty-six she was still as youthful as a teenager. Mariana cupped a hand to her mouth and whispered, "Better not keep the old ball and chain waiting."

The young men guffawed at Mr. Shannon's faux pas. "Indeed!" he replied over the laughter, then was off to find his wife.

Mariana turned to her husband. "It's *time*." Together they departed as Onofre escorted his wife toward the entrance of the veranda.

The three young men remained in the yard with the guests beneath the cottonwoods, two of them sharing good-natured jibes with each other, laughing and cajoling one another and discussing the exquisite collection of young ladies gathered among them in the season's most anticipated fineries to witness one of their own make her grand entrance into society.

The other young man barely noticed their childish banter, his heart racing as the front doors of the grand Vega home began to part.

ELEVEN

Present day

It was New Year's Eve.

In the kitchen I prepared an easy stir-fry meal and poured myself a glass of sangría as I listened to Stevie Nicks on my playlist. Wolfgang Amadeus Mozart—a/k/a Wolf—my five-year-old white Lab, lay stretched out lazily on the saltillo tile floor, so that I had to step over and around him to get to the stove, my cooking utensils, or the fridge.

"Hey, don't bother getting up or moving for my sake," I told him, my hands held up in protest.

He grunted and wagged his tail, *thud, thud, thud* against the tile. The only chance of that happening was if I held a delicious morsel in my hand from which his gaze never deviated, always hopeful that something—anything—might be tossed his direction.

"Oh, you sweet baby," I crooned at him, pouring a little teriyaki sauce into the sizzling pan. "You are the only man in my life who's ever paid me this much attention."

Thud, thud, thud, thud.

Relaxing felt good. The busy holiday season was just about over. There wasn't much to do aside from the semi-annual inventory Cedar and I were to tackle in a couple of weeks.

I thought of him at the small private party I agreed to let him host at the shop tonight, celebrating the New

Year with some friends from the music department at the university. An accurately self-described 'extraordinarily-handsome-senior-music-major-slash-flamenco-guitar-genius,' Cedar had more than one sorority girl vying for his attention who would surely be in attendance at the party tonight. He referred to them as his "muses." To them he didn't give much more than the time of day, in spite of flirtatious displays and a gallant effort on their part. This made him an anomaly, which didn't escape their scrutiny and only reinforced their aggressive attempts to woo him.

Much to their chagrin, however, Cedar was a tough nut to crack.

"I'm not nearly as interested in what could possibly go on between the sheets with them as I am interested in what's going on between their ears," he'd told me after a couple of freshman female admirers stopped by the shop for an impressive yet nauseating flirt-fest. It was hard to not notice the low-cut blouses that showcased their "extra padding."

"Sadly, there's just not a lot going on in there," he sighed.

There was only one woman for whom Cedar's heart beat longingly: Lacey. Tricia and Garrett's daughter had him wrapped around her finger since the moment I hired him almost four years ago at Old Town Music. *"She's the jelly to my peanut butter, Molly, the Catherine to my Heathcliff, the Bella to my Edward!"* Lacey was an incredibly focused artist and spent her time in her studio next door—or, more often than not, somewhere around the plaza, painting *en plein aire*—determined to carve her niche in the Santa Fe art scene. She had some of her work hanging in galleries there after a mixed-media piece she'd created when she was still in high school was hand-chosen by Michelle Obama on a trip to the Southwest during her husband's campaign. It hung in the dining room of their home in Chicago before being moved to the White House, where it was displayed thereafter in the First Grand-mother's bedroom. Garrett had an article written about it in one of the Condé Nast magazines clipped and framed and proudly displayed in the gallery.

Tonight, as I sautéed dinner in my robe and slip-pers, Cedar was no doubt awaiting Lacey's arrival, while he and his buddies entertained the intimate crowd on clas-sical guitar and piano. Surely by now the muses would be weak in the knees.

The days of staying up late and partying into the wee hours of the morning were bygone for me. The idea of lazily falling asleep to one of the star-studded, end-of-year countdown shows on TV from Times Square, knowing the shop was closed the next day, made me positively giddy.

I had come to embrace my "aloneness" in the early years of the divorce. As a mother, the loss of my children, if just for a few days or even hours, to the shared custody of their father absolutely shredded my spirit, violating the very thing I held closest to my heart. My children were so young when their dad left, and I was paralyzed by grief.

Physically and emotionally unable to continue to wallow in the mire of the depression being apart from them caused, it wasn't long before I realized the beauty that was to be found in spending time alone, without an-other human being vying for my attention. Every moment of every minute of my day had been preoccupied with chil-dren. As a music teacher, that fact was inescapable, and while I loved my children *and* my profession, I came to savor—and fiercely protect—my free time.

It was up to me to ensure that my son and daughter came through this predicament in which we had found ourselves. I was committed to doing whatever it took to be sure that they weren't "those kids whose parents divorced." There would be no acceptable excuses for bad behavior. They would never be allowed to be victims. So, instead of huddling in a fetal position on the floor, I decided on a healthier alternative, and vowed to be a better example to my children: I chose to embrace my time alone rather than be an emotional mess when they left to stay with their dad. Occasionally, well-intentioned, married girlfriends commented on my "free time": "Wow, I sure wish *I* time to breathe, but I never get a break! It would be so nice to have time away from my kids like you do."

Of course, I understood where these women were coming from. But they couldn't possibly begin to comprehend the haunting sorrow that had afforded my newfound "freedom." Being court-ordered apart from the most tangible expression of love of a mother's existence felt like having open-heart surgery without anesthesia. I would survive it, but but God, it was painful.

There would be some very dark nights along the path to healing. I remember yelling out to God, and telling God I hated Him (lightning strikes, be damned!). This God had told me He loved me, *and this is what a lifetime of serving and believing in Him got me?* I screamed it over and over again in the middle of the night—during the "witching hour," the blackest pit of darkness at night— when the children weren't home. I'd screech it as a teenager would before slamming the door on seemingly unfair parents. I was drowning in my brokenness.

Apparently, God was big enough to handle my shunning of Him, the meltdowns and name-calling. Before we knew it, days had turned into weeks, weeks into months, and then a year had passed. Then two years. Then five.

Through the lifting fog, joy returned.

Eventually, my children grew to see me not only as a survivor, but someone who *thrived,* as well. Over the years, and after much heart-wrenching prayer, I gradually let go of the bitterness that had consumed me in the dead of night.

After the path and life journey I had chosen had been irrevocably taken away by someone else's choices, it was time to deal with it. There was no amount of refusal, hatred and questioning that could change it. I had to let it go and get on with the business of living.

I had to forgive. So that's what I did.

When Paul walked away from our marriage, I metaphorically washed my hands of him, knowing I'd done everything I could—having turned over every possible stone to save it. I could only see him as a partner in parenting now, someone I needed on my side to finish the job we started when we brought those beautiful children into the world. I put all my trust in God to raise them with love and courage.

It paid off.

Years later, Paul and I became friends—a far cry from how I ever dreamed I would regard the man who violated the trust of a marriage I'd thought would last forever. And more importantly, our children grew into healthy, well-adjusted human beings. They were believers who clung to the faith they saw alive in their mother, having seen it proven true and loyal to two lost little children whose parents no longer loved each other. They learned that while life can deal some powerful, breathtaking blows to our spirits, we didn't have to stay down forever.

My most fervent prayers and greatest hopes had been answered; once I had desperately prayed that with God's guidance, I would give them "roots and wings." As a mother, I had now officially and successfully worked myself out of a job.

The song "Landslide" came on as I drew a bath upstairs and sipped my sangría. Walking through my bedroom I stood before the balcony. The French doors overlooked the sparkling city, tonight filled with celebratory partygoers and New Year's Eve revelers.

For a moment I was joyously expectant of what tomorrow might bring: A brand new year. I breathed in the sweet hope that filled my spirit and lungs, inhaling deeply.

As I listened to the simple guitar accompaniment of "Landslide," I wondered how the songwriter's passionate, poetic lyrics had come to be: What was the story behind them? Surely Stevie Nicks had to have experienced the wounds of some kind of separation, too; the heartache that comes from lost love, of raising children when one of their parents makes the choice to walk away...

> *Well I've been afraid of changing*
> *'Cause I built my life around you.*
> *But time makes you bolder,*
> *Even children get older*
> *And I'm getting older, too*

I marveled at how far I'd come, from the raw and

searing pain that accompanied the realization that the life-time investment of marriage and raising a family was not reciprocated in my chosen life partner; that everything I'd heavily invested in—with my entire being—was crumbling in somebody else's hands. Dissolving, like the adobe walls of the San Felipe de Neri church when the Rio Grande river tired of its borders hundreds of years ago.

The song's lyrics summed up the weeks and months following Paul's leaving, when I'd finally turned a corner in those tired days of mourning:

I took my love, took it down
Climbed a mountain, and I turned around
And I saw my reflection in the snow-covered hills
'til a landslide brought me down

While occasionally and momentarily I revisited the days of that sorrowful journey through the lyrics of a song, I never drowned in them anymore. *Thank God!* I was blissfully grateful.

As I dried off from the warm bath and slipped into bed, I was certain of one thing; that each of us on this planet have a cross to bear, our own paths to travel. Every single one of us on this planet is one of the walking wounded. The question I had to ask myself all those years ago was: Would I allow brokenness to *define* me, or *refine* me? I was no longer the woman I was at the start of my journey, fearful and timid, uncertain of who she was in the big world surrounding her. It finally felt as if the tide was changing for good.

"You remember that we have a merchants' meeting this afternoon, right?" Tricia reminded me.

I sighed. Clearly, I had forgotten. My plan was to take advantage of the unseasonably warm winter day and cut out of work early, leaving closing in the capable hands of my only employee standing beside me at the counter.

"*Crud*," I replied.

"So much for your bike ride in the Bosque," Cedar said, frowning. "Terribly sorry, m'lady."

"Well, I'm not," said Tricia. "This may be the only way I'm going to get you to do something about that lovely gentleman across the square from us."

"Mmm..." purred Cedar theatrically. "Yes. And what *of* said gentleman?"

"Uh, who writes your checks here?" I retorted defensively.

Cedar threw his arms up in protest. "Well, far be it for me to be concerned about the private life of my employer, who takes every opportunity to discuss *mine*," he said backing away, his long blond hair, previously tucked behind his ears, falling into his face as he gave me a mock curtsey. "Whatevs, m'lady."

"Go order some more staff paper. And don't you have a ponytail holder or something?"

He clutched his chest and fell to his knees on the floor, gasping for air. "Did you say, 'ponytail holder'? What am I to you, a seven-year-old girl??"

Garrett walked in with take-out from Del Patio and placed a cup on the countertop for Trisha, stretching his neck to see Cedar on the other side.

"Here you are, babe. Let's eat." As he headed back

toward the gallery, he removed the rubber band around the paper containing his burrito and aimed it at Cedar, who was regaining his footing behind the counter.

"Oh, thanks, dude," Cedar replied, catching it, and securing his long locks atop his head with the rubber band.

"Yeah, no prob, man."

Trisha and I giggled, witnessing the exchange.

"I'll see you at five, hon," she said.

"Cedar shall return to the grunt work," he said, saluting me, then headed to the back.

I walked to my office and stood alone, leaning against the doorway and trying not to think about the possibility of seeing Oscar Cardenas in a few hours. A nervous pang twinged in my gut.

It had been since before Christmas that I'd last seen him.

I really, truly thought we'd had a glorious evening together...clearly, I'd been wrong.

Cedar passed my office on his way back to the front room.

"Hey!" I yelled.

He backstepped to my door, arms full, raising an eyebrow.

"I'll be in here doing some catch-up work awhile. Could you mind the front?"

"No problem, m'lady," he bowed and continued on.

"Meant to ask you..." I hollered after him again. He returned and stood facing me in the doorway, both eyebrows raised this time.

"I haven't heard you mention Lacey in a while. Everything good?"

He leaned against the door frame and exhaled with

a *plbplbp* as the air escaped his lips.

"Ah. *That.*" His gaze averted to the floor. He examined a hinge beside him with his forefinger, balancing the stack in his other arm against his chest. "So I guess there's this new guy..."

Oh good grief, Moll. I'd forgotten that Trish had mentioned Lacey had a friend that she was spending a lot of time with these days—a pre-law student from the College of Santa Fe. At the time, I'd gotten the idea that they were just friends, that he was more interested in her than she was him.

From the look on Cedar's face, apparently that had been an incorrect assumption.

"Yeah," he sighed, "*Pete*, or *Fred* or something? She brought him here on New Year's Eve."

"Oh, that's right. Uh...I think it's Phil."

"Whatever." He shifted into standing, brows briefly furrowing.

"She brought him to your party?"

"Yep."

I gave him a slight frown and cocked my head to the side, not sure if he wanted to discuss the matter further.

"So, sure, everything's good." He nodded after a pause. "Well, duty calls!" He bowed, tipping a non-existent hat to me and smiling, then turned to head to the front, as if the momentary lapse in his disposition had been never glimpsed by either of us.

I heard him humming the tune of "Sad, Beautiful, Tragic" as he walked away, and watched his black-and-white image on the wall monitor above my desk as he strolled across the empty, open floor room to the register, where he now began belting out the lyrics:

We had a beautiful magic love affair,
What a sad beautiful tragic love affair...

I couldn't help but be transported back in time, re-membering my son, Jackson. Cedar had always reminded me of him—good looking, tall, blond, blue eyes. I learned when he was in high school that when he was having "girl trouble," his demeanor changed from his typically easygo-ing manner to a reserved quiet. Instead of talking about it, he did everything in his power *not* to. I had to give him his space. It made my "Mama's heart" ache a bit, listening to Cedar as he went about his work.

...a beautiful magic love affair—
What a sad beautiful tragic, beautiful tragic beau-
tiful—
What we had...

I sighed and grabbed a stack of invoices sitting on my desk, and set about the mindless business of entering data into the computer.
You and me, kid, I mused.
You and me.

My eyes scanned the room as the meeting proceed-ed to get under way.
There was no sign of Oscar.
I sighed to myself, and I could feel Tricia worrying on my behalf. She turned around and glanced at the door from time to time, trying to appear casual. Next to her, Garrett slipped on his readers, pulled out a pen from his

front pocket, and began to take notes on the itinerary we all had received at the door.

"There will be a group of surveyors out the last week of January, set up around the southeast corner of Rio Grande and Central," rattled Sylvia de Herrera, president of the Merchants Association, from the front of the room. "We're going to look at the feasibility of putting in a turning lane just past the Walgreens entrance into the parking lot.

"Now, traffic issues should remain at a minimum during this time, I've been assured by the city, but if you encounter any complaints from your customers, be sure and let me know."

She continued to drone on, and I looked over the minutes, making a note to myself about the post-holiday sale I'd planned for mid-month. I wanted to move out some of our inventory to make room for a Native American CD exhibit I intended to promote in time for Valentine's Day.

Tricia jabbed a hard elbow in my side.

"*Ow!*" I snapped.

The owner of the Rattlesnake Museum turned around and eyeballed me. I flashed a quick smile and he resumed focus on Sylvia.

Tricia was looking over Garrett's shoulder as he continued to jot down notes. But her eyes were wide, and she was oddly smirking.

"*Wha-*" I whispered, then noticed him.

He was picking up literature for the meeting at a table in the back of the room. Oscar glanced around, and seeing an empty chair in our row, headed toward it. I looked down as he directed his gaze down the row, just missing his eyes as they landed on Garrett, then Tricia, then me.

In a moment, a rush of air signaled Oscar had taken his seat. I didn't look up, pretending to be concentrating on note-taking as the droning Sylvia rambled into monotone.

Until Garrett reached across my lap, extending a hand to Oscar.

"Oscar," he whispered.

I looked up and feigned surprise when we made eye contact.

He took Garrett's hand, smiled, and apologized. "Sorry—there weren't any open seats left."

"Good to see you, man," whispered Garrett.

'Sorry'?

Wham! It was a blow to my ego, hitting me squarely in the gut: Oscar Cardenas is apologizing for sitting next to me.

I managed a tight smile and resumed the important business of note-taking.

Sylvia managed to draw out the meeting to an unbelievable hour and forty-five minutes. "Be sure and vote for your favorite color for the gazebo repainting!" she hollered as people began filing out, her pitch and volume rising: "Remember, it's *bright white,* or *Navajo white.* The sample chips are on the table at the back of the room!"

I stood and started to put my jacket on. Tricia pushed past me, trailing Garrett after her by the hand.

"Have you met my husband, Oscar?" she inquired, making her way to the aisle on the other side of him.

I started to explain, "Well yeah, he came in the store a while back—"

"No, I mean—yes, we've met...I wasn't aware that you two were married." Oscar smiled broadly.

"Oh, is that right?" she enthused. "I was sure Molly had mentioned it."

I had gathered my things and now faced him for the first time in weeks. He was standing facing me directly now. I smiled briefly and looked down.

"No," he shook his head. "No, she hadn't mentioned it."

I felt his eyes on me. I started to fidget with my purse strap, digging around inside of it, purposefully not looking him in the eye.

"So, you guys own the art gallery next door?"

"Yes," replied Garrett. "To showcase our daughter's work. She's an up-and-comer. You really should stop in—"

"You know," interrupted Tricia, tapping her wrist, "we've got an artist's demo in the morning and an oils workshop after that—right, hon? Lots to do. We should be going!"

She tugged a bewildered Garrett along. "Good to see you again, Oscar!"

"You, too." He watched them exit, then returned his gaze to me, just before Tricia gave me an exaggerated wink.

I cleared my throat. "Well. So...they're great," I responded awkwardly.

"Yeah," he nodded. We stood in silence as networking shop owners surrounded us shaking hands and visiting amongst themselves.

"So...he's Tricia's husband?"

I nodded.

"Wow, 'cause I thought the two of you..."

I furrowed my brow. "Wait, you thought...Garrett and me?"

He laughed and I joined him. "Uh, *no*. They've been married, like, forever."

"That day I came in the shop and you two were carrying on..."

"Carrying on?"

"You know, you were laughing hysterically about something."

"Hmmm...I see."

"Yeah...that was dumb, huh? Me, thinking that you guys were..."

"Yeah, that was dumb." I nodded, then burst out laughing. "Hey, say...you wanna get some coffee?"

Oscar smiled, that tender, familiar smile so warm it makes me glow. "Very much so." He extended his arm, and I looped mine inside it.

Together we walked outside. "I just need to walk over to the shop first," he said.

The weather was still warm this January evening although completely dark outside, and I felt safe in such proximity to Oscar. My heart was beating fast as we walked without talking, thinking of how the events of the evening had unfolded: This morning I'd practically written the man off, having not seen him in weeks, chalking it up to my lousy luck with men. I'd allowed myself to believe it just wasn't ever going to happen for me, that I would never find the "right" man. "Losers-100, Molly-zero," I had joked, forming the number with my hand in the shape of a circle, to a frowning Tricia.

"Not if you'd get your butt out there and give *someone* a fighting chance!"

105

"Clearly, he's not interested!" I had retorted, frustrated with her annoyance with me. More so, I knew deep inside my heart it was an effort not to feel completely rejected. To protect myself from feeling like the most repulsive, hopeless case. Again.

"Where are you parked?" Oscar asked, unlocking and holding the door of Book It open for me to enter.

"I rode my bike today, with the weather being so great this morning."

Inside, Bon Jovi was belting out *Living on a Prayer* from the radio behind the register counter. Just then, a young woman popped up from behind it balancing a stack of books in her arms. She had thick, shiny, shoulder-length dark hair cut into a bob, and a tailored denim shirt.

"Viejo," she greeted Oscar before looking up to see me standing in front of him. She raised an eyebrow fleetingly, smiling. "Oh, hello."

"Hello," I said turning to look at Oscar.

"Evelyn, this is Molly Lewis. She owns Old Town Music, you know—where Evangelyn is taking piano lessons," he said. "Molly, this is my daughter."

"Ah," she replied, taking a step around the counter toward us. She wore a long suede skirt and matching boots, and placed the stack of books she was carrying beside the register, extending a hand to me. "Nice to meet you, Molly."

Then glancing back at her dad, suddenly there was that spark I recognized, her grin broadening, her eyes shining brightly though almost squeezed shut. They were a deeper, richer brown than her father's, but they resonated with the same mischievous charm.

"Glad to see the old man's making some friends

around here," she said, looking back at me.

I laughed and shook her hand. "It's nice to meet you, Evelyn."

"My daughter's so excited to be starting lessons. And I'll be happy when she can bang out something other than 'Chopsticks' on the keyboard!"

"Where is my *jita?*" inquired Oscar, glancing about the small space.

"Just missed her. Raúl just picked her up. I didn't know when your meeting would be over and I had some sorting still to do here."

"Yeah, we didn't know when it would end, either. It was particularly lengthy tonight," I nodded.

"Glad you took notes," Oscar winked at me, then turned to Evelyn. "Hey, I'll leave you to your sorting then if you don't need me..."

He nodded and there was a pause as the two exchanged looks.

"Oh, yeah, sure—I'm good here. You two go. I'll see you tomorrow morning?"

"Okay," he replied. "Ready?" he asked me, gesturing toward the door with his head.

"Yes."

He held the shop door open for me.

"It was really nice meeting you," Evelyn sang as we headed out into the darkness. "I'll lock up, Dad."

He blew her a kiss. As she took the door from him, I heard her whisper loudly, "Behave yourself, *Viejo.*"

He sheepishly grinned and shook his head, looking at the ground.

"So!" he shrugged, smiling up at me as the shop door closed behind us. "Where to?"

We headed to Garduno's Cantina, just a block away inside the Hotel Albuquerque. By the time we arrived, there were groups of people huddled outside waiting to be seated.

"Uh-oh," I said loudly over the noise of the crowd and the mariachi band playing at a nearby table. "I just realized it's 7 o'clock on a Friday night in Albuquerque..."

Oscar nodded and approached the bubbly, young, auburn-haired hostess.

"How many?" she asked, tossing her waist-length locks around her shoulder and exposing a white, toothy grin. She had deep dimples and a glowing, natural complexion.

"Two," he responded. "How long is the wait?"

"Oh," she said perusing the list and tapping a pen to her bright red lips, "I'd say, an hour and a half?" She stared up at Oscar with wide, expectant eyes. I was overwhelmed by her odious perfume, and one couldn't help notice her blouse was buttoned down low enough to reveal a hot pink bra strap under her black blouse. She gave him a half smile, waiting for a response.

We exchanged looks, eyebrows raised.

"Never mind," he said politely to her. He reached down and grabbed my hand, leading us away from the hustle and bustle, out into the night air once again.

Oscar stopped in front of the Spanish fountain in the hotel courtyard and stood facing me. He held our hands between us, up to his chest. It felt natural, and yet completely electric. I felt alive and giddy. I was also thankful I'd been religious about using a hydrating oil on my hands recently since they become so dry in the winter months...

"This okay?" he asked.

I could only smile. I wanted to step closer to him, this beautiful man staring into my eyes. *How could this be?* How could he possibly want to be with *me?* This man who captures the attention of young women—*gorgeous* young women—what in the world is he doing standing here staring at me??

"Well, so much for that idea." He smiled.

"Tell you what," I said. "There's a cute little place nearby. Follow me."

This time I led him along by the hand. We exited the courtyard and crossed the parking lot, jaywalking to Blake's Lotaburger across the street. I glanced back at him and winked.

"Rebel," he shook his head.

"Right?"

Inside we ordered two coffees and two lotaburgers with green chile, to go.

"Sorry, they don't have red," I told him.

"Then I'll have to live dangerously," he winked.

I tucked the burgers into my bag slung across my chest outside my jacket. I handed Oscar his coffee and took mine, holding it between both hands to warm them, and headed toward the door.

Oscar grinned, a bit confused. "This isn't the 'cute little place' you were referring to?"

I backed into the door to open it and kept walking. "Nope. You coming?"

He followed after me as we strolled down Rio Grande Avenue toward my townhouse. We sipped our coffees and remarked on the unseasonable weather, and the moon in the clear night sky.

"Here we are," I said as we walked up the red brick walkway winding among chamisa and dusty purple sage to the front door. Instead of going inside, I crossed the porch and unlatched the *latilla* gate, leading along the side of the house, to the small back patio. Oscar closed it behind us, and followed the stepping stone path. It led to a porch covered by a small balcony wrapped in wrought iron and flanked with cobalt planters in various shapes and sizes. In the corner of the small yard, a water feature flowed from the high adobe wall above into a wide Talavera tile bird bath. Tucked into a succulent garden beside it was a statue of St. Francis of Assisi I'd purchased years ago at Jackalope in Santa Fe, his outstretched arms alight with birds. A climbing vine crawled across two of the three walls, with the moon casting its light over a large desert willow, bathing the patio in dappled shadows. I pointed to a built-in, cushioned *banco* across from a terracotta *chiminea*.

"Please. Have a seat."

Oscar obliged, nodding. "You're right, this is a *very* cute little place," he breathed, sitting down.

Suddenly, Wolf appeared inside at the patio doors, barking fiercely.

"I'll be right back," I said, shushing the dog as I let myself inside. I flipped on a lamp on the kitchen counter top and grabbed a couple of quilts my mother had made from a large basket on the adjacent living room floor. One was flannel and bordered in soft, southwestern hues, the other in a western motif framed by geometric patterned copper batik. On the way outside, I plugged in the string of mini-white lights that encircled the patio posts, and I tousled the dog's velvety ears.

The sizeable lab bounded joyously toward Oscar.

"This is Wolf," I said, handing him a quilt. "I can put him back inside if you like."

"Aw, he's a beauty," he gushed, rubbing his muzzle and scratching his belly, much to the dog's delight. I walked back inside to grab a lighter and the hamburgers. "So, Wolf, huh?" he called after me.

"Yes," I explained, reappearing to light a fire in the *chiminea*, "as in Wolfgang Amadeus Mozart."

I was pleased it lit quickly. I handed him a burger. Grateful for the warmth, I took a seat next to him and wrapped the quilt tightly around me.

"Ah-ha, Mozart." He smiled, staring at me. *Good Lord, those lovely eyes.* I was continuously startled by them. I took a deep breath and exhaled slowly, uncomfortable in the silent pause.

"What's the matter, don't you like cold burgers?" I said, attempting to fill the quiet. *Relax, Moll...you can do this. He's just a man, like Garrett or Cedar. Or Adonis.*

He looked down at the wrapper in his hand. "Who *doesn't* like cold burgers?"

We both unwrapped ours and started eating, I kept mine mostly under my quilt to keep my hands warm.

"So, Molly Lewis," he stated between bites. "You're *not* married to Garrett."

I nodded, covering my mouth as I attempted to swallow while laughing at the same time.

"Uh, you're looking at the only man in my life," I joked, glancing down at Wolf and patting him on the belly. "And probably the most loyal one I've ever met, aren't you boy?"

He grunted and rolled over for better tummy access.

"Okay, we've established that now," he continued.

"But what other mysteries are there to uncover about Molly Lewis?"

I wiped my mouth with the hamburger wrapper, realizing I didn't have a napkin.

"*Wow,* where to start..." I teased, narrowing my eyes. "There are *so many* mysteries."

He nodded and finished off the last of his coffee, turning to watch me intently.

"Do you want just the facts, or the urban legends, too?"

Oscar lifted his hands and shrugged. "I'm all yours." After the initial sniffing him out, Wolf curled up now and lay at his feet.

Not sure where to begin or how much to share, I started from the point at which I'd begun working as a music teacher, before opening my music store. I shared how much I loved my job, co-workers and students. Not being able to teach my beloved content any more, but rather training students to pass abstract tests and struggling for my professional life, it was time to retire.

"I didn't love it anymore. Unfortunately, that's the trend in education now, and they're losing tons of good, qualified teachers because of politicians who've never stepped foot in a classroom."

"Were you married when you started teaching?"

Relieved that he'd asked and opened that door, I told him about my marriage to Paul: a local churchgoing boy, he dropped out of college before we married and never went back, and was content to live in that small town on the Eastern New Mexico plains forever; that it was like pulling teeth to get him to contemplate leaving the tiny corner of the world where his farming family were rooted as deeply to the earth as the crops they planted in the dust, decade after decade, praying for rain. That I'd grown to realize it wasn't the size of the town that made it small, but rather their seemingly collective fear of anything "other."

I described our reluctant move to Albuquerque—I had wanted to move to Colorado, so this was our compromise; I was perfectly happy coming "home" as I'd been raised here in the Rio Grande valley, and my parents were still here. Then, five years after moving from the dusty plains, we had our son, followed two years later, exactly, by our baby girl.

"Then one day," I paused, breathing deeply, "after knowing in my heart for months that there was something wrong...one day I received a phone call."

It was from an angry man I didn't know, a husband demanding to know information about his wife and Paul.

"With that call came the beginning of the end of my marriage."

"I'm so sorry. How did you make it through all of that, with two little kids *and* teaching?"

I sighed. "With extremely strong family and friends. My parents were my oaks. And of course, my faith."

Oscar nodded toward the statue in the succulent garden. "I didn't realize you were Catholic."

"Oh, my Francis," I smiled. "I'm not. Just New Mexican. I attend City Life, downtown?"

He nodded.

"So, Oscar Cardenas," I turned and faced him, readjusting the quilt around me. "Your turn."

The fire was beginning to die down, the warm light illuminating the features of his face. It softened his already-pleasant expression as he stared into the light. He was angelic.

"Evelyn's mom and I were high school sweethearts," he began. "She didn't want to have kids, but I talked her into it. Then after Evelyn and Raphael, her brother, were born, Dolores said she wanted to go to college. I'd already graduated from New Mexico Highlands with an undergrad in business and was working on my Master's—we were living in Las Vegas, New Mexico, at the time. Not only did she want to go to college, she wanted to go to medical school. So, she completed her bachelor's there at High-lands, in three years—she was *brilliant*—then applied to medical school at UNM. Well, she was accepted, and we moved to the city.

"Our kids were still little, and she was definitely focused on her education and her career. So I worked as a stay-at-home dad during the day—oh, that made my fa-ther happy, you can imagine! A proud, traditional Mexican man?—anyway, on top of that, I had to make an income, but job opportunities just weren't presenting themselves to a man with little experience, and my hours working at home. So I took two jobs in the evenings over the next six years."

The firelight was flickering, the last flames burning into embers, flaring up, then dying down again.

"Are you cold?" I inquired.

"I'm fine," he smiled up at me.

"Go on."

"Well, after she was settled into her internship, she left us."

His face was drawn now, his eyes tired. He man-aged a slight smile. "It was the hardest thing I've ever done, raising two children after their mother walked out on us. After that, it was very difficult trying to find a regular job in the business world. I had kind of missed the 'window,' but after many years of climbing the ladder, I'd reached a plateau, professionally and emotionally. Once my children were raised, I decided to do something *I* had always wanted to do. I took a leap of faith and put everything I had into opening a bookstore." He turned to me, looking spent but satisfied.

"Sounds like you made the right move."

He closed his eyes and shrugged. "I sure hope so," he mused.

"What happened to Dolores?" I inquired quietly.

"Dolores met a psychiatrist and moved to Portland. They got married and divorced within a few years, and last I heard she still lives there."

"That's it? She just walked out of her children's lives?"

Oscar nodded slowly. "She took care of her financial responsibility, but she never attempted to contact them, ever again. I guess that's why my children and I are *very* close to this day."

I placed another log on the fire as Oscar continued. He told me about his son, a dentist living in Baltimore, engaged to be married though he hadn't yet set a date. How he hoped both of his children found genuine happiness in their relationships. I agreed that was what I wanted for mine, as well.

We talked about our failures and successes, the common experiences of single parenthood, at times wiping moisture from our eyes. It was refreshing and endearing to see a man, a strong, proud man, shed tears. To me, he was the definition of a *real* man.

Together, we mused over stories of raising boys, the trepidation that came along when our daughters began dating, the sorrow accompanying all the firsts, and lasts: The graduations and driver's licenses, college applications, the marriage of his daughter.

"Was that hard for you, after what you'd been through?"

"Yes and no," he recalled. "Of course it was terrifying that she might be cursed with 'the sins of the mother,' so to speak."

"I understand that," I nodded. "I mean, that's their experience."

"Yes, but I also realized that I'd raised her to not walk away from things. They were never allowed to quit something once they'd started," Oscar explained. "So I had to trust in that, that she'd make wise decisions."

I discovered through our conversation that while Oscar had been raised in a strict Catholic environment, adhering to catechism and all of the religious ceremonies along with a large extended family, somewhere along the way he stopped attending Mass.

"When Dolores left, everything I was raised to believe in the Roman Catholic Church seemed hollow to me. I think I lost my belief in God. I'm not proud of it, but I do still question if God is real."

I nodded, remembering those times when I'd felt abandoned by God when it appeared Paul's life was going on happily without me, as if I'd never existed at all.

"I know how you feel. I never lost my faith in God, but I sure was mad as hell at Him."

He gave a tired laugh. "You seem like such a joyful person, Molly. I remember thinking that from the first time I met you, when you came in my shop singing like nobody's business!"

I held a hand over my eyes and shook my head at the memory. "Mercy...please don't remind me...."

He laughed, then looked at me with a sincere expression. "It was beautiful."

I looked up at him and paused.

"Really?"

"*Really.*"

I smiled, exhausted yet deliriously happy.

Oscar yawned into a cupped hand and searched the sky with his eyes. He looked at me, then pointed up toward the east. The formerly ebony sky was slowly turning to deep purple. Somewhere along the bosque, roosters could be heard announcing daybreak into the early morning.

He smiled sleepily, his caramel eyes rimmed now with a tint of pink. He rubbed them and rose to his feet.

"This has been enchanting." Oscar breathed, inhaling the cool morning air in the quiet dawn appearing on the horizon above the Sandías. On the exhale he started laughing.

I smiled curiously, wrapping the quilt tightly around my neck. "Yes...?"

He shook his head. "I'm about to see my daughter in just a few hours," he laughed. "Boy, is she gonna think I've been misbehaving."

We both burst out laughing at the thought. The two of us "old folks" having stayed out all night, visiting the night away. That we had done something illicit was hysterical, and the thought doubled us over in our state of delirium.

Finally, we caught our breath.

I stood up. "*Who's* the rebel now?"

"Thank you," Oscar said as he folded up his quilt and placed it on the banco cushion. He bent down and stroked a sleeping Wolf's fur, then turned and headed down the stepping stones toward the side gate. I followed behind in his footsteps, and when he reached the end of the path he turned and moved toward me, taking the quilt by the edges around my neck in his hands and pulling me close to him. I looked up to his face, into his soft eyes, his lashes blinking lazily. He traced my cheek with the tips of his fingers and brushed some loose hair behind my ear. It felt so comfortable, so natural to be this close to him. My body went limp and warm, and I leaned my head against his chest. I could easily imagine inviting him inside; it was so tempting to think of having this man in my bed, even though I knew I wouldn't. I wasn't about to risk losing something wonderful and meaningful. Not after this night. I would wait. This man, this *gentleman*, was too important to me.

I breathed against his chest the sweet smell of his leather jacket, of Oscar. I was intoxicated.

"Stay warm," he whispered and pressed his lips against my head, then taking my hands and lifting them to his mouth, closing his eyes when I looked into his. He kissed them and turned to go. I ached watching him walk away. My insides were combusting, and I felt the flush of my cheeks.

On the way inside, I whistled for Wolf to come and picked up the quilt Oscar had just been enveloped in, holding it tightly to my chest. Gloriously, it contained his beautiful musky scent, and I breathed it in. Upstairs in my bedroom, the sunlight now peeking in through the blinds on the balcony, I undressed. Wrapping myself in his quilt I crawled into bed, blissfully drifting off into sweet slumber.

TWELVE

1891

She took his breath away in her pale, rose-colored, Atlas belle-toilette gown with festooned sleeves custom tailored for her in Paris, its pleated taffeta skirt flowing over her hips. It had a simple lace collar, with her rosary beads tucked underneath, her graceful neck adorned with a black velvet cameo choker given to her by her father just for the occasion. At the pinnacle of the stairs, she was the very vision of Aphrodite greeting her people from high atop Mt. Olympus as the crowd gathered outside her front door drew nearer, peering inside, voices hushed, expressions expectant, awaiting a glimpse of her entrance into the exclusive, polished world of high society.

Pilar was completely at ease, having practiced this moment in her mind over and over again, smiling back at the adoring crowd; she knew she was captivating, with all eyes on her, and felt a confident, heady rush.

Gathered at the base of the staircase were her parents, Onofre stoically on Mariana's left, and Padre Julien to her right, along with renowned photographer William Cobb. With a snap of her ecru lace-gloved hand, Pilar unfurled a fan emblazoned with claret roses and trimmed in coral satin ribbon. Placing her left hand on the finial crowning the wood banister, she awaited the nod from her mother signaling her descent.

Mariana, her heart pounding, locked her gaze on her father, Florencio, who was poised beneath the parapet with a violin tucked under his chin, a small group of mariachis flanking him. He winked, and she gave a slight audible sigh, then turned to Father Faustino, whose elbow, draped through hers, she squeezed. She returned her gaze to her daughter and flashed her a shaky smile.

The padre turned to the waiting crowd.

"Ladies and gentlemen, on behalf of our Holy Father in heaven who looks down on this, His Daughter, from on high and with whom He is pleased and offers His eternal blessing through the Blessed Virgin; and of her parents, señor and señora Juan Onofre Vega, and in the presence of all of you—her beloved friends and family—I present to you, señorita Pilar Maria Juanita Vega. *Con mucho amor, hoy en adelante, en el nombre de Jesucristo y Dios misericordioso.*"

At Mariana's nod, Pilar slowly stepped down.

Papacio lightly, fluidly dragged the horsehair bow across the face of his weathered fiddle. A mournful ballad slowly emerged, enchanting the audience. They watched as, step by step, she made her sure descent. Misty-eyed, her mother, with a prepared handkerchief, dabbed the corners of her eyes as the solo violin wept its lonely melody.

Reaching the wooden floor at the base of the stairs, Pilar took a few steps forward, her eyes scanning the rapt crowd as she breathed in the moment. They were all watching her—*as if their lives depended on it!* she mused.

He is out there right now, somewhere, and he will never *forget this...how I look at this very moment; he will remember me, just like this, for the rest of his life!*

Pilar took a deep breath. Placing one foot carefully behind her and bending at the knee, she reached around for the base of her gown with her left hand. Bringing it cascading forward, where it pooled before her, she curtsied; her right hand still clutching the fan, she brought it to her lowered face, all the while keeping her wrist in motion. Then slowly, slowly—as she'd rehearsed—she rose to stand as her grandfather's serenade came to a close.

William Cobb, his head tucked under the camera's black hood, gave the muffled instructions for the impending portrait: "Hold it right there—*don't move!* On the count of three..." After signaling with his fingers came the pop and crack of the illuminating flash bulb. "*Veeery* nice..." He cooed from below, then emerging, stood upright, nodding with a broad smile.

As if the stunned crowd had forgotten their

place, they now erupted in applause. Pilar bowed her head and smiled, ever the goddess accepting the praise of her immortals.

At his leading, Florencio roused the mariachis, costumed in the garb of Mexican peasant farmers, in an upbeat, traditional folk song. At its cessation, the guitar, stringed bass, and trumpet players stepped forward in preparation for the traditional father-daughter dance expected at a *quinceañera*.

And so began their waltz: Her father, handsome this evening in his black vest, cowboy hat, and boots, stepped forward in a brief bow, tilting his hat to her. She nodded and reciprocated with a small curtsy, then offered her hand to him, the now-closed fan dropping in place, fastened around her wrist. He stepped closer and took his daughter in his arms, where she stood on tiptoe to whisper in his ear: "Just like we practiced, Daddy."

As the music swelled, they spun gracefully in the foyer of the grand house, sweeping back and forth, as their guests whispered and smiled, sipping their drinks while the sun began to set behind them. The brilliant western sky was awash in strips of vibrant salmon and indigo. The brooding cottonwoods were now casting shifting, effervescent shards of slate over the home's façade, stretching, crawling inside as fingertips desiring to grasp its whirling contents, the ebbing sunlight twinkling through their shimmering leaves.

At the conclusion of the dance, there was more applause mingled with laughter and cheers. Father Faustino gave a pleased smile to Mariana and patted her arm. Her chin quivered as she returned a smile with a sigh, her shoulders giving in to a great heave while she dabbed again at her eyes.

The mariachis gathered their things and retreated out the back entrance of the house. Mariana turned to face her guests, who were momentarily quieted; Onofre and Pilar joining her on the veranda. Father Faustino closed the doors gently behind them.

"Thank you all so much for being here. This is a very proud day for us," she stopped and smiled, feeling the emotion in her wavering voice and afraid she might lose her composure, continued quickly: "Won't you join us around back for some food and dancing?"

Once again the clapping and boisterous laughter resumed as a huddle of preening, giggling young ladies descended on the belle of the ball, as laughing hyenas might on carrion. They stroked her hair, grasping for her hands and examining her gown, leaning in close-ly to whisper in each other's ears. Meanwhile lines of party goers snaked around the veranda, making their way to the back yard as directed by Mariana and the padre (*This way, please! Yes, just around the crepe myrtles...*).

Soon the mariachi band was in full swing again, having situated themselves around a set of several hay bales in the far corner of the yard, the syncopated rhythm of an added accordion, played by Papacio, competing with the beat of the stringed bass. Pilar looked out from around the bobbing heads of her admirers, her eyes scanning the horizon in attempt to find *him*. A few guests still lingered in the front yard.

"Your dress, Pilar...well I've never seen a fabric with this *sheen* before!"

"From the finest Parisian boutiques, I'm sure, isn't it?"

"This fan—I've simply got to have it—"

Then, in the distance she spied him standing there, practically in silhouette, under the canopy of the enormous trees with her brother Joaquin and some other young men, as the young ladies around her jabbered on. She was certain he'd seen her, too; in fact, she just *knew* that right then, he was looking directly at her. The residual light from the sun behind him made it official; none of the other boys in the valley had hair like his, practically angelic, the fading sunlight infusing it like a golden halo.

A half-smile curled on her lips. She looked back at the gaggle of peacocks surrounding her in their pastel gowns and finely braided and curled hair.

"Come on, girls!" she announced, pulling them and trotting off in the direction of the music. "Let's *dance*."

Oil lamps hung high in the stately branches

above the heads of revelers celebrating on the accommodating lawn below, where wide planks of plywood had been assembled together to form a large, rectangular dance floor. It was encircled by high-back oak chairs, and at its four corners, posts had been erected and laced together with rope from which dangled multicolored paper lanterns. A warm, effervescent glow cast its spell over one and all, while cotton shedding overhead wafted wraith-like around them.

The feast was impressive, stretched out on heavy wooden tables and dotted with massive cobalt vases brimming with sunflowers atop brightly striped *sarapes*. Each table was covered with half-empty baskets of corn tortillas and clay pots of salsas and spicy sauces; lining the perimeter of the yard, the festive tables ran the length of the statuesque, tin-roofed barn situated a few hundred yards away. By now, the guests had moved on to the desserts, having consumed untold amounts of posole, tamales, frijoles, and of course— sangría.

Mariana made the rounds among them with Father Faustino, exchanging hugs, accepting well wishes and laughter—in between trips to the kitchen refilling empty platters and trays, with Nicolas trailing behind them much of the night proudly toting a pitcher of ice water half his size and refilling the glasses of guests kind enough to lower them down to him as he passed by. Occasionally a generous recipient slipped small

127

coins into his hand, or if his hand was occupied with a pitcher, his jacket pocket.

Most of the time, he was unseen, meandering among the forest of grown-ups on his lawn, but could be *heard* making his way about the mass of folks making merry, the coins jostling along in his pockets revealing his presence.

At times he attended to grateful band members, who mussed his uncharacteristically copper hair after he brought them plates full of guacamole and taquitos to share between songs, returning the wink of his grandfather before he was gone again in a flash.

Onofre was no doubt in the carriage house, thought Mariana, smoking cigars and regaling his three brothers—all successful ranchers and businessmen, one the village mercantile owner—and boyhood buddies with tales of his prize-winning Appaloosa quarter horses. There was a very good chance they were indulging in a bottle of the 100% agave Mexican mezcal he kept on hand out there in the event of special occasions such as this, where the moment called for some boisterous machismo—and thinking his wife wasn't the wiser.

"Mrs. Shannon," Mariana greeted her neighbor with a warm smile. The woman remained in her seat, the scratchy lace collar of her dark, heavy dress buttoned up high on her throat.

Most of the women in attendance tonight embraced one another with kisses on the cheeks; not so

128

with Daniella Shannon. She thought it beneath her to take part in such an openly uncouth gesture, especially still being on informal terms as one ought with an acquaintance. It reminded her of how the Italians greeted her—a perfect stranger!—when she visited Venice during winter holiday some years ago, all bare fingers and expectant kisses. *Filthy.*

In response to her greeting she gave Mariana a curt smile, attempting to discreetly dab her brow, covered in a sheen of perspiration, with a balled-up kerchief.

Theophilus stood and shook the hand of the priest at his neighbor's side. "Padre! Excellent to see you, sir." Then turning to take Mariana's hand: "Job well done, I do say! Just capital, my dear."

Father Julien smiled warmly, then recognizing a clean-shaven gentleman at the next table sporting a salt and pepper goatee, stepped over and placed a hand on his back. "Señor Shannon, have you been introduced to my friend, Mr. Fred Harvey?"

Theophilus extended a hand to the gentleman now rising to his feet in acceptance of the gesture.

"I am certainly aware of the name, but I have not yet had the pleasure of making his acquaintance!" The two men grasped hands for a hearty shake. "Your reputation precedes you, sir."

"As does yours, Mr. Shannon," he replied in a distinctively British accent, having removed the cigar he previously brandished between his teeth. "I understand that you and I hail from the same neck of the woods, as it were."

"Indeed, we do!"

"Well, I insist on having you and your lovely wife over at your earliest convenience so that we can get to know one another properly."

"And there it is, the legendary Harvey hospitality I've heard so much about," Theophilus grinned. "Well, there you have it then, darling," he said, glancing toward Daniella, who was fanning herself rapidly. "We shall decidedly take you up on it."

"Very good," replied Fred. He turned to Mariana and kissed her gloved hand. "Now, if we could just talk this young lady into coming onto to the staff at the Alvarado House...her cooking is legendary in these parts."

She smiled. "*Muchas gracias.*"

"Stuff and nonsense, darling, we couldn't afford her!" Fred's wife, Betty, leaned into the conversation. "I most certainly agree, my dear. I simply must know your secret—these lime cakes are *divine.*"

Uncomfortable with the praise, Mariana laughed and averted the attention back onto her guests. "Once again, it's very good to have you"—glancing at Daniella—"*both* here."

Feeling forced into a corner where conversing was the only alternative now, Daniella looked about the yard. "My dear, wherever is your service this evening?"

At a loss, Mariana stared blankly into the pale green eyes accented under Daniella Shannon's upswept strawberry blonde hair. The stiff woman was battling streams of perspiration trickling from her hairline tucked beneath a tight-fitting boater hat.

"*Pardon*?" Mariana inquired of Mr. Shannon.

He opened his mouth to answer her, only to have his wife speak for him.

"Your *servants*, darling. Where are they?" she asked again, glancing around the lush landscape, then returning to her with raised eyebrows.

"Oh, *sí*," replied Mariana. "We don't have servants."

Now Daniella looked quizzically back at her. "You mean to say you don't *take service*?"

Theophilus looked at his wife, and back at Mariana.

It had sounded more like a statement to Mariana than an inquiry. "No. Well, we have hired hands who work for Onofre...the men who work the fields and the orchards."

Daniella continued to stare at her in incredulous disbelief. "Well, you can't *possibly*—"

"Yes, darling," interrupted her husband. "Mrs. Vega is an outstanding chef, isn't she? Why, she made

131

not only our dinner, but these scrumptious little confections, as well, didn't you, my dear?" He held up a fork impaling the moist, spongy cake.

Mariana laughed and protested, shaking her head. "No—" she started but was interrupted by her neighbor.

"You *see*, Theophilus? Why else would they have servants' quarters?"

"...My father," Mariana continued, "he helps me in the *cocina*. I could've never cooked all of this by *myself*," she giggled. "He lives there," she added, gesturing toward the carriage house.

Daniella Shannon looked right past Mariana Vega, *through* her really, as she did most of the people from this primitive little valley. Finally returning her gaze she managed a quiet, "Oh," then adding in a risen pitch, "*charming*."

Father Faustino bid a farewell bow to the table as they moved on to guests seated nearby. In all the years he'd known her, it had never ceased to amaze the priest—a good judge of character, he felt—how Mariana never allowed others to ruffle her feathers, if indeed she realized Daniella Shannon's words were intended to harm rather than praise.

And he was fairly certain she knew, very well, her neighbor's intent. However, one would never know it from the eternally angelic expression on Mariana's face. In fact, it had been many years ago that she had

132

made up her mind that she would not allow the judgment of a few steal her joy. It was that internal peace, thought Father Faustino, that made her so very lovely.

The girls assembled around Pilar on the back veranda, having already indulged in both some dancing (those who were over age fourteen) and copious eating, reclining on the assorted array of cushioned wicker furniture, fans waving, bouts of whispering mingled with bursts of laughter.

Pilar absentmindedly stroked the velvety orange fur of the Vegas' tabby, Havana, curled up in her lap. Her thoughts were elsewhere.

Why hasn't he asked me to dance yet?

"Mmm…" sighed a heavyset girl dressed in a gown matching Havana's coat, her plate piled with Mexican chocolates balanced on her knees. She wiped her glistening lips with a napkin, her crocheted gloves abandoned on the wicker side table to her right. "These are *so* yummy!"

"Aren't they?" agreed the platinum-haired Elza Shannon.

Elza was the very definition of *culture*, having had her coming-out party within the upper echelon of society circles in London not yet two years ago. There had been dukes and earls on the guest list—even their royal highnesses the Earl and Countess of Wessex— among those in attendance. The chiffon seafoam gown she wore on that most decadent of evenings was her

choice of attire for tonight, as well, much to the chagrin of Daniella Shannon. ("Mother, no one here has
ever seen me in this gown before. Why on earth should
I purchase a brand-new one? I mean, really, where
would I wear it again?")

But Elza was unlike her pretentious mother
("Well, you're certainly right about that, darling—
they most definitely have not seen anything of the sort
here!"). Pilar had never witnessed her new neighbor
and friend, *practically royalty* she'd presumed, putting
on airs. At this, Pilar Vega was highly disappointed.

However, it wasn't Elza Shannon whom she had
any interest in impressing.

She sighed and rolled her eyes, simultaneously
shoving the sleeping cat from its perch as she stood up.
"Better be careful, Henrietta," she said, smiling lazily
and looking down at her rotund friend, "or you'll never
be able to fit into your *vestido de quinceañera.*"

Still chewing, the girl gave a nervous giggle,
then wiped her mouth again. As she swallowed, she
watched Pilar grab Elza's hand as they turned to walk
to the opposite side of the porch. Henrietta replaced the
gloves she'd laid on the side table with her plate and
began the impossible task of pulling them back on in
the sticky heat of the night air.

On the other side of the veranda, Pilar pouted.

"I'm bored," she sighed, looking down and
tapping one of the railing spindles with the toe of her

Richelieu boot.

Elza grabbed Pilar's other hand, so that she was now facing her lovely, ebony-haired friend. She smiled, the corners of her ice-blue eyes crinkling a bit.

"Well, we certainly can't have that, now, can we?"

From across the lawn, Oliver Shannon and Joaquin Vega were stealing cups full of sangría from the enormous crystal punch bowl while the grown-ups nearby were engrossed in conversation.

Pleased with himself, the light-haired young man slammed his emptied cup (his sixth, or was it his *seventh?)* on the table with a *thud*, causing his inebriated friend beside him to convulse with laughter, his shoulders heaving as he tried to catch his breath and regain his unsure footing. Oliver could see his sister on the porch across the way, conversing with the intoxicatingly stunning woman of the hour.

Oblivious to Elza, Pilar had spied him staring at her, too, and smiled in her flirtatious way, her hips swiveling slightly now in an anxious rhythm. She looked down, then back up to the chatty Elza, then stole a glance directly at him again.

Blimey, what a vamp! Whether it was the sight of her or the alcohol that had his blood racing, emboldening him to take action, Oliver couldn't be sure. But he did know one thing with certainty: he *was going* to muster the courage to dance with Pilar Vega before the evening was over.

He stood there a moment with his thumbs tucked into his vest pockets, then slapped Joaquin on the chest, getting his attention. "I say, it's high time we give the ladies something to gossip about, don't you?"

Joaquin followed his gaze up the porch steps to the two young women standing at its top.

"*Hell*, yes!" he said, a bit too boisterously, as he received the disapproving look of an elderly woman from the village parish seated nearby. He gave her an apologetic tip of his hat, then returned his gaze to the radiant Elza, her alabaster skin breathtaking beneath the soft glow of the lantern-lit porch.

"*My*, but she's a saucy minx," shouted Oliver over the vociferous music and merrymaking, as the two began to wind their way through the landscape of chairs and dancers.

Joaquin paused to momentarily regain focus on his friend, then hauled off and punched him on the shoulder, barely hitting his target.

"*Ow!* What was that for?" chortled Oliver, rubbing his arm.

Joaquin nodded toward the veranda. "That's my *sister* you're talking about"—looking around this time—"*pendejo!*"

Oliver gave a belly laugh and continued making his way through the crowd. "I take it that's not a term of endearment, *amigo*!"

Joaquin followed behind him, shaking his head and chuckling. He was dizzy, and the ground was starting to spin. He closed his eyes tightly for a moment, and realized he'd bumped into something—a little girl was looking up at him. Her dance partner, Rico Ruiz, was steadying her.

"Are you okay?" Rico asked her.

"Um-hmm," the little girl nodded. Rico looked at Joaquin, who appeared a little green around the gills. He posed the question to him as well.

"So sorry—" he slurred his words. Rico caught him by the arm before he could teeter away.

"*¿Estás bien, hombre?*"

His brow furrowed, Joaquin jerked his arm away. He stared up at Rico, challengingly. *"Bien,"* he restated, posture softening now. *"Hombre."* He nodded and grinned at him and kept walking.

Rico, who had been popular tonight with the elementary school girls, watched Pilar's brother head toward the veranda, trailing Oliver Shannon. Oliver had hopped up the porch stairs, two steps at a time, bowing before Elza and Pilar. He watched as Elza stepped back, and the golden-haired boy stepped closer to Pilar, his hand outstretched.

She took it.

Rico felt the air being knocked out of his gut. He reached down and patted the shoulder of his dismayed-looking young friend, and walked away from

137

the dance floor to an arrangement of empty chairs gathering cotton beneath one of the shedding trees.

As he bent to sit, he exhaled deeply, his full cheeks deflating. He'd watched her tonight as she'd danced with her grandfather, with Nicolas, even several friends of his from the parish. But somehow, this was different; something had noticeably changed in her expression just now. Something in her demeanor... how she, smiling, had averted her gaze from *him* when he drew near, biting her bottom lip briefly—those full, blood-red lips.... Unlike those tarts in town in the red-light district near the railroad tracks, who brightly painted on their wry smiles and smoothed rouge over their cheeks, Pilar hadn't the need for any of that—she was naturally pretty without it—but of course, not just *pretty*, she was the most splendidly captivating woman he'd laid eyes on in his entire life.

Oliver was escorting her down the stairs now, leading her by the raised hand. People had stopped their dancing and visiting and were making way for her on the dance floor.

The mariachis played "Desierto Rosa Blanca," her grandfather on the fiddle again. Rico had to give it to Oliver: The grace with which he moved with her so fluidly over the lawn was practically *equine*, the likes of which he'd seen only in the graceful, exquisite movement of the horses he looked after and held in such high regard. It appeared as if they were gliding on

138

air. With each turn, he could see a glimpse of her back where her dress dipped and the hook and eyes came together, just above where Oliver's hand rested around the crook of her waist, her skin milky cinnamon.

Soon, others joined them again, and his view of her was obliterated.

He could still see Joaquin, who was now making his way down the veranda steps, Elza Shannon on his arm. At the top, he lost his balance and skidded on the heel of his boot to the safety of the next step, concern showing on the face of his would-be dance partner. He laughed and patted her dainty-laced hand resting on his forearm, and continued on to the lawn cautiously. There, they blended into the waltzing mob.

Suddenly, to collective gasps, the dancers parted, and Joaquin Vega appeared alone and bent over, hands on his knees.

The once undulating crowd was making a hasty retreat about him. A few feet away stood the erect and pale-faced Elza, staring wide-eyed at the ground before her, arms frozen and bent, fingers splayed, palms to the heavens. Some of the women covered their faces with handkerchiefs supplied by their partners escorting them from the scene.

By now the music had stopped, as had the jovial chatting of the evening's guests, everyone bewildered and unsure of what had just transpired on the dance floor. In unison, they turned at the brusque entrance of

Onofre Vega, who had been standing on the far side of the yard, now charging across the lawn like *el toro* advancing on *el matador*. He had only just arrived at the festivities a few songs prior from the carriage house, with his brothers in tow.

In an instant he had his teenage son by the collar of his shirt, and dragged him—half walking, half stumbling—to the barn. Before they could enter, Joaquin retched again, this time spewing the sour contents of his belly onto his father's boots.

The crowd then turned its gaze to Mariana Vega, who was staring, mouth agape, into the distance after her husband and son. Brows furrowed and her heart racing, she stood there, paralyzed and not knowing what else to do.

On the lawn there remained only the stunned Elza—still in stiff pose—and Oliver, his arm still encircling Pilar's waist, hers still on his shoulder. She covered her mouth with her free hand as the gaze of her guests volleyed to and fro between her mother and herself.

Rage began to roil in Pilar's gut as everything and everyone in her midst had come to a screeching halt, her utter humiliation rising to a searing level as she felt a wave of nausea sweep over her. She was horrified.

Pilar marched toward Mariana. *"This was* my *night!"* she screamed at her helpless mother. *"How* dare *he?!*"

Overcome by humiliation, Pilar gathered her skirts and ran for the house as quickly as her feet could carry her.

Having snatched the potato sack that former-ly housed his violin and instructing the stringed bass player—"*On my mark*!"—Papacio was coming from his hay bale perch in the corner of the lawn, when his granddaughter glided past him in hasty retreat. He dropped his arms to his sides and stood watching her briefly, then glancing at Mariana continued to the shad-owy spot on the lawn in front of Elza and, folding the potato sack in half, covered the mess before her.

He then addressed the gawking crowd.

"¡Please, everyone, *señores y señoras!* We've had only a minor setback," he laughed. "Come," he gestured to the grand tables around them, still laden with food, "and enjoy *más fiesta*!"

For a fleeting moment, violent, echoing bellows could be heard coming from the direction of the barn. At this, Florencio waved furiously to the mariachis, who struck up another high-stepping folk song.

"*Santa ma gania,*" he mumbled to himself, then turned to look at his daughter, still frozen on the other side of the yard. Standing beside her, Father Fausti-no whispered something in her ear. She gave a slight nod, and smiled at her guests, some of whom were still curiously eyeballing her, and departed to the house in search of her daughter. The priest then raised out-stretched arms, warmly inviting the partygoers to resume their visiting and feasting, a successful attempt in which to remove the focus from his beloved friend and back onto the festivities at hand.

As the beat of the band pounded once again into the night, and a few dancers began to filter out to the lawn, Daniella Shannon marched toward her teenage twins—careful to avoid the potato sack on the ground—and addressed her daughter, now in the comforting arms of her brother.

"*Please,* tell me that you did not get anything on your gown!" she hissed through a clenched jaw. Elza could barely look up at her mother. Oliver handed her a silk handkerchief from an inside pocket of his vest. She accepted it and dabbed the corners of her eyes, then pulled away and faced her mother angrily.

"No, *Mother*. My gown is fine."

Daniella was visibly relieved, sighing deeply. "We are leaving. *Now!*"

Elza stepped around her and raced away.

"For God's sake," Daniela spat, now addressing her son, "why can you never show any sense of *decorum?*"

"Of course, Mother," Oliver retorted sarcastically, with a laugh, "it is *I* who need to learn to control my liquor."

Daniella pointed the end of her closed fan in his

face. "You *will* learn to control yourself in a manner that is respectful and decent, do you understand?" She lowered the fan and composed herself, her eyes scouring the newly assembled dance partners nearby them. "We may not be in Cambridge anymore, but this family will retain a sense of *standards* in this savage place, I can *assure you of that.*"

She smoothed the bodice of her dark dress and caught her breath, tugging to straighten each of the tight sleeves at her wrists, then turned on her heel for home.

Somewhere in the dark and early morning hours after his sister's fifteenth birthday party, Joaquin was startled awake in a sweat and sat upright in the back of one of his father's wagons in the carriage house. Blinking as if coming to from a trance, and feeling the weight of a heavy blanket surrounding his body, he scrambled to his feet, stumbling backward but managing to catch himself on the tailgate of the wagon before going over the side.

He was suddenly aware of the fact that he was alone in the pounding silence of the stifling summer night, and as he realized that there was, in fact, no blanket on or anywhere near him, he began to pant breathlessly, feeling through the darkness with his hands and feet, his head whirling as images from the previous night began to hazily resurface.

Straining to see about him, Joaquin peeled off his wet shirt and slung it to the floor. Swirling in the air, overhead appeared nebulous aphotic vapors. They began to form demonic shapes, sparking and flashing in and out of the wooden planks of the ceiling. Derelict and screeching, the necropolis legion dove toward him before vanishing into the walls and floor around him, then reappeared again and again.

"What do you want with me?" He attempted to scream but merely managed a breathy whisper, tearing haphazardly at the inky images with his fingers.

Joaquin's head pulsated, white pain slicing through his brain like knives, his gut broiling with the remnants of the prior evening's indulgences. He stumbled backward into the floor of the wagon, his back striking the wood and sending him writhing, as splinters pierced the flesh still raw from his father's beating. Unable to catch his breath, and mustering the remaining strength he had, Joaquin jumped over the side of the wagon and dove beneath it, his eyes darting to and fro in search of the sinister shadows that taunted him. He felt a suffocating, nefarious presence about him as he attempted to slow his racing heartbeat.

The stifling summer heat pounded in his ears as he waited.

Silence.

He once again resumed normal breathing, and after what seemed forever, Joaquin emerged from underneath the wagon and stood on the dirt floor of the carriage house. He shook his head and began cursing under his breath.

He made his way through the darkness to the door. Hurling it open, he stood in the doorway and took a deep breath, relieved at the sight of a sliver of the moon in the night sky, and inhaled the sobering, cool breeze. He left the door ajar, which lit the carriage house well enough for him to find a path to the cabinet containing his father's alcohol. Feeling hastily above his head for the mezcal he knew awaited him on an upper shelf, he knocked over a bottle of liquor, sending it shattering on the countertop below, then splashing sticky liquid on the earthen floor at his feet. At last he grasped the treasure he was seeking, loosened the lid, and emptied its contents down his throat, the burn of it as he swallowed the only thing giving him a semblance of peace in the remaining hours before dawn.

THIRTEEN

Present day

"So, did your daughter give you a hard time this morning?"

On the other end of the line, Oscar exhaled with a delayed laugh.

"Poor guy, you sound exhausted."

I was grateful that Cedar had convinced me he needed more hours after the holidays, and that I needed some time off. It had felt lazy to sleep in and not get out of bed until after noon.

"Yeah," he sighed. "I am. Guess I can't keep up with you young party animals."

I laughed. "Well, what you need is a good night's sleep then. Listen, I'll let you go, and you go to bed."

"Okay," he said, stifling a yawn. "I'll take you up on that. But I just wanted to call and tell you...it was worth it. Today was exhausting, but last night was wonderful."

I felt a rush of adrenaline pulse through my veins, taking my breath away. I was at a loss for words.

"Anyway, call you tomorrow?"

"Yes, that'd be great," I managed.

"I'd love to take you on a *real* date. But maybe not so late at night," he laughed.

"I'd love that, as well, Oscar."

"Bye, Molly."

The next night, I was locking up the store when I glanced across the plaza toward *Book It*. Even knowing Oscar wasn't there, I couldn't help being drawn toward that side of the plaza, to this place he'd put his heart and soul into and where he spent much of his time. He'd taken the day off and reported that he'd had a good night's rest when he phoned me at noon. We'd made a lunch date for the next day, and I couldn't wait to see him again. It had felt like an eternity since the long night spent out on my porch wrapped up in quilts.

I caught a glimpse of a woman exiting the front door of *Book It* before turning to head toward my car. Doing a double take, I watched as Evelyn closed up shop across the way. She was adjusting her bag and a stack of paperwork in her arms, then stepped off the sidewalk and glanced over at me.

Feeling a little embarrassed that she'd caught me standing there staring at the bookstore, I gave a tentative wave. She smiled, turned, and walked in my direction. I headed her way.

We met up near the gazebo facing La Placitas restaurant. There were always people milling about there, moving in and out of the restaurant, waiting for tables to open up. Evelyn approached, appearing apologetic for the bundle she was carrying.

"I'd shake your hand, but..." she smiled warmly.

"Wow," I responded, "I'm having flashbacks of my teaching days when I took home music compositions to grade!"

"Yeah, well, I'm not a fan of working here alone at night. And Pop is such a slave driver, he expects these invoices to be done tomorrow." And then there were her father's eyes, friendly and unassuming.

"A child laborer...wow. Who'd have ever thought it of Oscar Cardenas? He looks so innocent."

"Right? He even recruits his granddaughter!" Evelyn laughed. "I understand you crazy kids stayed out all night long the other day."

I paused, looking down and wondering what she assumed about me. I must've blushed.

"Oh, you have nothing to worry about," she reassured me. "He doesn't tell me everything, but I know he respects you very much. That, and you had green chile cheeseburgers for dinner."

I grinned remembering.

"The truth is, Molly, he hasn't told me about a woman since...well, *ever*. That's kind of a big deal."

I knew I couldn't hide the pleasure her words brought me—it was written all over my face. "I really think your dad is a very special person."

"He is," she said quietly, nodding. She looked down and readjusted the pile of folders in her arms. "Well, I'd better run."

"You know you can always call over here at night before you leave, by the way," I said, gesturing behind me toward *Old Town Music*, "and Cedar would be more than happy to walk you to your car."

"Oh, I appreciate the offer. It's not the walking to my car that freaks me out..." She rolled her eyes. "It's silly really."

My brow furrowed. "What's silly?"

She shook her head. "Ah, you'd think it's weird..."

I wasn't sure if I should pry, but I was curious as to what she was referring to. "Try me," I smiled.

"Well, okay," she sighed. "Do you believe in ghosts?"

Ghosts. Hmmm, well I wasn't expecting that.

"Uh...I'm not sure," I said.

The easiness in her expression changed a bit, as if she regretted having brought it up.

"But I *do* certainly believe in the existence of the spiritual world," I added, hoping to put her at ease.

"I do, too."

"You know, I actually took the ghost tour here last summer," I said.

"Well, then you may remember some of our local poltergeists," she said, raising her eyebrows.

"Yes," I nodded. The story that Sandra the Tour Guide had told us about Scarlet came to mind. I could picture the description of her in an emerald green flapper dress, walking up the stairs of the saloon.

"So...I've *seen* one," said Evelyn.

I lowered my chin and squinted my eyes at her, my interest piqued. "You have?"

She nodded her head. "Yep. Sure have. It was one night around the beginning of November last year. We'd hadn't been open long, and we were getting people in the store, tourists, interested in literature on Dia de los Muertos—you know, the Day of the Dead?"

I nodded.

"Well, I'm sure that had something to do with it. They'd already had the parade here in Old Town, and I'm sure the *calacas* and *calaveras* were still hanging around somewhere in the recesses of my psyche." She laughed, waving toward the back of her head. "Anyway, like usual we were working late into the evenings most nights, and I had told Dad to take Evangelyn home around six, that I'd finish up and lock up the shop.

"So of course, not long after they left—and I was there all by myself—the power goes out."

"Of course," I laughed, shaking my head.

Evelyn continued: "Everything was pitch black. I'm standing there in the dark, and I carefully make my way to the counter and feel my way to my laptop—battery powered, you know—and run my finger over the mouse, and the screen lights up. I decide that even though I can't finish whatever I was doing with the books, I could stay and at least do some work on the computer. I thought maybe the power would come back on while I worked.

"There wasn't another light source anywhere outside around the plaza. Things were silent, too, not even the usual buzz of the neon lights—nothing. Soon I was engrossed in doing some accounts payable, when from the corner of my eye there was a flash of red. Well, more like an orange—coppery colored. I was startled, and I quickly turned to look in that direction, but my eyes weren't adjusted to the dark, and all I could see was the bright white of computer screen when I blinked my eyes.

"But I *heard* something too," she said. "It was the laughter of a child."

I felt a chill between my shoulders. I took a deep breath. "Nicolas Vega."

Evelyn nodded her head slowly, her eyes wide. "Yes."

I stared at her, expectantly.

"In my haste to comprehend what I'd just seen, or *hadn't* seen—I wasn't quite sure—I must've jumped back or something, and knocked the computer off the countertop.

"So now, I was standing there in complete and utter blackness. And I couldn't see a thing, or hear a thing. After the clattering of the laptop hitting the floor, I couldn't move, either. It was like I was completely stunned or something. It was truly petrifying. But I knew one thing for sure: I *knew* for a fact he was still in there with me. I could feel Nicolas there in the room, somewhere in the dark.

"And there's something else," she continued, knowing she had my full attention. "It was freezing. Not like in any way I'd ever experienced cold before. And oddly enough, although I was totally terrified, I wasn't afraid of *him*."

We stood staring at each other for a moment, my mouth agape.

"So what happened?" I asked breathlessly.

"Well...that was it," she shrugged. "After I managed to get my hands on my laptop and open it back up, I used it as a light and shined it around the room. Of course, by then he was gone. And so was the intense chill. After that," she laughed, relieved, "I told my husband I was never working at night again! He calls Nicolas my '*amigo pequeño*'—my little friend."

"Huh..." I said, my voice trailing off.

Evelyn and I just stood there for a moment, contemplating her experience with the ghost of little Nicolas Vega together in silence. I was becoming a believer in the supernatural, things that couldn't be explained or understood from an earthly perspective. I knew from the Ghost Tour the six-year-old had fallen out the window of his home, which was now La Hacienda restaurant just around the corner from where we now stood. It was interesting to

152

me that Evelyn hadn't been scared of the presence of the small apparition...was he trying to tell her something in his appearance to her that night? If so, I pondered, what could it be?

We parted company with the usual pleasantries. As I turned to walk home, I couldn't help but be a little apprehensive in the growing dusk. Shadows lengthened in the waning daylight as I hastened my pace home.

FOURTEEN

1891

She *had* to get out of the house.

Pilar wasn't exactly sure where she wanted to go, but she knew it was *anywhere* but this place.

She had slept fitfully the night before; her only solace was knowing that her idiot brother was banned to the carriage house, staying there with Papacio for the foreseeable future. That was the only way that she'd agreed to her father's pleas against her threat to run away, to take the train and go live with her older sister, Elena, attending teachers' college in Colorado. "You want me to be an old maid, just like her, don't you?" she'd screamed. She also wished to pacify her pathetic mother, whose weeping was seen by Pilar as a ridiculous attempt to appease her father's rants threatening to wring his worthless son's neck.

It had nothing to do with the fact that her party—*fifteen years* in the making—was completely ruined. That the satin Richelieus imported from Paris that she'd worn the night before barely missed a spattering of *vomit* was nothing short of miraculous. But her mother, no doubt, mourned for her precious son now purged from beneath her roof.

Onofre had himself spent the night on the porch, coming inside only mid-morning to spit curses in his native tongue about the uselessness of his eldest son before the hand-wringing Mariana. She knew eventually his wrath would pass. For now, she would sit and endure.

She was also sure that their beautiful but humiliated daughter would be able to show her face in public again one day. That, while it wouldn't happen right away, Pilar would be able to look past this tainted memory and even possibly forgive Joaquin. True, she was the clearly over-indulged daughter (*spoiled rotten!* according to old Florencio) of a wealthy and influential rancher here in this beautiful valley. From birth, Pilar had been granted her every whim, her heart's desire: her father had never spared any expense for her, indulging her exorbitant taste for fashions, and as far as Mariana was concerned, this extravagant behavior had only served to encourage her daughter's never-ending thirst for more.

But perhaps, Mariana reasoned, the events of last night just might provide the structure with which to build some strength and character inside her daughter's pampered little heart, that Onofre's darling *mija* might benefit from not having everything go her way all the time.

Pilar wandered aimlessly for a while, kicking at the dusty ground on the banks of the irrigation canals along the bosque. She was encapsulated here along the curving path by tall, willowy groves of salt cedar, forming an impenetrable thicket on either side. She could breathe deeply now, and as she meandered with her parasol casting a violet shade about her, she could feel her anger toward Joaquin begin to soften slightly and start to give way to sorrow.

All my planning...all my hoping...

She could picture Oliver leading her down the veranda last night and over the lawn, to the dance floor, her hand in his. *Finally, finally! He asked her to dance.*

But the vision dissipated like an apparition, vaporizing before her eyes; she could barely feel the strong, protective arms around her, whirling and spinning carefree across the ground...

Then the sting of her tears springing into her eyes took her by surprise, angering her once more.

Halted in the unbearable afternoon sun, Pilar cried out and stomped her foot.

She dropped in a crumpled heap, weeping, the plumes of her skirt billowing about her.

She had not really mourned until now, her rage so intense toward her brother and her perfectly ruined *quinceañera*. Now she wept for the lost opportunity, the hopelessness; after last night, she doubted the cultured Oliver Shannon would ever want to see her or her family again.

Pilar used the cotton clutch she was carrying

to dab at her eyes, wiping her wet cheeks. Blinking, she looked up to see the blurry image of a young man standing a few yards in front of her.

Startled, she awkwardly scrambled to her feet.

Using her palm, she wiped her eyes in attempt to better clear her vision. He began walking toward her.

"*Rico?*" she managed to squeak.

He had never heard her speak his name. He began to apologize as he slowly approached, his stained, crumpled hat now in his hands. He raised them slowly. "I didn't mean to frighten you…"

She wheeled around, embarrassed anyone would see her like this. She tried to shake off the dust that had accumulated around her crinolines. She breathed in deeply, smoothed her skirt, and turned back to face the young man, assuming a stance with her head high. Only now, she was flustered and once again, angry.

"What are you doing here?" she demanded of him.

He looked around apologetically, as if he didn't have the same right to walk in the bosque as she did.

"I'm so sorry, Señorita—"

"Why are you *here*," she reiterated. "Here, right now, this time of day! Shouldn't you be working?"

At a loss, Rico looked up, as if the placement of the sun in the turquoise sky would provide an answer and relief from her accusation of him—although he wasn't sure of what, exactly, she was accusing him. It did remind him, as he replaced his hat to shield himself from its terrible summer torment, that he was indeed on an errand of his employer.

He started to explain, stumbling over his words, but Pilar bristled and attempted to walk past him.

"Señor Shannon sent me to speak to your father."

She stopped on the other side of him.

"Whatever for?" she turned on her heel to face him now, her tone slightly less perturbed.

He couldn't look her directly in the eye. Rico was keenly aware of his lot, even here, between just the two of them on the dusty bank of the canal: He was a laborer for her wealthy neighbor, a hired hand; she, the daughter of the most pre-eminent family in the Rio Grande valley. And even more distracting to him, she was utterly striking, here in the unforgiving midday heat. He glimpsed the glint of tears she hadn't been able to erase in her hurried attempt to wipe them away. By contrast, a trail of perspiration from his brow dripped down his face and through the residue of clouds kicked up by hooves of the animals in his charge. "I have an invitation for him."

She waited impatiently for him to continue. "Well?"

"Señor Shannon would like to meet Señor Vega at Mr. Fred Harvey's Alvarado House for drinks this evening. He says, it's...he called it an 'olive branch' for the events of last night…"

Pilar stared at him quizzically for a moment. Rico looked up at her.

"Huh," she finally stated. She was pondering how this might mean that reconciliation between her family and the Shannons might be possible after all. He took the opportunity to savor her exquisite features up close, her pouty mouth and furrowed brow. The sparkle in her lovely mocha eyes. Her black hair, in a thick braid, swung over her shoulder.

The moment was interrupted by the distant pounding of a horse's gallop and a resonant, labored grunt. The odd sound was repeated every few moments and echoed hollowly beneath the cottonwoods beyond the salt cedar cathedral surrounding the two of them.

Pilar smiled to herself upon realization that Oliver Shannon was practicing fencing. *On horseback.*

She turned her attention to the young man staring intently at her. "Well then, let's go."

She kept her gaze on him but turned in the direction of the Vega home. Rico offered her his arm, which she took expectantly.

Oliver Shannon's linen shirt was soaked, as in a fury he spurred the horse on, his distinctive golden hair flashing with every fervent stride.

As they approached each fencepost topped with a watermelon, he mustered all of his strength now at a steady lope, digging his heels into the horse and grunt-

160

ing with great force as he wielded the sword and swung it into the fertile red fruit, effectively slicing it in half. Without slowing, he was on to the next.

The fence divided the property line between the two great houses. At the base of each post were the remnants of melons filleted by prior runs. By the time he'd finished at the last post, Oliver was spent. With a guttural howl, he plunged the sword into the earth at the feet of his steed and dismounted with a leap. He took a canteen from a pouch attached to the saddle after tying the reins to the post, and doused his head with it. He wiped his eyes with a rag from the side pocket and caught sight of Pilar Vega beneath her purple parasol being escorted up her veranda by the likes of his stablehand, Frederico.

He shook his head and gave a hearty laugh. *Lucky stiff*, he mused.

She pretended not to notice him off in the distance in the shade of the ancient trees across the bosque, but Pilar had not once taken her eyes off him as he'd made his way up and down the fence line, while Rico carefully steadied her arm at her side.

At the top of the veranda she turned and nodded down to Rico, smiling. "Thank you for the walk. I'll get Papa."

Rico's heart soared. *"Gracias, Señorita."*

As he waited in the shade of the veranda, his hat again in his hands, he couldn't believe his good fortune of coming across Pilar like this at the very moment he was sent to deliver the message from his master. When he first saw her there on the banks of the canal, cotton drifting hazily around her in the stagnant air, she appeared to him a vapor, a taunting vision from his imagination sent to haunt him.

But she was real.

And she was right there with him, if only for a moment. And after taking his arm, she'd smiled at him.

It was fate—Rico was sure of it.

FIFTEEN

Present day

Oscar was waiting in a booth at the Backstreet Cafe on the east side of Old Town where I had just walked in the door.

When I arrived, he stood and waved, a warm smile spreading across his face. We embraced one another briefly and he helped me out of my jacket.

"They have the best street tacos in town. Evangelyn loves the shrimp tacos."

"Mmm, sounds great," I smiled, taking a seat. I was consciously making the effort not to allow myself to be so distracted with this man. There was no way I could contain my resolve if I allowed myself to focus on his physical attributes. It wasn't going to be easy...the fact that the smell of his cologne continued to linger in my nostrils after our greeting proved that it was going to be easier said than done.

He was leaning across the table toward me with his hands folded, looking me in the eye and grinning. I flashed him a smile and grabbed the menu. *You're a forty-plus-year-old woman. Stop acting like a teenager! Have a little self-control.*

It was frustrating; it had been so long since I had been in the presence of a man that I was so attracted to. *Come on, Molly! Pay attention....*

"So...what's *barbacoa*?" I asked, intent on scrutinizing the menu.

"Uh, it's a marinated meat. A blend of chiles, cumin, garlic, cloves, with a bit of vinegar and lime juice."

I raised my eyebrows at him without taking my attention off the menu. "Impressive." He laughed. "Yeah, well I've learned a few things in my bachelorhood over the years."

I continued my perusing of the menu. "Do you like to cook?"

"Love it."

"Really?" I asked, sounding more like a statement than a question. I looked up at him now, surprised by his answer.

"Yep."

Great. A man that could cook. A gorgeous, sweet man that could cook. *Just great.*

I felt my brows crinkle. "And I fed a *chef* green chile cheeseburgers from Blake's."

This made him laugh out loud. "Hey man, Blake's is an institution."

"Yes, the least I could have done was get you a Lota Combo."

"With onion rings?"

"Heck, yeah!"

"Then you're on next time," Oscar said with a smile.

The waitress came and took our order. We made small talk for a while until our food came, which I was thankful didn't take any time at all. I had chosen the shrimp tacos, and Oscar offered me a bite of his *carne barbacoa.* Self-consciously, I took the offering off his fork and into my mouth, dabbing with my napkin as the juices spilled down my chin.

I nodded, savoring the spicy concoction. "Yes," I approved. "A little warm, but very good. Is it like yours?"

"Close, but mine has a bit more chipotle in it."

"Wow. Any chance I'd get to sample it some time?"

"I'd say there's a really good chance of that happening." He looked me square in the eye.

My heart fluttered into my throat. I watched him and took a sip of ice water. *Waitress?? I'm going to need something stronger than this!*

"You know," Oscar continued. "I've been needing to talk to you about something."

"Oh yeah?" I replied casually in my most feminine voice. *I'm beginning to get into this flirting thing,* I mused feeling confident. I stopped short of batting my eyelashes at him.

"Yeah," he said. He put his fork down and wiped his mouth. He averted his eyes now, taking a drink of water.

"I thought about not telling you," he said after a pause.

He was still not looking directly at me. I was getting a little nervous now, my stomach starting to churn. I took a deep breath.

Oh no, please no. Please don't let this be what it feels like...

I put my hands in my lap and waited for him to continue. "Then I told myself I had to tell you. It wasn't fair not to, if we're going to have..." now he glanced tentatively into my eyes, "...whatever this is going on here." He gave me an unsure smile. It vanished quickly.

"Ok..." I steeled myself, ready for the proverbial shoe to drop.

He sighed. "It's just that it's not easy, and I'm embarrassed. You see," he began, this time holding my unsteady gaze. "I may have taken on more than I bargained for with the shop."

I inhaled deeply, listening. He looked down again as he began to explain. "I sank every last penny into that place. I mean *everything*. As you know, it's not cheap to lease here...."

I nodded, loosening up a bit. "Right."

"Well," now his hands were on the table again, fingers interlaced. "I was too optimistic figuring sales the first quarter. I really thought I'd planned carefully, thoughtfully, coming in on the holiday season and all. I'm not an accountant, but I thoroughly went over everything before investing in the shop, all of the overhead, all of the expenses—the utilities, my vendors—I'm not even taking a salary..."

His eyes were imploring mine. I sat silently, not sure of what to say.

"I'm struggling. I'm struggling," he repeated, anger and disappointment in his voice. "My accounts receivable are just not what I'd envisioned them to be. And I'm so mad at myself! How could I do this? I thought I was smarter than this! How could I do this to *my daughter*..." He shook his head and gazed out the window toward the velvety purple of the Sandía mountains in the distance.

I exhaled, not realizing I'd been holding my breath. I was relieved and a little ashamed for thinking the worst, that in an attempt to protect myself I'd gone too hastily to that place in my heart where I had been spurned so dismissively in the past.

I reached over and took his hands in mine. He squeezed them but continued to avoid eye contact.

166

"Oscar. Thank you for telling me," I said softly. "I'm sure that wasn't easy to do."

He shook his head, eyes still searching the horizon beyond the cafe.

"That means a lot to me. But surely there is something you can do. Surely there's something to be done to save the shop."

He turned back to look at me seriously. "What? What is there that I can possibly do? I mean the place is a broom closet as it is!" he laughed. "Every time I turn around I'm bumping into Evelyn. And yet I can't keep up with the bills. How on earth you run a place the size of *Old Town Music*, I don't know."

"It's a good market, for the tourists and the locals," I offered. "Listen, Oscar, there is no shame in having a hard time getting a business off the ground. I knew the guys that owned the place before you did, and they put blood, sweat and tears into it. For the first two years I owned *Old Town Music*, Garrett did my books for me. It took me years to run things on my own, and I still have to consult him and Trish any time I make a change or have a big purchase for the store. Clearly it's not easy, and whoever says it is doesn't know anything about running a business!"

He nodded. "Well," he sighed, "I haven't completely run it into the ground, thankfully. But it's just a matter of time."

He looked directly at me. "I owed it to you to tell you. Obviously this is big, and it's on my mind a lot." Now he took my hands into his and leaned in once again. "But *you* are on my mind a lot, too. You mean a lot to me, Molly. I used to not be very good about discussing things that were difficult, and about how I feel. But I want to be open

167

with you. I want you to know what's going on in my heart. I hope..." he appeared sheepish. "I hope I haven't disappointed you."

I shook my head and began to laugh, shocked at the prospect. This man had just spilled his heart out to me, shared with me his inmost fears. How could I be anything but *more* attracted to him, here with his heart laid bare before me?

I tightened my grip and leaned in toward him. "You have not disappointed me, Oscar, just the opposite! I have so much respect for you. You followed your dreams of opening a bookstore. That in itself takes so much courage!" I shook my head. "No, I'm not disappointed, I'm honored that you shared this with me. And *we* are going to do something about it. Okay?"

"Wow," he smiled, taking a deep breath. "I was so scared to tell you. I don't know what to do—what *we* can do—but I'm sure glad you're here with me."

He smiled warmly and stared into my eyes.

"Well I'm not sure either, but we'll figure it out."

We just looked at each other a while.

"Right now, your barbacoa is getting cold. Finish your food!"

He chuckled and picked up his fork. "Yes, ma'am."

We discussed possible options for the bookstore as the meal progressed. "What about maybe reconfiguring the layout of your store, redecorating or remodeling?"

He nodded in agreement, complimenting the design style of the music store. I suggested the possibility of his shop going from its outdated state to maybe "new west," perhaps even implementing a coffee bar and snack menu. "Maybe a patio?"

Oscar's expression became more relaxed over the course of our conversation, even hopeful. We both became animated at the plethora of prospects.

"I'm not sure about the covenants here...what would I have to do to renovate?"

I told him we'd pay a visit to the president of the merchants association tomorrow. As the conversation wound down and we finished our meal, we agreed to revisit our plans daily until we came up with a viable option for the rebooting of *Book It*.

We walked back across Old Town and to his store. From outside on the red brick walkway, we could see Evelyn chatting with a prospective customer. In spite of her jovial conversation, the visitor left the store empty-handed, holding the door open for us.

As he walked past us on the sidewalk, I watched Oscar sigh.

I was purposeful in my upbeat tone. "This is going to be fun. I'm excited."

Oscar turned to me and took my hand.

"Molly, you are such a breath of fresh air."

I smiled. Before I gave in to my temptation to kiss the lovely, grateful smile on his lips, I stepped backwards and waved.

"And I will see you tomorrow."

At home I reflected on the gut-wrenching prospect that our conversation momentarily brought me, that Oscar might've been giving me "the kibosh" in the cafe, and the relief I felt when I realized he wasn't. What a sense of peace I had knowing that my world was safe from being pulled out from underneath me like the proverbial rug.

Could the storm have truly passed? The days of

feeling unsure and insecure in a relationship be over?

I recalled the time when, in the blurry disbelief that my husband was in fact not the person I thought I'd married, I arrived at the courthouse for divorce proceedings nauseated and weak with the thought of having to appear in front of a judge. Against my husband...the *defendant.* As I was being wanded like the others in line at the cavernous entrance of this steel and concrete cave, I looked up to see Paul standing at the railing of the balcony. For a split second, I actually felt a sense of relief—*There he is, thank God! My husband is here. I'm safe...* And then, in the resulting despairing realization that followed I could barely stand upright and not buckle to my knees: The man standing at the railing was not my savior. He was now, in fact, my *enemy.*

Aside from how my children were going to be affected, this was the single worst memory that had haunted me during those days. It was an epiphany that eventually led me to turn a corner on the reality of my life, my "new normal." Nothing I'd ever experienced before or after that day had broken my spirit more.

But that was not what happened today in the cafe with Oscar.

Shaking my head, I breathed a sigh of relief. *Thank you, God, for your great blessing!*

It used to be that I couldn't bear to recollect such devastating memories without feeling overcome by grief. *Well,* I thought with tears of gratitude stinging my eyes, *not anymore.*

Gratefully, along with the haunting memories of those days also came the single most helpful piece of advice I received: In the days that followed the court visits, unable to drag myself out of bed and face the school day, I called my dear friend and vice principal, Glennys.

"I can't do this. I can't even get out of bed," I managed through tears.

"All right," she said gently. "I'm coming over. Until I get there I want you to do something, though."

I wept, unable to reply. The thought of *doing something—anything—*at that moment aside from curling up in a ball forevermore was incomprehensible.

"I need you to get yourself up and just put your shoes on. Put on your shoes, throw on your sweats. Then I want you to take a walk. You can go around the block. That's it. Okay? I'll be there soon."

I couldn't manage to go for a walk that dark morning. It had to suffice that I drag myself out of bed and, a step at a time, go downstairs. I propped myself upright on the sofa and awaited Glennys's arrival.

I met her at the door with tears streaming down my face. I couldn't muster the strength to even offer her a greeting. She came in and sat down on the couch with me, assuming a firm tone of voice.

"You have *every right* to be angry. You have every reason to be sad and devastated. What Paul did was the ultimate betrayal one could survive in this lifetime. Of course you're going to be down.

"But Molly," she said shaking her head, her tone becoming more intense. "You cannot *stay* there. You have children."

I sobbed, thinking of their sweet faces diligently working at school, having been dropped off after the new timeshare parenting agreement with their dad. And yet here was their mother, a pitiful *mess* who couldn't face the thought of a new day. I owed it to my babies, these angels from Jesus gifted to me, to try.

"You've undergone a tremendous loss, almost like a death—but worse in my opinion. Your husband is still out there in the world, carrying on, searching for *something*. But he's empty, Molly. He's trying to fill an empty void inside. He doesn't have any idea what he wants or what on earth he's just thrown away," she reached out and grabbed my hand.

"You're going to get down in the dumps sometimes. But don't stay down here too long, okay?" she said softly. "You owe it to yourself and those kids."

A strong woman of faith, Glennys prayed over me, a helpless puddle on the sofa desperately needing hope.

The next day I awoke, again depressed after another night of fitful sleep and the usual dosage of Tylenol PM. But that morning, I sighed and sat up, reaching for my tennis shoes, and went for a walk.

SIXTEEN

1891

"Psst! Let's *go!*"

The loud whisper startled Oliver in his room upstairs. He looked up from his desk, where he was sitting alone with a book.

The cavernous house was otherwise quiet. A dim oil lamp cast a shadow across the open door. He could barely see his visitor. Momentarily puzzled by *how* he got upstairs in the first place, Oliver sat up straight in his chair and squinted his eyes. "Go *where?*"

Joaquin ignored this and sauntered into the room, leaning against the doorway and folding his arms. "Amigo, my parents are gone, as are yours." His eyes glistened in the darkness. "The evening is ours to do as we please."

A grin curled across Oliver's face. "Oh no," he shook his head. "Didn't we get in enough trouble last night? I'm frankly surprised you're standing upright."

Joaquin laughed. "Don't be such a *pendejo.*"

Oliver rose, closed his book with a sigh, and shook his head again.

"So then...where to?"

Joaquin gestured through the open door and

looked back at his friend with a smirk.

"Hell's Half Acre."

As they neared the ramshackle building beside the railroad tracks, they could hear music being pounded out on a piano and a lone masculine voice attempting to entertain the rowdy crowd inside. It was more of a glorified barn, really, than it was a saloon. Certainly nothing of the sort of drinking establishments the likes of which Oliver Shannon had ever frequented. The gentleman's clubs in London he'd visited on occasion with his father sported fine leather and mahogany furniture, lead glass windows and bronze lettering on the front of the building. The sign out front of this establishment was painted on a wooden board above its swinging doors. It read "Vine Cottage." The two seventeen-year-olds tied their horses to the hitching post and made their way inside.

No one noticed the two teenagers. They stood at the entrance for a moment, soaking in the raucous scene, leather-faced frontiersmen staggering past them while "gentlemen" not a couple of years their senior sat at tables dressed in fine tailored suits puffing on cigars, and intimately studying the cards arranged in their hands. They had recently stepped off the train platform, having come west in search of their fortunes.

There was a dimly lit stage in the corner of the room, or rather an elevated perch where the landing of the stairs rested before proceeding down to the first story. This is where the piano player sat on a crate crooning "After the Ball," bent over a precariously placed instrument missing its entire front panel. If you watched closely enough, you could see the small hammers striking the strings inside as its player's fingers danced to and fro over the black and brown keys. Oliver seriously doubted anyone else in the room had vision clear enough to focus on details that precise. Revelers jumped from the balcony above the piano player to get to the steps below, most of them not landing on their feet, and cursing at the musician on their way to the bar.

Oliver made a note of the enormous chandelier in the middle of the room, composed of antlers, which offered little illumination to the crowded tables below. This, he reasoned, was perhaps to take one's attention off the "ladies" attending to the gentlemen behind the bar. They were a gangly crew, to be sure, donning heavily applied rouge and lipstick. Their laughter was punctuated with language just as colorful, often accompanied by a well-placed slap across the face of a gentleman who had neglected payment for services provided below stairs in anticipation of services provided above. Once the tab was paid in full, however, the plumed women led their tipsy patrons upstairs, past

175

the piano player, and with the approval of the enormous dark-skinned gent whose job it was to ensure that the ladies of the house weren't left empty-handed, into one of the rooms down the hallway whose door wasn't latched.

"¿*Como están,* gentlemen?" said a breathy voice in a southern drawl behind them.

No sooner had they turned than the sultry woman had them both by the hands and was leading them toward the counter. She slammed her fist on it, getting the attention of a hefty young woman on the other side. She smiled warily and snatched Joaquin's hat off his head. "Have a drink, little Mr. Vega." She tossed it at him, and he caught it in midair.

He slid onto a stool and saluted his hostess as she meandered through the thick crowd away from them. "Yes, ma'am, Miss McGrath!" he hollered after her.

"Who was that?" yelled Oliver over the noise, as he sat down next to Joaquin.

The young woman in the too-tight bustier behind the counter grinned at them. "*Cerveza?*"

Joaquin nodded.

"That, my friend," he said, turning back to Oliver, "is Lizzie McGrath. The owner of this fine establishment."

"The Lily of Copper Avenue," as she was known, owned what was by far the most illustrious and frequented of the brothels that had proliferated in the new part of town since the arrival of the railroad more than a decade earlier.

Oliver looked at his friend with mouth ajar. "Well aren't you the ladies' man?" He patted him on the back heartily and laughed.

Joaquin took a swig of the beer placed before him by the portly painted lady. She winked and looked at Oliver out of the corner of her eyes.

"And you can be, too, shooger, if the price is right."

"Thank you kindly, Madame—*er, Miss*—for now just a beer, please."

"Suit yourself." She turned to fill a glass she wiped off with her skirt. "We never close."

"I'll take another, Magdalena!" Joaquin yelled after her, slamming his now-empty glass on the countertop. He turned around, propped his elbows on the bar and leaned back. Oliver watched him, wide-eyed.

"Whoa there, big man. You had enough alcohol last night for the both of us. You sure you're up for more?"

Joaquin narrowed his eyes, and they flared in anger at him. Oliver had seen this look before on the face of Onofre Vega. He decided it probably wasn't a good idea to push the issue. But he also knew that if Joaquin's father found out that he was here tonight...he shuddered to imagine the consequences.

"Here y'are, darlin'," said the barmaid. Oliver smiled and nodded, and began sipping his beer.

"Oliver Shannon," hollered Joaquin over the crowd, bringing the refilled glass to his lips. "I thought you were an educated man."

Oliver nodded. "I am, sir."

"I don't think you are, at least not in the *ways...* of the *world...*" he drew out the words mockingly, gesturing at the motley gang assembled in the expanse of the room before them. "Look at all this! You're telling me you've read in one of your books about *this*?"

Oliver laughed good-naturedly. "I can assure you that in *all* the books I've read, I've never come across anything like this."

"Well then! It's time that you get yourself a whole new education." He finished off the drink and hopped off the bar stool. "Come on."

Oliver braced himself with his boot, digging it into the wooden floor before him and leaning back in his stool. "Hang on now, I'm not...what are you doing?"

Joaquin guffawed. "Come on! We're going upstairs to visit the ladies, *big man*."

Oliver pushed himself onto his seat. "No thanks."

The look once again flared in Joaquin's eyes. "What the...you *scared*?"

"Only that your father will skin you alive if he

finds out what you're up to."

Joaquin stepped closer to him, leaning into within an inch of his nose. "Yeah? And who's gonna tell him?"

Oliver held Joaquin's stare, then put his arm around his shoulder, patting his back. "Relax, amigo," he smiled. "I have no interest in telling him anything. But I also have no interest in these...*ladies*, either." He glanced up and watched as Magdalena led a particularly inebriated gent past the piano and up to the top floor. At the other side of the balcony, Lizzie yelled for the giant praetorian looming in the shadows.

"Jonah!"

At this, the volume in the room dropped dramatically and the pianist ceased playing. She pointed toward a doorway, where a scantily clad Chinese woman stood with her arms crossed. Beside her was a seedy looking character wearing only pants and suspenders. His boots were in one hand while he pled with the other for leniency as the massive Jonah approached him.

Lizzie continued with composed calm.

"This gentleman says he doesn't have the necessary funds to properly reimburse Genevieve here for her time. Would you please see him to the door?"

In one stride, Jonah had the man dangling over the side of balcony railing like a rag doll, his boots dropping to the ground below as he clawed in vain at the air around him. "Stop!" yelled a man wearing a champagne-colored silk vest with his sleeves rolled up. Not taking his eyes off the hand of cards he was holding, he fanned them out on the table to the chagrin of his tablemates. "Put it on my tab."

"Aw, that's awfully neighborly of you, Ben." She nodded at Jonah who pulled the man back over the railing and stood him upright in the hallway.

"You'll be on your way then," Jonah informed the man, who knew he'd just escaped certain death. He quickly made his way down the stairs, fumbling for his boots as he skittered out the door.

The piano player started back up again. This time, Lizzie headed a rousing rendition of the chorus, and the crowd joined in with her:

> *After the ball is over,*
> *After the break of morn,*
> *After the dancers' leaving,*
> *After the stars are gone.*
> *Many a heart is aching,*
> *If you could read them all—*
> *Many the hopes that have vanished,*
> *After the ball.*

Oliver smiled and shook his head. "I'll give it to you, amigo. You do know how to live it up."

Joaquin gestured at Lizzie, who started to make her way toward them.

"I respect you, Oliver. You're a good man. But I'm seventeen, and my father thinks I'm never going to amount to anything...I'm going to live *la vida loca* while I can." He smiled and punched his arm.

"So you're really going up there?"

"Not sober, that's for sure!" He grabbed the refilled drink on the counter and slammed it back. As Lizzie approached him, he removed his hat. A weathered but still beautiful woman wearing a burgundy gown trailed behind her.

"Mr. Vega, have you met Clementine?"

"Pleasure to meet you, ma'am," he said, kissing her hand. She smiled with her dark eyes and began to head upstairs, with Joaquin following after her. He quickly turned back with his hat held high in one hand, and sang one of the verses of the familiar melody:

"Long years have passed, child, I've never wed, true to my lost love though she is dead!" He laughed heartily and replaced his hat with a snort. "Go home, *pendejo.*"

Oliver raised his glass to him and watched his friend make his way to the harlot's room.

He dropped a handful of coins on the counter and departed.

SEVENTEEN

Present day

It wasn't going to be easy.

"These are historically preserved buildings, as you know," reminded Sylvia de Herrera, president of the Old Town merchants' association. "To begin with, you'll have a never-ending stack of paperwork that comes with its fair share of red tape built in by the city, and a whole slew of inspectors. After you have your refurbishing plan from a contractor, you're still not guaranteed approval by the historical society. There can't be anything that interferes with the structural preservation of the building. Then you'll have to present all of this along with your completed paperwork and revision forms and get consent from the merchants' association's transition committee. *If* they approve your plan to renovate—and that's a *big* if—you're in the clear to make your changes. But I warn you now, they're sticklers for historical preservation and how it affects our community of merchants, and the greater Albuquerque community at large, with Pueblo architectural accuracy, and so forth. And I can assure you that this process will not come cheap."

Oscar and I exchanged furtive glances.

"So," he asked with a sigh, "where do we start?"

"How are you going to do it, Dad? I mean financially, how *can* you do it?" Evelyn gently implored. "I don't

183

mean to be a buzzkill, but seriously. Where are you going to come up with the money required to do the remodeling?"

"I've already secured a loan through the Small Business Administration. Their rates are more than competitive, and I have time to pay it off once we're seeing a profit."

"But isn't it risky? What if we *don't* turn a profit soon? What if you can't pay it off in time?"

Oscar grabbed his daughter's hand. "*Mija,* I know you're scared. You don't think I am, too? Of course it's risky! I knew that long before I opened the store, that there'd be risk associated with the whole thing. That's not the question here. What is in question is whether I can afford *not* to. I got the loan because I'm a calculated risk, and they believe the store can succeed. They wouldn't have approved it if I didn't have a solid business plan now. Working with them on a business plan was imperative for funding. Without it I wouldn't have secured the loan. Before, I was lacking a solid game plan. Now we have that. And I feel really good about it. Besides, Evelyn, what other choice did I have? If I'm going down, then I'm doing it with guns blazing."

"Nice wild West metaphor, *abuelo,*" she smiled in approval. She took his hand holding hers and shook it. "Okay, business *pardner,*" she said in a western drawl. "I'm hopeful."

"I'm *more* than hopeful," he said, turning to me. I'd been seated on a stepladder next to a bookshelf in his shop, listening to their exchange. "I'm downright excited. Molly used to be a decorator, and she's got some great ideas for this place."

"Yeah," I laughed, "starting with comfortable seating."

I rose, rubbing my rear, and walked toward Evelyn's outstretched hand.

"This *is* exciting, you two," she smiled, taking my hand. "I feel like we need to pray over this place right now, is that okay?"

Oscar and I held hands. "Of course, *mija*. Thank you."

"You deserve this, Dad. You deserve good things to happen. And I think they will."

We stood there in the dark of the evening while Evelyn prayed. She squeezed my hand when she was done, and I added my own requests for blessing for the shop, for Evelyn and her family, and for Oscar. I squeezed his hand.

"Father, God," he said with a sigh. "I just want to say *thank you* for these women in my life. Thank you for their strength and examples. We ask for your blessing as we work together in this place. Amen."

EIGHTEEN

July 1891

"Comment t'appelles-tu?" the chorus of children repeated after Father Julien.

*"Je m'appelle...*say your name," his hands gesturing in the air for them to complete the sentence.

Amidst the giggles and garbled French, they did exactly that, copying him verbatim.

"Non, non, non," he feigned a pained expression, placing his palm to his brow as their laughter continued. "Let's try this again. Listen to Señora Vega and me."

Mariana stepped up to the front of the room from her small chair in the back and perused the faces of the children smiling back at her. She winked at them.

"Let's pretend that we are meeting for the first time on the street."

The padre turned to her with a bow.

"Bonjour."

"Bonjour," she replied with a curtsey.

"Comment t'appelles-tu?"

"Je m'appelle Madame Vega," she smiled, looking directly at the children.

"Mon plaisir, Madame." He took her hand and
187

kissed it, which elicited stifled giggling from the class. He turned back and looked at the children. "Your turn. Choose a partner, and we shall practice our greetings outside in the courtyard."

The cool of the morning was quickly turning too warm inside the classroom in spite of the windows flung open wide within their thick plaster walls. At least outdoors there might be a breeze, and the walk to the other side of the parish house would help invigorate all of them.

The children of the orphanage, housed in an adobe building to the west of the church, were eager to learn whatever it was the good father wished for them to. They longed for Tuesdays, for it was then that the nuns who worked at the school got caught up on the weekly tasks of cleaning and cooking for the week ahead. And it was Tuesdays when Señora Vega, whom they loved for her affectionate nature—and her sugary *biscochitos*—volunteered at the school.

One of the children, an older boy, waited for Mariana's arrival with great anticipation. Always, he watched for her from the window looking out onto the plaza. At her appearance he hollered *"May-anna!"* and rushed in his broken gait outside to meet her, one foot seemingly leaden, often failing him and causing him to stumble. As she approached, he wailed with glee, his words indecipherable to many but their sentiment unmistakable.

188

She could momentarily embrace his twitching body, its spasms uncontrollable, before he wriggled out of her arms. Tightly he would then grasp her forearm, escorting her inside the school building, by which time she had produced for him a cookie. He took and ate it with a wail, and she wiped the drool from his mouth with the cotton cloth that had contained the sugary treat. Sometimes, Mariana would come to visit him on other days of the week, as well, and just the two of them would enjoy a lovely slice of *dulce de leche.*

Now as the class hurried outside, she offered her forearm to him, and they walked to the courtyard together. They sat on a banco beneath the shade of a balcony overhang, where the late summer roses and dying hollyhock wilted lifelessly beside the red brick pathway.

"Je m'appelle Mariana," she told him, as the other children tried out their best greetings on their classmates. "And what is your name?"

He grinned up at her, his black hair falling into his eyes. She wiped the corner of his mouth, where there seemed to be a never-ending leak.

"May-anna!" he squealed.

"No," she gently corrected. "*I* am Mariana, comment t'appelles-tu? Who are *you*?"

He continued to smile up at her, the innocence of his expression heartbreaking to her. She knew he would never comprehend much English or Spanish, much less this bizarre new language the priest wanted him to learn.

She took his hand in hers and placed it against his chest as she leaned down to him.

"'Je m'appelle Ramón.'"

He squeezed her hands and pounded himself with them. *"Rone!"*

She nodded her head. "That's right. Your name is Ramón."

One of the sisters appeared at the open doorway and summoned the children to lunch with the clap of her hands. As they joyfully gathered to go back inside, Father Julien reminded them to practice their manners. *"En français..."*

"Merci, Sister Isabel," they sang in unison.

He smiled and nodded. "Ah, *trés bien, les enfants.* Now go eat!"

Mariana received hugs from some of the children as they proceeded to the kitchen. "They didn't need much prompting that time," she observed. "They're getting better."

"Oui. I'm proud of them."

As the two stood in the courtyard in the midday sun, the lull in conversation prompted the padre to bring up the unfortunate events of the previous week.

"Mariana," he started quietly, turning to face her. "We haven't had a chance to speak since Pilar's...How is everything?"

190

She was nodding, ready for the uncomfortable inquiry to be over. "She's going to be just fine, *Merci,* Father."

He reached up and touched her elbow. "It's not your daughter I'm so concerned with."

Her gaze fell to her feet.

"Onofre was very angry," he stated.

A resentful breath escaped her lips before she could turn away. In Father Julien's compassionate efforts, she felt unable to hide the flood of emotion simmering precariously below the surface. However, she could not afford the luxury of falling apart, not after all these years. She inhaled deeply.

"Mariana, I know you're resigned to keeping up a strong front concerning your husband, but you don't have to. Not with me—"

Holding up her hand to silence him, she smiled and turned toward him. "I will be fine, Julien. I will deal with Onofre. I have before, and I will continue to. You know very well this is my lot in life."

The padre nodded and looked away. She reached for his kind hand and squeezed it. He covered her delicate grip with his other hand.

There was nothing more to say about it.

She turned and went inside.

NINETEEN

Present day

It was March.

Two months had passed since the merchants' association committee had approved Oscar's application to remodel *Book It*. They'd been impressed with the plan for its revitalization, with minimally invasive intrusion to the original structure. Demolition was to be restricted to one small corner, where a fireplace had once functioned but was later bricked over and sealed with stucco, and it would now be enjoyed both inside the shop and outside, courtesy of a glass insert. A small patio area would be erected into a small courtyard with a partial wall composed of traditional adobe. In warmer weather, tourists and locals alike could enjoy a book and a cup of piñon coffee outside by the toasty glow of the newly converted fireplace.

Oscar was kept busy with the hustle and bustle of construction. Anticipating his desire to be constantly present there, I took to bringing him lunch from time to time. The shop was still open for business, and his and Evelyn's goal was to minimize the impact of remodeling on their customers.

A buzz had been generated amongst merchants and shop visitors, who looked forward to the project's completion, anticipating a special niche in the area designed for book lovers and coffee aficionados as well.

Evangelyn's excitement was bubbling over. "Guess

what, Molly?"

"*Ms. Lewis*," chided her mother.

"Tell me, darlin'." I responded to the little girl the way I often referred to my students.

"Abuelo said I could make *empanaditas* for the store when they have the grand re-opening." She grinned up at me.

"I think that's an excellent idea. Honestly," I turned to Oscar. "I think they should be on the menu after the opening, as well. A sweet traditional Mexican treat."

I'd learned to make the little fried fruit pies myself as a teenager. We had apricot trees in the vast backyard of our house in the bosque when I was growing up.

"Why not?" said Oscar, still visiting with Jose, one of the construction workers. He was installing electric wiring this week.

"Yay!" she clapped. "Did you hear that, Mama?"

"Yes, baby. We need to get you home for lunch, because you have your piano lessons this afternoon." With no customers in the shop at the moment they shuffled out the door. "See you later, Dad."

He nodded, intent on the conversation he was having with Jose.

I placed the plastic bag containing the drink and quesadilla in Styrofoam containers on the counter next to the register, then walked over to the corner to inspect the status of the fireplace demolition. It was partitioned off with a plastic curtain hanging from the ceiling.

Oscar and the electrician stepped outside to further discuss the lighting and outlet placement for the new patio area. I pulled back the plastic and looked at the assemblage of adobe bricks that had come out of the fireplace and were now piled carefully against the wall. They were going to be set in place again once the electric and gas lines had been installed, as per agreement with the preservation committee that original materials be used whenever feasible. The zoning wouldn't allow for the traditional wood-burning fireplace now, although before the walls that divided the shops were erected, at one time it had enabled a much larger space to be heated, likely a dwelling for a family a hundred years ago. Soon, with the gas lines in place, the fireplace would offer more ambience than practical heating.

I kneeled down and picked up a brick, probably made by men or boys of the village. It was cool to the touch and heavy, with hay compacted into the rectangle block. I imagined it must've taken hundreds of thousands of these little mud bricks to compose an entire building. I realized I was holding a unique piece of history in my hands.

The opening of the fireplace wall was a dusty, gaping cavity as it underwent the transformation process. I turned on the flashlight on my iPhone and shone it into the darkness.

What appeared to be piles of ash and dust covered the earthen floor of the interior. I caught sight of a metal hinge at the roof where the flue might've been. Curious if it would open after all this time, I pulled the lever toward me with the full knowledge I might unearth an ancient cloud of soot, and who knows what else.

It didn't budge.

Undeterred, I gave it a hard yank, and to my surprise the entire base of the roof of the flue gave way, landing on the floor with a dull thud and exhuming a cloud of dust in its wake.

I landed on my backside and waved the billow of gray ash and dust from my face. Choking, I scrambled to my feet and coughed, taking a few steps back and covering my face with my sleeve. After a moment, things cleared, and I peered back inside at the mess on the floor of the fireplace. There in the rubble were pieces of wood, the metal handle of the hinge to the opening, and perched on top was what appeared to be a filthy bag of some sort, blackened by time and soot.

At one point in time it had served as a piece of textile tapestry, a carpet bag or purse, perhaps. I could make out what appeared to be a wooden handle at the top.

I reached for it. As I attempted to lift the bag from its earthen tomb, the wooden handle detached itself from its weighty contents. Untold decades of rot and decay had taken its toll, and where the handle had once been stitched to the tapestry, it had now disintegrated with my touch.

I was determined to retrieve this relic lost to history from within the walls of the fireplace. Whatever it turned out to be, likely insignificant in the overall scheme of time, I was going to salvage it from further reckoning of the demolition process. I walked over to the countertop and took Oscar's lunch out of its roomy plastic bag, and brought the bag back along with a stack of napkins to the opening in the wall. I reached in carefully, placing my hands covered by napkins beneath it. It wasn't as heavy as I thought, and lifted it effortlessly into the plastic bag.

Whatever was inside had been painstakingly wrapped in an outer linen cloth. I touched the outside of the bag, and instead of disintegrating further, I was pleased it stayed intact. Except for the ashen appearance, the bag itself appeared to be in decent condition.

No telling what I was going to find inside. I gingerly carried it to the door and looked out. Oscar was still in deliberations concerning the electrical work. I wanted to tell him of my discovery, to explore the contents together. I had always been fascinated with history, especially of this unique corner of the world. Maybe it was merely a handbag, full of nothing more than years of accumulated debris. Or maybe it held secrets otherwise forgotten by time. Either way, I was fascinated by the prospect of this aged object, and the fact that it had been sealed away like a hidden treasure.

"Mr. Cardenas, I think we can accommodate what you're looking for out here and keep it within budget. I just need to run it by my foreman."

"Excellent. So you think it's within reason to have a sound system out here too?"

I wasn't going to interrupt him. But I couldn't wait. My curiosity won over, and I decided to have a peek inside before I left. I walked to the other side of the register and gently put the bag on the floor. Kneeling beside it, I opened it and delicately pulled the wrapped contents out, inhaling a whiff that reminded me of visits to my grandmother's house and its stale, dusty attic.

I pulled out a stack of folded papers—*letters, perhaps?* They were bound with faded, blue-gray velvet ribbon. Rather than untying it and risk damaging the ribbon, I coaxed out one of the folded papers and carefully opened it. It was indeed a letter, written entirely in French. From the residual college French I hadn't used since, I made out a few words:

"Toujours"
"au revoir"

"Amour"

It was signed simply, *M.*

In spite of my excitement and curiosity to learn more about the mysterious contents, I had to get back to work. I'd call Oscar later when he wasn't so busy. I placed the bag in the tiny storage closet behind the register and headed back to the music store. Oscar winked at me as I stepped outside, he and Jose debating styles of punched-tin wall sconces.

Several days had passed since I made my discovery in the fireplace, and Oscar and I hadn't had a whole lot of time together with the whirlwind of remodeling Book It. He was as fascinated as I was about where the letters could have come from and who could have written them, but between both of our stores, we were kept busy until today.

"Ready to go shopping?"

Oscar held the door of Old Town Music open without stepping inside.

"Be still my heart," I said, fanning my face with my hand. Cedar and I were standing behind the counter going over the new sheet music inventory. "The four words that make every woman weak in the knees."

"Well then, come on, *woman!*" he replied with a mischievous grin.

Cedar snorted, then glanced at me and covered his mouth. I glowered at him as I grabbed my purse and made my way toward the door.

"Sure she can't make a sandwich for you before you

go?" I reached across the counter in an attempt to smack him, but he jumped out of the way.

"Who writes your paychecks?"

Cedar dropped his head remorsefully. "I pray m'lady has a wondrous day in Santa Fe."

Before I made it to the door, a young woman entered carrying a guitar case. She was wearing a gauzy summer dress, and her strawberry blonde hair was piled atop her head. She propped her sunglasses against her hair clip and smiled at Cedar.

I turned back and gave him a quick I'm-watching-you gesture with my fingers.

"Always, m'lady."

Oscar and I drove uptown to the Rail-Runner station. It was housed at what was once the thriving Alvarado Hotel and still retained the name as a main stop along the railway line from Belén to Santa Fe.

I'd always loved this building along the tracks as a historical hub in the city. This morning the train would be full of commuters and sightseers on the way to "The City Different." After we found what we wanted for the new Book It, we would momentarily become tourists as well and visit some much beloved historical sites around Santa Fe Plaza.

The train approached, emblazoned with its giant roadrunner in red and yellow, the traditional Zia colors of the New Mexico state flag. Oscar and I stepped on and took a seat upstairs next to the window. As the Rail Runner prepared to pull out of the station, the train doors closed with a "Meep meep!" sound from the Coyote and Roadrunner cartoon.

"That never gets old." Oscar smiled at me.

I giggled.

We talked about the vibe we were looking for in the newly remodeled space.

"I have some ideas," I grinned mysteriously at him. "There are some great shops on the plaza I think you'll like."

"I'm putting my trust entirely in you with the decorating," he said, grabbing my hand and pointing out the window. His touch was thrilling. I savored holding his hand as he chatted about the landscape speeding past us.

When we got into Santa Fe, we took the short walk from the downtown depot to the plaza. I breathed in the surroundings: While Old Town had its share of adobe buildings, Santa Fe was unique in that every cloistered street was lined with authentic Pueblo-style architecture. Every quaint, narrow village thoroughfare showcased the flat-roof stucco businesses and homes, with their turquoise door frames and window casings, sprays of sunflowers and hollyhocks bursting from terra cotta pots. They lined red brick pathways undulating like waves from the overgrown roots of cottonwood trees.

Arm in arm we strolled past art galleries and museums, stopping to gaze upon the woven fineries and silver jewelry created by Native craftsmen beneath the balustrade of the Palace of the Governors. Located directly on the plaza, it was a historic landmark, the oldest continually occupied building in the United States, constructed in 1610. Along with throngs of tourists, we meandered slowly, admiring the conchos, bolo ties, and wool blankets displayed on crushed velvet sheets.

I grabbed Oscar's hand, and we crossed the plaza to a favorite interior decorating boutique of mine. Before going inside, he pulled me abruptly to a halt, drawing me close to him next to a column festooned in piñon branches. He placed his hand behind my neck and pressed his lips to mine. It was warm and wondrous, and I felt my body go limp, a delicious jolt running through my veins. After a moment I pulled away and looked into his eyes, squinting as they smiled back at me.

Oscar shook his head. "Wow," he breathed.

I kissed him again, then smiled back at him as I walked into the boutique.

As my eyes adjusted to the dim lighting inside, I took a deep breath to steady my giddiness. Oscar stepped in behind me and we were greeted by the rich fragrance of leather, and a gentleman dressed in yellow jeans and Italian calfskin shoes. His closely shaved hair was coiffed and gelled in the front. He winked at me.

"Hey, y'all," he grinned with a drawl. "I'm Jovan. Can I help you find something today?"

"Yes, please," said Oscar, placing his hand on my back and taking in the atmosphere. "This young lady is outfitting my new bookstore in Old Town Albuquerque. If you would show her everything you've got."

"Oh, honey," said the trendy young man, replacing Oscar's hand with his around my shoulders. "Let's *do this.*"

He ushered me to the back of the shop and up a wide, elegant stairway. Hanging from the ceiling overhead were lanterns of all shapes and colors, evoking a cosmopolitan feel. Designers had staged breathtaking bedrooms, offices, and living rooms bedecked with rich Indian embroidery, dhurries and kilims from across the globe, intermixed with "new West" themes. My eyes landed on a unique cowhide rug dyed in turquoise at the top of the landing.

"Mmm..." I purred pointing to it.

"Right?"

It was set at the base of a heavy, traditional Southwestern wrought iron and wooden seating arrangement accented with warm, mocha leather cushions.

"I've never seen this before, only the traditional rawhide."

"It works, though, doesn't it?"

"Yes," I said nodding. "I would've thought it was gaudy on its own, but I love it paired with this grouping!"

Jovan and I looked at Oscar for approval. He raised his hands in protest. "She's the boss."

"Do you like it?" I asked.

"I do," he said, nodding. He stepped in closer to me and interlaced his fingers in mine. "Like I said, I completely trust you, Molly."

I trust you....

I smiled back at Jovan. I was over the moon.

Jovan led us around the shop as I *oooo*ed and *ah*-*h*ed over the furniture and *objets d'art*. Arrangements of cream-colored calla lilies adorned tables laden with colorful textiles alongside Nambé bowls and candlesticks.

"Do you have the butterfly bowl?" I inquired.

"Oh yes, give me a sec," he said, meandering through distressed Portuguese armoires, and returning with a contoured silver work of art in hand.

"Don't you just love Nambé?" he crooned, handing it to me.

"So much!" I turned to Oscar. "For the mints after coffee."

"Better make that two," he said to Jovan, who obediently turned to fetch another. "For the 'Book It' matchbooks and business cards."

I smiled. "Now you're talking."

I spied a cobalt Venetian glass lantern hanging in a bedroom suite nearby.

"Wouldn't this be a great accent in a corner of the store?" I said, walking toward it.

"And this little Spanish colonial loveseat would be perfect tucked in underneath it," offered Jovan, his fingers trailing the arm of the sofa. "With a couple of Moroccan pillows, I could *so* see myself curled up with a good book in it."

Oscar furrowed his brow, intently scouring the piece. He nodded. "Oh yeah. It's perfect."

I pulled out a measuring tape from my purse, mentally appraising the piece.

"Maybe with this lamp on a side table nearby?" Jovan gestured to one with a stitched leather shade.

"Speaking of pillows, we'll need some cushions for the bancos outside," I reminded Oscar.

After choosing a few accessories and getting care instructions for the rug, we were set. Garrett had promised several framed works by Lacey for display on the walls of the newly remodeled book store that would also be available for purchase. I could imagine the placement of all our new purchases alongside the artwork. Everything was coming together beautifully.

"Now before we ship, I'll double check the measurements for you again."

"Excellent, since there's not a lot of room for error," laughed Oscar.

"How much is shipping?" I inquired.

"Oh, it's free for orders over $2,500 within the state."

I raised my eyebrows at Oscar, hoping I hadn't just run him into the poorhouse.

He nodded and smiled. "Perfect. So we'll get it within the week?"

"That's right, Mr. Cardenas," he said handing back Oscar's credit card. Oscar took it and headed toward the entrance.

"If it's going to be later I will call you, but typically you'll get everything in less than a week. You wanted to take the Nambé ware with you, right?"

"Yes. Thank you so much, Jovan," I said watching him carefully wrap each silver bowl in sheets of paper before placing them in a large gift bag. "You were *really* helpful."

"And you two are *so cute*," he said handing the bag over the countertop to me. He leaned in, looking over the top of his glasses and whispering. "Girl, he's a *hottie*. I saw y'all out there before you came in."

I laughed and blushed at the memory of Oscar's kiss.

"*So* cute," he shrugged. "Have a good one, now."

Together we crossed San Francisco street toward the La Fonda Hotel and stopped inside The French Bakery. We ordered crepes and coffee and ate quickly in the crowded cafe.

Back outside on the street, we were now facing the façade of the exquisite Cathedral Basilica of St. Francis of Assisi. Originally erected of adobe in the New Mexico Mission style, it had been destroyed in the Pueblo revolt of 1680. The massive structure now stood in its stately grandeur at the end of the street dwarfed a statue of the first Bishop of Santa Fe, Father Jean Baptiste Lamy. He welcomed visitors through the front doors in the portico in the shadow of the cathedral.

Inside the cathedral, the nave soared overhead, with vivid stained glass windows flanking the perimeter below. At the entrance, I grabbed a brochure as Oscar dipped his fingers into the font of holy water beneath a crucifix and, dotting his forehead, made the sign of the cross.

It was buzzing with tourists talking in hushed tones. I read in the brochure that Archbishop Lamy brought in architects from his native France to build the basilica, and it was where the stained glass windows depicting the twelve apostles were located as well. They cast a brilliant kaleidoscope of color over the cavernous walls of the nave. The effect was awe inspiring. Oscar and I strolled the perimeter of the cross-shaped structure, which held such history for this region of the Southwest, so deeply beloved by its first archbishop. According to the brochure, he had been buried in a crypt beneath the cathedral floor in 1888.

Above our heads to the left of the sanctuary, the words to a prayer for the stations of the cross were carved: "We adore you, oh Christ, and praise your name."

I knew from growing up in the Rio Grande valley that the Catholic church had its fair share of scandal here, beginning in territorial times. From what I recalled of New Mexico history in school, Bishop Lamy's presence in the diocese was a turning point in the way priests were viewed among the native people here. He was beloved and trusted, a far cry from others who preceded him, posing as representatives of a higher calling, but instead living lives far removed from the true vision of Lamy's Roman Catholic church. While at first there was a deeply ingrained suspicion of him, Lamy became revered and respected among the culture he embraced.

We stopped in what was the original portion of the structure, which housed "La Conquistadora," the oldest Madonna in the United States. The shrine held the 3-foot wooden statue of Our Lady of Conquering Love, and according the literature it was not seen as a relic capable of creating miracles, but more of a symbol of hope held fast by the religious Spanish colonists after the infamous Pueblo Revolt of 1680.

Oscar was peeking over my shoulder at the brochure, eyebrows furrowed.

"What is it?" I whispered.

He walked around me and stood before the shrine.

"Huh," he said, still intent on the display before us. "I've always been aware of the history of the Catholic church—you know the Spanish and Native cultures of its past..."

I nodded, looking up at the strange doll encased in the wall above us. She represented the bloody revolt and return of the Spaniards to their faithful parish in Santa Fe from what is now El Paso, Texas.

Oscar turned to face me. "But until now, it hadn't really occurred to me that Lamy brought with him his European culture, as well." He pointed to where the brochure stated that *French-Romanesque* was the architectural design of the church.

"I mean surely he didn't simply assimilate into our culture. He had to have brought certain traditions and practices with him, including his language."

My eyes widened at this epiphany: The letters I'd

found enclosed in the fireplace. "I wonder if there's a connection...?"

"Yes...to our mysterious *M*." He nodded and raised his eyebrows.

We left the basilica pondering the possibilities. Someone the archbishop knew, perhaps? Somehow, there must've been a relationship to the San Felipe de Neri parish. After all, Albuquerque was within the vast diocese of territorial New Mexico, and the closest most populated settlement to Santa Fe. But *what was the connection*?

For the moment, the city was beckoning us once again. Out in the bright afternoon sun, we ducked into the courtyards of the buildings surrounding the plaza. To the north we found ourselves in the hidden enchanted gardens of cafes and shops, where ancient cottonwood trees burst forth to the heavens. White lights barely visible in daytime snaked up thick trunks and branches, while whiskey-barrel pots of petunias overflowed on pathways below. Nearby sat patio tables where the waitstaff unloaded margaritas and mimosas from large platters for well-attired diners.

Later, we sat on a painted wrought-iron bench on the patio of The Shed, awaiting our summons to a late afternoon lunch from the maître d'. In the distance, bells from the cathedral chimed as we chatted and enjoyed the ambiance. Once Oscar's name was called, we made our way inside, ducking so as not to hit our heads on the low-hanging door frames original to the 1690s hacienda. We were led past the cantina and into rambling rooms brightly painted in hues of orange, lavender, and hot pink. Consistent with Santa Fe style, punched aluminum lighting fixtures and retablos hung on walls alongside murals depicting rural peasant life along the Rio Grande. "This is the first place I ever had blue corn enchiladas, back when I was a kid," I told Oscar.

"Really? I grew up with the ones my grandma made." He smiled.

The Shed was a popular eatery with locals and tourists alike. Both of us had been here many times before, yet this time with Oscar, it felt new and exciting.

I ordered stacked green chile enchiladas with a fried egg on top.

"Impressive," winked Oscar at the waitress. "I believe I'll try the same, but with red."

As we sipped our drinks—his Dos Equis and my sangría—we discussed the day's events; the fantastic finds for the shop, the possible connection to the letters we'd found. It was exciting, and we looked forward in anticipation to what the future might have in store for us as we enjoyed the delectable feast, complete with chips, salsa, and honey-drenched sopapillas.

Stuffed to the point of drowsiness, we made our way back to the depot, stopping along the way to listen to a street musician playing folk music on her guitar. She wore a white poet's blouse and long, prairie-style patchwork skirt. There was a small crowd gathered, swaying to her lyrical ballads, while an elderly couple danced together in the closed-off street by the plaza. Two children joined them, and soon among the smiles of onlookers there developed an ensemble of free-spirited souls dancing in the splendor of the waning day. Perhaps feeling heady from the sangría, I raised my eyebrows at Oscar, beckoning a dance partner.

He wiggled his back at me, then grabbed my hand.

"I warn you, I'm no good at this."

I laughed. "Me neither!"

The singer strummed the opening chords of Paul McCarthy's "Blackbird," and we joined the moving crowd as he pulled me to his chest, his arm around my waist. As I held him close, I softly sang the lyrics into his ear, breathing in the scent of his lovely cologne mixed with the masculine emissions from his soft skin after the hot day of exploring Santa Fe. I wrapped my arm around his shoulder, and he buried his head in my hair. I could feel his breath, warm and even in my ear.

> "Blackbird singing in the dead of night,
> Take these broken wings and learn to fly...
> All your life
> You were only waiting
> For this moment to arise.
> Blackbird singing in the dead of night
> Take these sunken eyes and learn to see...
> All your life
> You were only waiting
> For this moment to be free.
>
> Blackbird, fly...
> Blackbird, fly into the light of the dark,
> black night..."

TWENTY

Autumn 1891

Such informal reference of "Padre *Julien*" by some of the church members to the kind-hearted priest was acceptable to him in light of the still-recent and deeply troubled history of his infamous predecessors; it wasn't that he was opposed to the moniker, only that his superiors would prefer him to insist they address him by his proper surname, Father *Faustino*—which most of the elderly members did—but he also knew very well that change was slow in coming, and that his important work in this valley and in the larger diocese of its outer regions would take some time.

Today he was off on his humble burro to make the rounds of some of the Indian pueblos on the fringes of the desert towns. He had refused the use of the carriage and driver appointed to him upon his arrival at the San Felipe de Neri parish by order of the Santa Fe basilica. What with the hypocrisy and corruption brought forth by the priests who served the peoples of the New Mexico territories prior to the arrival of Archbishop Lamy, he preferred the simple transport and solitude provided by the old but reliable burro, Faya, who was now his constant companion.

While riding, he could dwell upon the image of the emaciated figure of the crucified Christ. Somehow, the purity of it brought him peace. He kept close to his heart the words of the apostle St. Paul, who warned against the evils of a life of sin, "shunning even the very *appearance* of evil." He wanted nothing more than to honor the memory of his mentor by leading a life commensurate with that of his hallowed friend.

As Faya carefully plodded on, past bare penstemons and Apache plume, beyond the yucca and prickly pear, over the sandy ground where the landscape morphed from the lush green of the valley into the sandy beige of the rising mesa to the west of town, the padre grew more resolute in his commendation by the archbishop. They had had many late evening conversations, reclining in the courtyard of Bishop Lamy's adobe living quarters in the shadow and resplendent grandeur of the basilica in Santa Fe. There, with vivid pink, paper-like petals of the bougainvillea overflowing the walls to his back, the aging priest reflected upon his first encounters with the Indian parishioners spread across the vast space of the Vicariate Apostolic of New Mexico.

At that time, it comprised the entire New Mexico territory. Enormous as the landscape was the task set before him by the Vatican: Lamy had been deeply saddened by the treatment of the native peoples at the hands of the Spaniards and then later, the secular priests, prior to his arrival from France. He had labored alongside them to rebuild their parishes as well as relationships, in hopes that their hearts would be once again fertile to the Catholic message.

With grave intensity, he gave Julien the charge: *"C'est la Grande Commission!"*

He oft repeated the Spanish proverb, *"No hay mal de que por bién no venga,"* which neant "There is no evil from which good cannot come." The bad blood caused by the Pueblo Revolt centuries prior to Lamy's arrival in the New World remained deeply steeped within the pueblo cultures. Reconciliation was still a top priority to the archbishop, and therefore it was also with Julien Faustino. He was profoundly aware of the high expectations that were bestowed upon him by this man of God; he who had dared explore this remote and seemingly forsaken expanse of the Spanish empire in the name of the Holy Trinity, "to spread the gospel into all the world, making Disciples of all nations."

It was a mystery to his congregation, still reeling from the memory of its sordid past and suspicious of Father Faustino: Why had this young priest chosen to take his holy vows to heart, when many of those before him had chosen a life of debauchery, greed, corruption, and even sexual promiscuity instead? What made this "man of the cloth" different from any of the others?

Julien Faustino's earthly father had died when Julien was a boy. He clearly remembered his mother's drive, when he was just seven, to carry on with the duties of a small sheep herd in the absence of her husband. Their shack with an earthen floor and roof situated to the north of Bernalillo along the Rio Grande offered little more than shelter. But he could clearly recall the warmth of a mother's love, a mother who had pounded corn into meal every day and cooked in an *horno* outside, then served the bread alongside a simple soup of pinto beans for every meal.

Alongside her, Julien led the sheep to the river daily, to drink after grazing in the abundant fields of the river valley. He would help her mend fences mown down after a storm had riled the flock, milk the ewes, shear the sheep in the spring, and turn tallow into soap and candles. Every night she would "read" to him from the holy scriptures—that is, she opened the tattered book and searched its pages diligently for the only letters she recognized: *M, A, T, T, H, E, W,* and the numbers *1: 18.* Spreading the pages carefully across her lap with her calloused hands, she would then gather her rosary beads and massage them between her fingers. "*San Mateo, uno, dieciocho,*" her eyes intently scouring the page. "*Este es el relato del nacimiento de Jesús...*" she began, then closed her eyes and recounted the story of the birth of the Christ child she'd memorized from the visits of the priests to her village since her childhood. Her voice was quiet but resilient in the retelling of the story, and by the end, tears were always

214

streaming down her face.

"Un día, mi bebe, tu serás un hombre de Dios," she would tell him, tucking him in safely beneath layers of wool blankets, and covering his face with kisses. This provided more comfort to the small Julien than he could possibly ever desire.

Just before sundown, the padre would arrive in the pueblo along the Rio Puerco and be given a traditional bowl of mutton stew with squash and beans, and a warm cot on which to sleep for the night. Before sunlight, he would be up in preparation of the blessing of Feast Day.

TWENTY-ONE

Autumn, present-day

I had to find out more about the "Mysterious M," as Oscar and I referred to our enigmatic author. While he was keeping busy in Book It as the holiday season drew nearer, I was able to do some research of my own. Cedar was carrying a light load in his final semester at the university and had requested more hours at work. He would be graduating next month and was saving up for his entrance into graduate school in the spring. His almost continual presence at the store afforded me the opportunity to do some digging and find out whatever I could about whoever it was that had written the secret letters.

I began to take extended lunch hours at the Albuquerque Museum. Having undergone a recent renovation of their own, the museum now had extensive, archived memorabilia from Albuquerque's past on display in addition to the many varied styles of artwork created by some of New Mexico's most celebrated and eclectic artists.

I wandered the hallways of glass-encased collections of textiles, pottery, and adobe bricks unearthed from long ago, studying the linotypes and black-and-white photos of prominent members of society long past. There were objects and vestments and tools from different time periods of the city's history, prior to the 16th century, when the Spanish conquistador Coronado was exploring the area in a quest to find gold and the Seven Cities of Cibola. As my eyes scoured the expressionless faces peering back at me, I wasn't even sure what I was looking *for*. They were almost haunting, their eyes vacant, like posed mannequins eternally captured in time.

One group of photographs caught my attention. They were taken at the Alvarado Hotel soon after the arrival of the Atchison, Topeka & Santa Fe Railway in Albuquerque in the 1870s. An assembly of men and women posed on the platform of the Alvarado train station alongside conductors and Pueblo Indians reclining on Navajo blankets.

I recognized the women in the photo as some of the Harvey Girls, with their famous hairdos piled high and loosely gathered on top of their heads, wearing crisp white uniforms with black aprons. The placard underneath the grainy photo read:

> *The Alvarado Hotel lodged train travelers from all over the country, introducing them to the Southwest through first-rate Fred Harvey customer service. Harvey and the AT&SF promoted Albuquerque in its railroad excursions to the "exotic Southwest."*

Many of these photographs were taken by William Cobb, who had come to Albuquerque, as many did over a hundred years ago, for its higher elevation and climate more conducive for folks suffering from tuberculosis. He was Harvard educated and documented much of what we know about the early days of Old Town through his photography, as another placard had informed me.

As I rounded a corner I was instantly struck by the

image of a stunning young woman wearing what appeared to be a wedding dress. Her jet black hair was upswept on the sides and fastened with a silver barrette on top, soft ringlets framing her face. A lace collar showcased the cameo necklace hanging from a black ribbon around her neck.

"Striking, isn't she?" I heard a man's voice from behind me say.

A stocky man in his late twenties, with curly brown hair and a moustache, had slowed to a stop on the other side of me and hugged to his chest the stack of folders he was carrying. Intently studying the image through thick-lensed glasses he added, "I think she's my favorite work of art in here."

He turned to me with a smile and a wink.

"Who is she?" I asked. He shook his head and sighed. "*That* we do not know."

"Well, she is very pretty, isn't she," I commented, admiring her flawless complexion. Unlike most of the other photographs flanking the hallway walls, she had a poised smile on her face. I was reminded of the Mona Lisa, and the secret she was hiding behind her famous smile.

"She is, indeed."

"I'm assuming from the dress this was taken on her wedding day."

"Well, it isn't her wedding day. That we do know. Oh, sorry—Marcos Del Toro," he said extending a hand to me. "I'm slide librarian. I go through and record all of the collections and exhibit donations, so I'm familiar with most of the history of the objects and images on display here."

"Oh, very good. Molly Lewis," I said shaking his hand.

"Hi, Molly." He grinned and turned back to the photograph. "You see here?"

He pointed to what appeared to be a beaded necklace barely visible underneath the lace collar of her dress.

I squinted my eyes.

"It's her rosary."

"Oh," I nodded. "So this must be her..." The word wasn't coming to me. Less familiar with the rituals of the Catholic church than I would've liked to admit, I knew it was an event symbolizing a rite of passage of its young people. "Holy communion?"

"If she were quite a bit younger. She appears to be in her teenage years, right? And if it were her holy communion, her dress would be white, as a bride's, representing the Bride of Christ. But if you notice too, the shade is a little bit darker...it's hard to see in these old black-and-white images, but it's likely either a very light peach maybe, or some other color, not white. So we believe this is from her *quinceañera*."

"Oh, that makes sense." I recalled my daughter, Annalise, attending several of her high school friends' fifteenth birthday parties while growing up here in the Rio Grande valley. Some were lavish affairs, where families spent a fortune on the celebration, exorbitantly catered affairs with parents renting out entire dance halls or hotel ballrooms for their daughters. Others were simple family gatherings where grandmothers and "aunties" traditionally cooked authentic Mexican fare.

"Typically, brides wore bridal veils—new to this time period when Queen Victoria had made them popular in Europe after her wedding—and maybe a pearl necklace. We really don't see rosaries worn other than when they're associated with traditional religious festivities, which is what a girl's fifteenth birthday celebration really was about, especially in those days."

I nodded. "It's fascinating what can be deduced about someone by just studying an image like this."

"Well I'm pleased to help," Marcos smiled at me again. It was obvious he took joy in his job and could quite possibly be a big help to me in my search for answers about our Mysterious M. "So, are you just visiting Albuquerque, or do you live here?"

I wasn't ready to divulge more information than I had to yet about the letters I'd found. I wasn't sure what protocol there was concerning ownership of our discovery in the carpet bag. After all, the letters didn't technically belong to us. Eventually, Oscar and I had discussed, we'd turn the letters over to either the museum or perhaps the University of New Mexico History department.

For now, they remained our shared secret.

"I'm just doing some looking around. I own Old Town Music, and I'm on my lunch break. Don't get over here as often as I'd like."

"Ah," he nodded and turned to face the photograph again. "Well, one more thing about this lovely work of art here. This isn't your typical party gown. Her mother didn't purchase the fabric and a pattern from a local mercantile and sew it up for her. It was ordered from a catalog from a Parisian department store. We have some catalogs in the back with this very dress in it. So she was undoubtedly the daughter of one of our wealthier families in the village at the time. Plus, this is a William Cobb portrait. That her parents could afford to commission a photographer of his caliber meant they weren't sheep farmers. We think we have another of this stunning young lady along with her family somewhere in the archives, but it's been damaged over the years and not fit for exhibit."

I looked closely at the breathtaking girl in the portrait. "Wow. This is great information. Thank you so much, Marcos."

"Any time. My office is just right around the corner," he added before heading down the hallway.

TWENTY-TWO

1891

The nights were beginning to turn cooler as it was nearing the end of October. In the mornings before Mass, the women in the neighboring Vega and Shannon households donned shawls to ward off the chill before heading to church.

Filing into the pews among the murmur of the congregation before the liturgy, the older of the Vega siblings paired by gender with their twin neighbors and engaged in lively discourse. Once the service got underway, they practiced the rites as they'd been taught in catechism, crouching on the kneeler during the Eucharistic Prayer, rubbing their rosary beads between their fingers, making the sign of the cross along with those of the congregation who had done so for generations before them, yet still unsure of their elders' convictions and rituals.

The youngest Vega sibling in his starched cotton shirt and scratchy tweed breeches could hardly contain himself throughout the homily, which seemed to stretch out forever. Nicolas knew when Father Julien was *finally* done he'd be announcing the All Saints Day festivities coming up at the end of the week.

"All of us are anticipating the celebration of our dearly departed in just a few days."

On cue, the child clapped in mime and cheered silently, his toes tapping as they barely skimmed the floor, grinning up at his mother beside him. Mariana smiled and bent over to kiss the top of his bronze head.

"It is a tradition we cherish in this valley, one passed down through the generations, and in which we feel an everlasting connection with loved ones who have gone before us." The padre's voice echoed inside the stoic walls of the San Felipe parish as the announcement was made. "We will journey to the cemetery on Friday evening. It's once again time to start decorating the *ofrendas*"—then he added with special emphasis—"and baking plenty of *pan de muerto*."

There was hearty laughter from the parishioners.

"Whoo-hooo!" squealed Nicolas through cupped hands before his mother, whose arm was resting around his shoulder, covered his mouth with a *Shh*.

"I'm looking forward to seeing all the lovely *catrinas,"* Father Julien smiled. He gave a slight bow in conclusion. "Peace be with you."

"And also with you," the congregation responded resonantly in turn.

The heavy wooden pews creaked collectively, and jovial voices begin to rise as churchgoers made their way into the aisles to greet one another.

"Papacio! *Papacio!"* Nicolas squealed loudly

over the noise, jumping up and down with the back of his grandfather's vest in his grip.

The frail old man turned and smiled. "Yes, Nicolas. What is it?"

"You promised we would make *pan de muerto* together this year! And you said I could help you decorate The Lovely Leonor's *ofrenda*."

Florencio laughed. Of course he remembered. Hardly a day had passed since last year's festivities that his grandson hadn't brought it up to him.

He feigned a confused expression. "I *did*?"

Nicolas didn't miss a beat. He knew his grandfather, always teasing and playful. His favorite phrase was a made-up term he used to express exasperation, and Nicolas yelled it at him over the crowd. "*Santa ma gania,* Papacio!"

Several elderly women gathered nearby frowned in consternation when Florencio burst out laughing, dismayed that he would find comical his grandson's apparent use of a curse word.

By now, Nicolas was giggling too, seeing his grandfather attempting a reprimand before his audience. Florencio cleared his voice.

"You watch your tongue, young man," he chided, shooing him toward the door as he followed close behind.

Outside, the old man lightly smacked the child's behind with his flat cap before replacing it on his head.

Nicolas snickered.

"Don't embarrass me in front of my girlfriends."

"Sorry, Papacio."

Always dapper in his tweed trousers with suspenders, linen shirt, and sable brushed cotton vest, Florencio was sincerely pleased that his little grandson desired to pay homage to the grandmother he never knew. What Nicolas did know was that "The Lovely Leonor" was how his grandfather always referred to his one and only true love, and that in the twenty-seven years since her death, Papacio had never remarried.

"And yes, *mijo*," he said, ruffling his copper hair. "I will teach you how to make her bread."

At this the child grinned and skipped ahead of Florencio. "The marigolds are looking good this year! I'm going to check on them."

"Don't pick any yet—they need to be fresh for the *ofrendas*!" he hollered after him.

Later in the *cocina* alongside Mariana, Florencio assembled ingredients required to make the customary bread: lard, sugar, flour, eggs, anise seed, and an orange. Nicolas sat eagerly on a stool close by.

He watched as his grandfather curled back the peeling of the orange and ground it with the anise seed with a mortar and pestle. In a large bowl he combined the dry ingredients, setting it with a wooden spoon before his grandson on the countertop.

"Here, mix this real good."

In a small *talavera* bowl he dissolved the yeast in water. Combining the dry ingredients with the eggs and animal fat, he then added the sweet flavorings and a pinch of salt. The batter was thick; flouring his hands, Papacio removed it from the bowl and placed it on the countertop where he proceeded to knead the dough for what seemed a lifetime to Nicolas, who continued to patiently observe.

His grandfather picked up the dough one last time and dropped it with a *plop* on the countertop, covering it carefully with cheesecloth.

"And now, we wait." He turned to Nicolas and smiled.

"For what?"

"For the dough to have a chance to rise."

The boy's expression turned downcast. "How long will that take?"

"Not long. We'll check back in a few hours."

"A few *hours?*"

Disappointed, Nicolas knew if he could just be patient, it would be worth it. He leapt from his stool and sprinted outside.

"Don't you want to punch the dough for me?"

"Yes!" he yelled, never slowing down.

"Then don't go running off," his mother called after him. He stopped short of the screen door and turned to head upstairs. Punching the fat, warm dough was his favorite part of making the bread, after the

227

dough had risen and doubled in size. It was the only part his grandfather had allowed him to do—until today. He certainly wasn't going to miss that!

He wondered where his siblings might be, although he knew very well they wouldn't be even the slightest bit interested in playing with him. He quietly ascended the wooden staircase, his sister's room directly at the top to the left. Tiptoeing now, he sneaked up to Pilar's door and, opening it silently, spied her intently brushing her long black hair at her vanity. Just as she caught sight of her little brother in her mirror through the sliver in the doorway, he burst in screaming, "*Augh*!!"

She leapt in her chair and slammed her fists into her lap, her hairbrush clattering to the wooden floor.

"Tarnation!" Pilar bellowed. She jumped up and in two strides had her now-regretful brother by the collar, squeezing it tightly around his neck so that his face became red as he struggled to free himself. "You little *ass*. I'll kill you if you do that again!"

Finally squirming out of her grasp, he managed a laugh as he glanced back down the hallway, making his escape. Behind him, he slammed the door of his brother's room, panting for air.

He turned to look around, but Joaquin was nowhere inside. His window, however, had been flung wide open. Walking to it, Nicolas placed his hands on the casement and looked out. He caught sight of his

228

brother in his peripheral vision bracing himself on the sloped roof outside, waving frantically.

At first Nicolas started to wave back in reply. He realized quickly, however, that Joaquin was not greeting him. Rather, he had something he was shielding from his brother on the other side of his body.

"What are you doing?"

"What are *you* doing? Get the hell outta here!"

"I want to come out there and sit on the roof, too."

"No, Nicolas!" Joaquin snarled.

Nicolas put his head down. Once again he was being shooed away. He started to leave, then looked back at his brother. "What is that you're hiding out there?"

"None of your business, *entremetido*," he replied through clenched teeth. "I told you, get lost!"

A trail of smoke was drifting up from beside him in the fall breeze, wafting toward the open window.

"No problemo, I'll just go tell Mama you're smoking, then."

He started away from the window.

"Stop!" shrieked Joaquin. "Wait!"

Shaking his head, he inhaled deeply from the glowing cigar, mumbling to himself on the exhale. He softened his composure. "You can come out here. Take off your shoes and socks, though"—adding with venom—"and *be careful*."

Nicolas quickly removed his boots and knee socks and hopped over the window casing.

Just what I need, to babysit my little brother. Joaquin simmered, taking another puff of his cigar and staring off into the cottonwood canopy outside his window. Its remaining autumn leaves were shimmering gold, with rust-colored piles forming mounds on the cool ground below, their thawing aroma heavy in the early mornings after the nights' frost.

"Where did you get those?" Nicolas inquired, as he sat beside his big brother, who clearly resented his presence at this moment. Joaquin was his only brother, though, and Nicolas worshipped him.

Joaquin held the dwindling butt to his mouth and inhaled, not taking his gaze off the ground below. "Where do you think?"

Nicolas watched him, nodding. He knew he'd taken it from their father's stash in the barn. "A dandy."

Expressionless, Joaquin faced him. He exhaled a large puff of smoke into his face. Nicolas blinked and choked, fanning his face with his hands.

"Better not ever try it if you know what's good for you."

Both of them barefoot with their legs propped against the tin roof below them, they sat for a while in silence.

"So, what did you do to piss off Pilar?" asked Joaquin.

Nicolas snickered. "Anything I want, I guess."

His brother briefly nodded his head. "That's true enough of both of us. You better be careful. Someday she's really going to kill you."

Nicolas watched as Joaquin took a final puff of the stubby cigar, tapping its glowing end on the cool roof to extinguish the light. He pulled a small leather pouch out of his pocket and unwrapped a handkerchief, exposing a stash of several bound cigars and a box of wood matches. He returned the "evidence" to its container and concealed them once again, standing carefully, thoughtfully placing his footing to match the angle of the steep incline. Beneath the wood frame of the dormer there was a loose bit of metal flashing that Joaquin pried back, and he tucked the pouch where it wouldn't be noticed by passers-by below.

As he made his way back inside, he turned to his little brother.

"And if you tell anyone about this"—he glanced at the leather pouch— "you will only wish it was Pilar that got to you first. Now *get the hell out of here!*"

Back at his post atop the kitchen stool, Nicolas intently watched as Papacio gently picked up the soft dough and carefully molded it within a greased and floured cast iron pan.

Bent over the smooth, cool concoction, he then took a paring knife and began to carve the image of bones representing those who had passed over, but who

231

were not quite gone from this world. When he was done, Nicolas saw him scrawl a word he couldn't decipher into the delicate dough.

Papacio was ready to place the cast iron pan into the metal cook oven. "Time to open the gates, Nicolas!"

Entrusted with the task, the child carefully pulled open the heavy steel door and stood back. His grandfather slid the bread inside and nodded for his grandson to close it. He dusted the flour from his hands onto his apron and sighed. "This one will be ours to enjoy this week, and we'll make another for the altar in a few days, for the Lovely Leonor."

Nicolas nodded and smiled. "You carved a name into the loaf, Papacio. Whose was it?"

"I'll do it again with the next one, too," replied Florencio with a smile. "'*Gordita*'."

Nicolas returned a wide-eyed expression to his grandfather, who laughed.

"It was a term of endearment for her."

Onofre, who was seated at the *cocina* table polishing his Colt Dragoon revolver, grunted with a smirk. "*Hmph, y*our grandmama was fat, *mijo*, but damn she could cook." He turned to his wife and, addressing her in Spanish, asked her, "When are we going to eat, I'm starving!"

Finally, it was Friday! thought Nicolas as he bounced out of bed.

Still in his pajamas and socks, he didn't bother putting on his boots like his mother nagged him to wear whenever he went outside. He bounded down the stairs, careful to balance himself using the railing, and ran through the kitchen, sliding to a halt at the screen door. Slamming it opening he gave Mariana, already cooking over the steaming stove, an obligatory *"Hola, Mama!"* without even glancing in her direction before resuming his pace, sprinting across the yard toward the carriage house.

She shook her head at her messy-haired boy and chuckled. It was barely light outside, but Nicolas didn't care if Papacio hadn't yet got himself dressed. There was no time to waste—tonight the whole town would be celebrating *Día de los Muertos*, and they had to make ready the decorations for the altars.

Just before he reached the door, it swung open.

He skidded to a stop inches prior to it smacking him in the face.

Grinning, he waved joyously to his grandfather. *"Hola, Papacio!"*

"What were you going to do, *pequeño*, break it down?"

Florencio pulled his loose suspenders over his shoulders and reached for his flat cap, allowing his

233

grandson to catch his breath.

Panting, with his hands on his knees, Nicolas stood upright and grabbed the old man's hand, tugging him toward the house.

"Rápido, rápido!"

After breakfast and lunch were over, Papacio, Mariana, and Nicolas were once again busy in the kitchen, creating loaves of *pan de muerto*. As the day wore on and the evening sun began to sink below the horizon, a beehive of activity was taking place both inside and out.

Walking toward the Vega home arm in arm were Pilar and Elza Shannon.

"Do you want to wear a *catrina*'s mask?"

"Hmm, I don't know...I think I'll just watch this year," Elza sighed. "Mother isn't very happy about any of this as it is. She may come unhinged if she sees me wearing one."

"That's the point, silly. She won't know it's you!" laughed Pilar. "At least try one on."

"Is it scary?" inquired her soft-spoken friend.

"What, the masks? They're just skeletons; that's all. It's all in fun."

"And, tell me again, why do you dress as a skeleton?"

The cultural celebration equally baffled her mother, who pouted as she stood before a mirror in the Shannons' Victorian parlor. For the life of her, Daniella could not understand why these primitive villagers practiced these morbid traditions, dancing around as skeletons and bringing food and gifts to their dead relatives. She couldn't imagine tomorrow's mess mere feet from the church building; she shivered at the thought of coyotes and other scavengers having a field day gorging themselves in the early hours of dawn. And on holy ground!

This was their religion?

As her husband made his way down the staircase, he stopped at the landing and gazed at his wife standing in the dark room. He smiled in an attempt to cheer her obviously foul mood.

"Well, aren't you a sight, darling."

Frowning, she glanced up at him and sashayed to the parlor window, moving aside its heavy silk curtains to watch the darkened forms of "spirits" dancing in the night.

"Explain to me again, Theophilus, why on earth are we to attend this...*dirge*?"

He laughed softly, wrapping his arms around her waist and attempting to kiss her neck. She stiffened, and he stepped beside her instead.

There was a bonfire in the distance beside the church, and the boisterous laughter of revelers in the night air carried to the Shannons' ears.

"Daniella, this is where we live now. These are our friends. No, they are not *le bon ton*"—at this she exhaled sharply and rolled her eyes— "but they are our neighbors, and this is their culture. I'm willing to bet that you'll fancy yourself having a jolly good time if you'll just try to enjoy yourself."

A maid entered the parlor carrying a black fringed shawl as Theo turned to pour a shot of brandy from the crystal decanter on the sideboard.

"Thank you, Eudora," said Daniella as the shawl was placed across her shoulders. "You may retire for the evening. Mr. Shannon and I shall be returning very soon."

Eudora curtsied. "Very good, ma'am."

Daniella swept past her husband to the entryway of the grand house.

Theo slammed the drink down his throat and reached for his walking stick, tapping the brass ferrule on the floor as the brandy smoothly burned its way down, clearing his sinuses. He took a deep breath and started toward the front door.

Long live the Queen.

The girls giggled behind their painted masks, dancing skulls with marigolds crowning their foreheads. The bright orange blooms were everywhere, seemingly blossoming from the *ofrendas* carried by loved ones of the dearly departed, sprouting from the buttonholes of bedecked spritely *calacas* and adorning braids of the dark and mysterious *catrinas*. Onofre and

236

Mariana walked ahead of the family toward the church. In his arms, Onofre carried a large basket of fruit, the *pan de muerto,* and clinking glass bottles of mezcal and tequila. Mariana had donned the veil from her wedding day as she had every year for the stroll to the church and, as a bride, carried a spray of marigolds.

Scampering down the veranda steps behind his family was the youngest of the Vega children, rushing to keep up. He spied his grandfather ahead of him, carrying the flour sack that held his fiddle, which he would be playing later in the evening along with the other mariachis at the cemetery. Catching up to Papacio, Nicolas reached for his hand; while he was giddy with excitement, he wasn't yet confident of what surrounded him in the darkness. He was safe here beside his grandfather.

Papacio bent to whisper in his ear: "Ready to awaken the Lovely Leonor from her eternal sleep?" He squeezed his hand tighter and skipped alongside him.

The breeze in the evening air softly whistled through the cottonwoods overhead as the caravan rounded the corner to the cemetery. The others who had joined them along the way were forming a hushed crowd gathered before the whitewashed picket fence encircling the resting place of their loved ones.

"Can you hear them?" Florencio leaned down to his grandson.

"What?"

He touched a gnarled finger to his lips. "Listen... *los angelitos*."

Nicolas peered up into the blackened sky, mouth agape, straining to hear the tiny wings of babies fluttering overhead.

He held his breath.

"Do you hear their little wings?"

His grandson squinted harder into the darkness, intent on seeing one of the baby angels—the spirits of infants captured for eternity in their passing from the earth—perhaps lighting in the ancient trees above their heads.

"Yes, Papacio..." he whispered, nodding faintly, as remnants of autumn leaves were tickled by the passing wind. "I hear them."

Father Faustino was standing before the gate at the entrance of the cemetery. Behind him flashed shadows of crosses and headstones in the firelight from the bonfire nearby. He made the sign of the cross and raised his palms in the air.

"We welcome you, beloved friends and family, who have gone ahead of us, not yet into the arms of Jesus. Tonight is yours, and we honor you! We beckon you to our altars. Come, eat. Drink. And make merry, for the night is fleeting!"

The rickety gate squeaked on its hinges as the padre flung it open and stepped aside.

From the back of the crowd, Daniella Shannon

238

watched with brows furrowed as the mass poured into the cemetery, snaking through rows of headstones with piles of dead-headed flowers and the faint, tinkling sound of glass liquor bottles as the revelry grew louder. Her farmhand, Frederico, meandered with his mother along the throngs of wooden crosses and carved saints festooned in ribbons and beads. He placed the *ofrenda* he'd been carrying at the foot of one of the mounds as his elderly mother sat and rearranged what Daniella surmised was part of the garish sacrifice to Frederico's late father.

There is no reverence here! she assessed smugly. *This isn't religion, it's blasphemy.*

Soon the mariachi band struck up a raucous number, the trumpet and stringed bass echoing off the adobe church walls. Partiers drank tequila and danced in the street after erecting shrines to their loved ones buried six feet underground.

In the distance, she observed a gaggle of preened "ladies" gathered around the bonfire, prancing around in their colorful skirts with masks of the macabre hiding their faces. One stood out to her amongst the rest, with porcelain hair gathered in ringlets at the nape of her neck.

Daniella marched toward her daughter and grabbed her by the arm, spinning her around.

Elza's giggling waned at the sight of her furious mother. The mask she was wearing dropped to her side.

239

"You're making yourself ridiculous!" hissed Daniella.

Elza glanced around her at the other girls, who were presently consumed in gossip, swaying to the beat of the deafening music. She was simultaneously engulfed in embarrassment and rage. She felt her face flush as she jerked her arm out of her mother's grasp.

"If I'm such a disappointment to you, Mother, then *go home!*"

Daniella calmly appraised the ignorant crowd engrossed in their merrymaking and raised an eyebrow at her daughter. "Well, of *that*," she leaned closer to Elza with a smirk upturning the corners of her mouth, "you can be sure."

She whirled around and pushed her way through the crowd, attempting to find her husband. Before long she spotted him next to the imposing silhouette of Onofre Vega.

"I'm going home, Theophilus," she spat.

Onofre began to tip his hat to her before she spun on her heel in a hasty exit. Instead, he raised the bottle of tequila to her backside, then offered it to his speechless neighbor. After a moment, Theo burst out laughing at the gesture.

"*Sí, amigo,*" he said, slapping the expressionless Mexican's back.

"*Gracias!*" Theo grabbed the bottle. Turning it upside down, he took a generous swig.

240

"De nada," Señor Vega responded with what sounded to Theo like the closest thing Onofre ever came to expressing amusement.

Leaving the pounding of the awful music in her retreat, Daniella wondered how on earth she would find sleep tonight with it resounding throughout the valley. She halfway expected her husband to be trailing her, but when she glanced back, he was nowhere to be seen.

She shivered and picked up her pace, the atmosphere around her suddenly closing in as she thought she heard the faint sound of footsteps approaching. She stopped and turned around, heartbeat pounding. Her eyes searched the dim figures in the distance as fireworks exploded behind the cemetery walls, being quickly obscured in the distance.

Daniella gathered her shawl closely around her neck and continued in haste toward her home. Keeping her head low, she was sure she could make out a dark figure crouching in the shrubbery of the Vega home in her peripheral vision as she passed by.

Her heart now thumping in her chest, she began to run.

A foolish thing to do if it's an animal.... The thought came too late, as whatever it was in the darkness darted toward her.

A piercing cry escaped her lips as she froze and closed her eyes.

"Augh!" came the screech of a neighborhood

child.

As she heard it scampering away, she took a hesitant glance in its direction.

Adrenaline coursed through her veins as she thought she caught a glimpse of copper-colored hair disappearing into the blackness.

"It's time I say *buenas noches,*" said Father Julien to Mariana. For a moment they stood side by side, observing the festive scene before them. Tonight the children of the orphanage had been given the opportunity to partake of the festivities, and they ran through the rows of decorated tombstones, each piled high with flame-colored blossoms, food, and memorabilia.

"You know," he remarked, leaning in to her, "these children don't have any idea who their families are. They know nothing of their bloodlines, their pasts...their histories."

She nodded, watching them play, darting in and out of the shadows cast by the crackling bonfire. They were unabashedly blissful, without inhibition.

"It makes me sad for them," she replied. "That is why they need *this*, to be a part of something. To *belong.*"

The padre nodded. "I think they feel loved here."

Mariana turned to him. "I know they do, because

242

of you."

He smiled and reached for her hand, enveloping her fragile grip within his, bringing it up to his face with a gentle kiss.

"The sisters should be collecting them soon. I'm sure they will all sleep soundly tonight."

"Buenas noches," she said, smiling, and walked away.

He turned and made his retreat toward the rectory.

In the courtyard, Julien heard the scurrying of feet behind him. He stopped momentarily and looked about, then seeing nothing suspicious let himself inside his modest quarters.

When the door was closed, Pilar burst out in nervous giggles.

"You almost got us caught!" whispered Oliver.

They had jumped into the Castilian rose bushes planted along the arched portico walls to escape notice when the padre had approached.

"Oh, *sí*?" she responded coquettishly. "It was *you* chasing me!"

As she stepped away from him, her black lace shawl remained in the thorny embrace of the rosebush. She threw her head back in a gale of laughter as Oliver shushed her and attempted to gingerly extricate it, carefully handling the intricate fabric so as not to pull the threading. Once he freed it, he turned and held it

243

out to her.

The moonlight was shimmering on her face, enhancing her beguiling features, her black eyelashes sweeping over her wide, dark eyes staring back at him. Her blood red lips were enticing, beckoning him.

Pilar spun around, whirling her ebony braid from where it lay across her spine. Her white cotton poet's blouse was worn off the shoulder, exposing her smooth skin, milky in the moonlight. She glanced back at him.

Oliver stepped toward her, replacing the shawl. She turned around to face him again, her eyes fixed on his gaze.

"You're simply enchanting." He breathed, inhaling the sickeningly sweet scent of the marigolds encircling her hair. It was intoxicating. Lifting her chin with his fingers, he leaned down and gently pressed his mouth against hers; it was dewy and warm, and the sensation sent a bolt of electricity through Oliver's body.

Suddenly, Pilar shoved his chest violently away from her, jolting him from his moment of ebullience and causing him to stumble backward.

She stared at him tauntingly, her chest heaving.

Stupefied, he raised his hands in protest, regaining his footing. *Surely I hadn't read her wrong—*

Teasingly, a smile started to form in the corner of her mouth as her eyes narrowed. Gathering her skirts in one hand, she replaced the skull mask with the other, laughter cascading from behind it as she darted away into the shadows.

He shook his head. "Oh, no you don't!" he yelled after her, forgetting his previous fear of discovery and chasing her into the gardens beneath the terraces outside of the courtyard.

She danced around the stone fountain with Oliver close behind. She swung behind the safety of a cottonwood trunk, peeking around the other side, making a dash for the fountain once again as he was closing in on her.

At the sound of the close of a gate on the far side of the courtyard, the pair froze just as Oliver had captured his giggling runaway in his muscular embrace. Unaware of their presence, two nuns were making their way to gather the children from the evening's festivities.

As they passed, Pilar and Oliver stood close together, his arms encircling her waist, hers on his pounding chest. She was keenly aware of the power she had over him in this moment, and she was dizzy with excitement. This was more than she had hoped for in the months since she had met this tall, fair Brit. He was exquisite beyond compare.

For a moment the two simply breathed together, motionless, embracing the fiery heat of their shared proximity.

Then Pilar stood on tiptoe, leaning against his

firm build, her mouth searching once again for his.

He took her hands and stepped away from her.

She exhaled a laugh and again moved toward him.

This time she stood confused as he took her hands and kissed them, then turned to walk toward the jubilant crowd.

"But," she smiled, stepping closer again, "I'm not playing now."

He breathed deeply and glanced behind him. "Neither am I."

Stunned, her heart sank as she watched him disappear into the shadows. Fireworks crackled and echoed against the thick parish walls in the distance.

Oliver walked purposefully ahead, passion burning within him. He knew very well if he had wanted to, he could have easily had her. He knew he had not been wrong about the signals she'd been sending him for months now, that had he so desired, she was ripe for the plucking.

However, ingrained in his very being, Oliver was a gentleman first. Perhaps it was because it had been instilled in him all of his life, or maybe it was that she was too willing; this desert rose who'd taunted him from afar for so long was also the friend of his sweet, innocent sister. He would never allow Elza to be treated with such wanton disregard as he had been tempted by this evening by the likes of Pilar Vega. She was a rare beauty, to be sure, but he couldn't take advantage of her. It was too easy, and his urge was powerful. Yet, somewhere deep inside, Oliver knew that regardless of her aggressive flirtations, she was somebody's daughter, a sister; he would not compromise her reputation in a moment's folly.

TWENTY-THREE

November, present day

"We are never going to find anything out about the Mysterious M as long as we keep it to ourselves," Oscar said one night over steaming, oversized mugs of posole after Book It had closed. We were sharing the Spanish Colonial loveseat we'd picked out on our shopping excursion to Santa Fe in the spring.

"This is excellent," I said, taking another spoonful. "I'm so glad you're making it for the Holiday Stroll next week."

"Thank you." He smiled. "I'm serious, though."

"I know you are," I replied, blowing into my cup to cool off its contents.

Oscar looked at me as we continued to eat in silence.

"I know they're your baby."

I looked up at him. "What, the letters?"

He just smiled at me.

"I guess you're right."

"You don't want somebody else to get their hands on something you want to figure out all by yourself."

"That's not all of it," I frowned. "I mean, yes, I'm stubborn."

Oscar laughed, then began to whistle and avert his gaze.

I gave him a soft jab to his calf with my foot.

"It's just, I feel like this is *ours*. Well, obviously they're not really *ours*, but we found them right in the middle of remodeling—"

"—the store, I know, but—"

"No," I interrupted with raised eyebrows.

He stared at me expectantly.

"Right in the middle of remodeling our *lives*."

Oscar grinned. "As a literary lover, I can appreciate how that is symbolic for you." He put his empty cup on the side table and waited for me to finish.

"Yes, it is, thank you." I nodded, handing him mine. "You know, Paul would have never understood that."

"Well, beautiful—" He leaned forward and kissed me softly on the lips, then looked deeply into my eyes. "I'm not Paul."

"And I'm so grateful. " I leaned over and kissed him again. "You do make me feel beautiful. But you don't know how much *you* completely take *my* breath away."

Oscar sighed and placed his hands gently around my face.

"Molly," he said, looking intently into my eyes. "You have to know I love you."

I felt those now familiar tears of gratitude burning as they sprang into my eyes. I blinked them back and squeezed his hands.

"Oh, Oscar," I managed to whisper. "I love you, too." We kissed once more and embraced each other. I was blissful.

"You know," I said, with my arms still around his neck. "It's almost been a year since we met."

He began to giggle and pulled away. "Yeah, I was thinking that *Good King Wenceslas* should be 'our song.'"

I burst out laughing.

"Well," I said standing up to leave. "We'll never forget it, that's for sure."

He stood up with me.

"Okay then, I will go to the museum tomorrow, then to talk to Marcos, and take the letters with me."

"I think that's a good idea."

I reached up and put my hands around Oscar's soft neck, pulling his head to mine. We stood with our foreheads together and just breathed for a few moments.

Feeling him breathing on my skin, the scent of his cologne, the comfortable familiarity—he had just told me *he loves me*, for heaven's sake! I was heady.

"This is getting harder and harder to do, saying goodnight to you," he said.

I took a deep breath. "I know."

He took a step backward and held my hands between us, kissing each of them. He sighed. "Goodnight, my darling."

TWENTY-FOUR

November 1891

"*Madre,* I'm going next door to visit Elza."

Pilar swept past Mariana on her way out the door. She was carrying her violet parasol and pulling on a pair of gloves.

"*Un momento, por favor,*" her mother's voice rose. "You didn't ask to go out."

She stared blinking at her. "Well, I am now."

"Young lady, you're welcome to *ask* if you may go visit your friend—"

Onofre's voice boomed from his seat at the kitchen table upon which his feet were propped. "Of course you may go, Jita."

"Thank you, Papa," Pilar smiled and headed out the door.

Mariana's mouth ajar, she helplessly shook her head at her husband.

He yelled at her in Spanish. "What the hell, Mariana? She can go see her friend!"

She took a deep breath as she had countless times before. "*Sí,* Onofre. But your *bebe* doesn't need to go running around the countryside unaccompanied."

He snorted. "*Muy bién, Señora* Shannon. If you

say so."

She silently returned her work.

Rico Ruiz was diligently laboring in the shade of the corral, using a beveled broad axe to at once chop through the slender spruce branch in his grip, then remove its rough outer bark. With each swipe, the blade blithely stripped away the tree husk, as a butcher would fillet venison from the bone for a stew. The splintered pieces accumulated in a pile beneath his boots.

In spite of the fact that it was November, he was working up a sweat. Peeling off his shirt, he flung it over a low-hung rafter, stopping momentarily to rest.

When he looked up, Pilar Vega was standing across the corral, watching him.

She gave him a nod, beckoning him to come speak to her.

Suddenly self-conscious of his roughshod appearance, Rico retrieved his shirt and wiped his face. He slung it over his shoulder and approached her. She twirled her parasol over her shoulder, knowing somewhere on the premises Oliver Shannon might be watching her right now.

"Señorita." He looked up at her, eyes squinting from the tiny bits of debris and dust he'd inadvertently now wiped into his eyes from his shirt.

"Do you know if Elza is home?" she inquired, knowing fully all she need do was knock on the front door to find out for herself.

He shook his head. "I don't know—sorry..."

Mostly he was apologizing for disappointing her, and it made him feel more aware of his inability to bridge the class barrier between them—especially standing here like this, covered in perspiration and likely smelling like one of Theophilus Shannon's short-horn cattle.

Pilar couldn't help but notice the sinew in his arm muscles, his well-defined chest heaving to catch a breath. She noticed the axe still in his grasp.

"What are you doing?"

"Oh," he turned around toward the pile of *latillas* and the scattered shavings surrounding the barn. "Señora Shannon wants a winter garden, and so Mr. Shannon wants me to build her a little *puerta....*"

He continued explaining as Pilar's eyes scoured the landscape, searching for a glimpse of Oliver.

"Uh-huh," she smiled when they turned to face each other again, having no knowledge whatsoever of or interest in what he had just said. "That's nice."

She began to head for the Shannons' front door.

"I never figured out which *catrina* you were," he called after her. "You know, the other night."

Pausing, Pilar turned and glanced at him, batting her eyelashes and giggling. "I was the prettiest one, of

255

course!"

"*Of course,*" he repeated, his confidence swelling. "By far, *la más hermosa.*"

He watched her walk away, his pulse soaring. He pondered why she hadn't gone to the front door in the first place.

Could it be possible? he dared to hope. *Had she wanted to see me?*

Elza was in the library of the great house, reclining on a leather sofa reading *A Christmas Carol.*

"Listen to this, Mother," she said, reading aloud from her novel. "This sounds like something you might say:

> "There are some upon this earth of ours," returned the Spirit, "who lay claim to know us, and who do their deeds of passion, pride, ill-will, hatred, envy, bigotry, and selfishness in our name, who are as strange to us and all our kith and kin, as if they had never lived. Remember that, and charge their doings on themselves, not us."

"I would fancy you feel the same way about the goings-on in our little village. What do you think, do I have you pegged?" Intent on her embroidery from her chaise longue, Daniella raised an eyebrow.

"I would think your Mr. Dickens a thoughtful assessor."

"Now, how did I know?"

Daniella fumed internally at the memory of her experience during the All Saints Day fiesta. Somehow, she was going to bring a little culture to this paganistic valley if it killed her. She inhaled sharply and announced to her daughter, "I was thinking of hosting a Christmas party."

Elza slid herself upright and put her book down beside her. "Oh, Mother! Truly?"

Eudora appeared in the doorway and quietly cleared her throat.

"Miss Pilar Vega here to see you, *Miss*."

"Oh, you came!" Elza squealed at the sight of her friend. She jumped up to greet her, grasping Pilar's collapsed parasol and handing it to the maid. "Thank you, Eudora."

"Pilar," acknowledged Daniella with a terse smile.

"Mrs. Shannon," she curtsied in response. "Did I hear you mention a party?"

"Yes!" gushed Elza. It was the first time in days Daniella had seen her daughter express joy in her presence. Elza took her friend by the hand and led her to the sofa. "Tell her, Mother!"

Daniella lowered the sampler she was working on to her lap. "Well, I was thinking something like the ball we hosted in Derbyshire—oh what was it—about four seasons ago, I believe?"

"*Oh*, how could I forget," swooned Elza, her hands clutched at her chest. She turned to Pilar. "We had turtle soup, and *mmm*...the pastries—oh they were *divine!*"

Pilar, sitting as erect as she could make herself, tried not to balk at the mention of "turtle soup," but she couldn't help but squirm a little.

For the first time since Pilar had known her, Daniella Shannon's face lit up. "It was the most wondrous evening, such gaiety! Perhaps we can find some Christmas crackers here for pulling and do some wassailing." She turned to Pilar. "Young lady, have you ever had Christmas pudding?"

"No," she shook her head. "I've not."

"Well, then, we shall remedy that. I'll send out invitations with our Christmas cards."

TWENTY-FIVE

November, Present day

I sat down at Marcos Del Toro's desk with the carpetbag of wrapped letters on my lap concealed inside a gym bag.

"It's nice to see you again, Molly," he said reclining in his office chair with an expectant expression on his face. "So, what is it that you wanted to see me about?"

I took a deep breath and began my story of discovering the letters concealed in the fireplace, starting with, "I wasn't completely honest with you when we first met..." and ending with how the disintegrating carpet bag was unearthed in the demolition process of the shop renovation, and that I was now on a mission to discover who wrote the mysterious letters.

"We think they may be love letters. They're written in French, and I can't completely understand them. The last time I took French was in college many moons ago," I laughed nervously. "But I could make out some phrases that seemed to be the writer's expression of affection to the intended recipient, whoever that is. Of course *that* is the $100,000 question, right, who they're written by and who they're written for? By my account, they appear to be pretty much in chronological order, but I haven't looked through them all. They were written starting in about the mid-1870s. And they're signed with simply one letter: *M*."

I wasn't completely convinced he would be accommodating in helping us solve the mystery yet and studied his expressionless face after I finished speaking.

He looked at the bag in my lap, and back up to my face, then down at the bag again.

"So, they're inside there?" he asked, his eyes growing wide and looking up at me again.

"Well, yes," I said. I felt myself tightening my grip on the strap of the gym bag.

Marcos's face evolved into a goofy grin. A laugh burst out of him. "Well, heck yeah, I'll help you figure out who wrote them. Let's take a look!"

I thought he was going to leap out of his chair with enthusiasm. Feeling a flood of relief, I stood to place the bag on his desk in front of him. He rose and carefully unzipped it, reaching into his desk drawer and pulling on a pair of latex gloves with which to extract the fragile contents. After placing the carpet bag atop a nearby table, he flipped on a swivel lamp for further inspection, adjusting it to shine directly inside.

He used some sort of tweezer type of instrument to undo the ribbon on the first stack of letters, then gingerly unfolded the letter on the top of the stack before placing it onto the tabletop.

"Hold on—I'll be back in a sec. I'm going to get Charlize. She's our intern from Belgium." He wiggled his eyebrows at me and exited the room with his hands raised in a 90-degree angle at the elbows facing toward him, like a freshly scrubbed surgeon prior to surgery.

Soon he returned with a trendy, fresh-faced grad student in tow, his arms still in the air. She was wearing ripped jeans, a plain white t-shirt, and platform heels, with a bandana covering a head full of cornrows.

"Charlize, Molly. Molly, Charlize."

"Bonjour," she said cheerfully.

"Hello," I smiled.

"Okay, Charlie. We need you to do something for us," he instructed, pointing to the letter on the table. "*Read.*"

As she reached for it Marcos screeched.

"*Wait*, wait, wait! You need these," he insisted, fetching another pair of latex gloves.

We both jumped at his outburst and exchanged looks.

"Sorry," he said. "I get a little excited at the prospect of fascinating, new discoveries."

"A *little*?" said Charlize, pulling on the gloves and hesitating before attempting to pick up the letter again. She glanced at Marcos.

He nodded, "Go ahead." She smiled and shook her head. "Merci beaucoup."

"*De nada*," he laughed.

Charlie rolled her eyes. "Not the same."

"I know," replied Marcos impatiently. "*Andale!*"

At first Charlie scanned the contents of the letter, quickly reading aloud at a barely audible whisper.

"Holy cow, I love it when she talks like that."

Charlize shook her head. "Focus, *s'il vous plaît*. Ok. This one is dated 1871. It says:

'My dearest angel,
God blessed me with you the day He put us together. Despite the fact that we cannot be together every moment, I cherish your love over all others. You are my heart and soul. I cannot take a

breath without knowing you are walking the face of this earth along with me, for you are the air that I breathe.

Forever yours, my sweet love.

~M'

She handed it back to Marcos and picked up the remaining letters from the bundle, carefully leafing through them and unfolding some to peruse. Charlize nodded as she mumbled the contents to herself, folding them up and replacing them neatly in the bunch.

"Can you open another group?" she asked Marcos, who obliged with painstaking care.

She unfolded the one on top and lifted it to her face.

"1875," she remarked and continued to read quietly to herself.

Finally after opening and refolding several batches of the bundles she said, "They pretty much say the same thing. While the language is expressive of deep love, there is nothing in here that I've read so far that appears overtly passionate or sensual in nature."

"Huh," I remarked. "But you don't think they may be simply platonic love letters between close friends?"

"No, I don't think so," said Charlize. "The phrases used here for 'love'—"*Je pense toujours à toi,*" 'I always think about you,' et "*J'ai besoin de toi,*" 'I need you,' and so on are less passionate than say, "*Je suis amoureux,*" 'I am in love with you,' which I'm not finding in these letters. However, there is no denying that there is something deeper here. The writer is definitely expressing his deep personal feelings toward the reader."

I looked at Marcos, who shrugged.

"So you think the writer is a man?"

"Not necessarily, however, a man during this time period was more likely to be educated, or at least more literate, than women.

"Additionally, there are some sloppy syntax and grammar errors in what I read. My guess is that this is not a person for whom French is their first language."

"You know, that other photo I told you about, the one with our quinceañera girl," said Marcos. "It had a priest in it and some other folks. I have a hunch about him and the only tie I can think of to the French-speaking community in the middle of territorial New Mexico. Let me do some digging and find out who they were."

Later that afternoon, Cedar buzzed me in my office.

"A phone call for you from one 'Marcos of the Bulls,' line two, m'lady."

"Thank you, Cedar," I said and picked up the other line. "Hello?"

"So, Molly, I know who our priest is. And I was right about my hunch: He did speak French."

By 5 o'clock that afternoon, Oscar and I were seated in Marcos's office, along with Charlize. Marcos was on the phone wrapping up some other work for the day. We exchanged looks in anticipation of what he might be sharing with us.

He hung up and held out a hand to Oscar to introduce himself.

"Okay, so of course everything we collect now is

processed digitally."

He started typing on his computer, and the screen behind him on the wall lit up. "So here's the image I told you about."

On the screen appeared the partial image of an old black-and-white photo that, from the ragged edges, looked as if it had been torn in half. There were several Hispanic people who appeared to be possibly related and dressed to the nines.

They were gathered together on a porch in the tightly cropped scene; on the right, a young man was standing behind a little boy in knickers; then beside him was a priest in traditional vestments with a pleasant expression on his face. His hand cupped the elbow of a beautiful woman beside him, and next to her presumably her husband, a very serious-looking man to say the least—he was intimidating in his hulking stature, enormous compared to the other figures in the photo. In spite of the deep-set lines in his stoic expression, he had likely been handsome at one time and looked dapper in a dark leather vest and hat. These were the clearest figures in the photo because to his left, a young woman could be seen only from about the jaw up.

The photo had been ripped just below her nose and cheekbones, diagonally from the top right. She did appear to be facing the camera directly, whereas the others were turned to the left a bit to face her. Had the photo been intact, I imagined the emphasis would've been entirely on her. "We think this was taken early in the 1890s. It's a Cobb image, as well," continued Marcos. "The priest at that time here at the church in Old Town was a gentleman by the name of Julien Faustino. It was pretty easy to find out that information, and I also got my hands on the church ledgers and so forth. There's a plethora of information on the religious celebrations and history of the church well before this time period forward, and also the identities of many who worked at the church, including the nuns of the Sisters of Charity. They ran the orphanage and school at the San Felipe de Neri.

"One thing we know for sure is that Father Faustino just so happened to be a prodigy—and the dear friend of—Archbishop Lamy of Santa Fe. Of course we all know Lamy was from *France...*"

Oscar and I looked at each other with raised brows.

"Father Faustino. That's the Old Town connection," smiled Oscar.

I smiled and nodded recalling our visit to the Santa Fe basilica.

"But no *M*?" Oscar asked Marcos.

He shook his head. "Not yet, anyway. Now, interestingly, you guys found the carpet bag while doing your shop renovation, and Book It is located in what was once that very orphanage, so it's conceivable that perhaps the recipient of the letters might be someone who worked or lived there...you know, often young women would join the convent as a means to a stable future for themselves, or some to escape home life. Not necessarily because they felt divinely called to be the brides of Christ. It's not inconceivable...who knows?" Marcos implored us with his eyes.

We all sat silently taking in the implications of this new-found information. I began wondering if finding the letters and their author might be the unwitting opening of Pandora's box. Could there possibly be a secret, perhaps *illicit* relationship between the writer and the recipient?

My eyes scanned the photograph again, landing on the priest and the woman standing next to him. I found it odd that he was touching her arm whereas the man on the other side of her didn't seem to display any connection to her whatsoever aside from proximity. Assuming, of course, that he was in fact her husband. But clearly the imposing figure standing head and shoulders above the rest was completely detached from the others physically and, at least by appearances, emotionally. "Look up here," Marcos jumped up and circled the image at the top right above the girl's head with his fingertip. "See that? I think it's the same silver barrette and hairstyle that we see in our *quinceañera* girl down the hall."

We all nodded in agreement. "It does look like it could be her," I remarked.

"Give me some time to do a little more research, and I'll get to the bottom of who these other people are, okay?" Marcos asked, assurance in his voice.

"Great. Well this is exciting!" I said, turning to look at Charlize. "We definitely could not have done any of this without your help. Thank you."

She nodded. "And I will continue to read through the letters, as well."

"Yes, thank you both," said Oscar as we rose to leave.

"Of course. This is what we do," said a beaming Marcos. "It may take us some time, though. We've got our big annual museum fundraiser during the Holiday Stroll next week. Both of us will have our heads buried until that's over. But Molly, I think we just might be able to find your '*Mysterious M.*'"

TWENTY-SIX

1891

It was mid December.

Mariana and Florencio were busy once again in the kitchen, making preparations for the arrival of the eldest of the Vega children.

Elena would be coming home for Christmas break from teachers' college by train that afternoon.

The nineteen-year-old had always yearned to attend college and one day return to the Rio Grande valley to become a teacher there, much to the chagrin and disapproval of her father. Onofre had made it clear that along with a fancy degree, Elena would be rendered unfit to become a good wife and mother. *What woman has time to take care of her own children when she's busy raising those of other people?* Unwilling to change her coursework to "Domestic Science" at his behest, she had only another year to go before graduating and running a rural schoolhouse of her own.

He was to pick her up at the Alvarado Station and deliver her promptly home to change quickly into something fitting for a festive gathering. It was to be held at the estate of their new neighbors she had yet to meet, but whom she'd learned quite a bit about in

269

letters her mother had written her at school.

Elena was aware of the Shannons' standing as "squirearchy," the discovery of which had highly impressed her younger sister. Her mother had informed her of the close attachment between Pilar and the seventeen-year-old daughter of the Shannons, Elza, and the friendship of Elza's twin brother, Oliver, with Joaquin. Elena thought it the perfect match.

"Papacio," said Nicolas coming into the kitchen. "I thought you said my sister was named after the Lovely Leonor."

"She is."

"But how can that be? Her name is *Elena,* not Leonor."

"Well, Elena is like a nickname. Both of them come from the name *Eleanor.*"

"Oh…" he nodded slowly, unsure if the distinction was clear to him now.

His mother carried a platter of *tres leches* carefully over his head and placed it on the table nearby. Crossing back to the cookstove, she leaned down for a quick peck on his coppery head. "Now go upstairs and get dressed. I laid out your clothes for the party on your bed."

Nicolas rolled his eyes and groaned. "Do I *have* to?"

"Yes, you have to. *Go!*"

"But I can't breathe in them…" he moaned,

slouching over and dragging his feet as he left the room.

At the same time, Onofre entered the kitchen on his way out the back door. He stopped and grabbed a sugary churro from a basket on the table.

"Are you off to get our girl?" She smiled and danced toward him, wrapping her arms as far as she could around his middle. "I can't wait to see her!"

He grunted with the pastry in his mouth and headed out the door.

"He needs to pace himself," remarked her father, stirring a pot of *posole.* "Too much holiday joy, he could have a heart attack."

"Papacio," Mariana clicked her tongue at him and laughed, untying her apron and hanging it on its peg inside a narrow pantry. "I need to go change!"

Upstairs, Pilar was preening herself in front of her mirror. Her mother walked in and admired her new ballgown, a splurge she had begged her father for. No telling how much it cost him, but money seemed to never be an object of concern for the fifteen-year-old daughter of Onofre Vega.

"Well, let me see," she nodded and gestured in a circular motion with her finger.

Pilar stood and twirled around. Her gown was a deep emerald velvet, gathered at the waist with a cream satin sash. There were three tiers of ruffles on the skirt edged with handmade bobbin lace applique. The neckline was looped with rhinestone rosettes. Mariana approached and lightly touched it, then reached up and brushed the side of her daughter's soft cheek. "You are lovely," she smiled.

"Do you like it?" Pilar laughed, sashaying from the mirror to her window. Through the barren branches of the cottonwoods she could see the warm ochre glow from within the enormous paned windows of the Shannon household.

"Yes, *mija*. It is beautiful."

She returned to her cushioned chair and brushed her long, ebony hair. "Oh, I'm so excited, Mama! I can't wait to see my sister, too. She's going to be so impressed to see their house...Oh, wait 'til Elena sees the pianoforte! She's never seen a pianoforte before."

Mariana giggled. "It won't be long now."

She was reminded of Elena's love of music at Pilar's mention of the instrument, something she'd inherited from her Papacio. As she hastened to her room, Mariana pondered how it had been such a long time since she had heard her oldest daughter sing and play her guitar. She was sure there would be an occasion for her to do so, soon.

All of her children would be home under her roof, *a perfect holiday!* She was overjoyed.

The sound of her little brother bounding downstairs at half-past six alerted Pilar to Elena's impending arrival. She listened as the back door slammed open and Nicolas squealed as he no doubt leapt into her arms. Elena was far more accommodating to their little brother's antics than was Pilar, often riding horses with him along the bosque and racing him barefoot in the backyard when he was smaller.

As Pilar made her way down the staircase, Elena was being ushered into the entryway with her mother and Nicolas surrounding her, Papacio and Onofre trailing behind. Joyful banter ensued as Joaquin slid down the banister past Pilar, jumping off at the base of the stairs to the applause and laughter of his siblings.

Landing before his older sister, he planted a loud kiss on her cheek. "So, did you get real smart yet?"

Elena laughed and looked up to see her sister descending the staircase toward her.

"Look at *you*!" she said, mouth ajar.

The two girls giggled as they embraced. "And look at *you*..." Pilar assessed her up and down with less enthusiasm. In her travel attire, Elena was sporting a long, dark coat over her modest wool skirt and western boots. Her curly brown hair was tucked beneath a crocheted snood. It did nothing to accentuate her perfectly angelic features, thought Pilar.

"Yes, I know," Elena replied to her sister's disapproving frown. "I need to get ready! Won't you help me?"

"Well, come on then!" Pilar took her by the hand and escorted her back up the stairs.

Nicolas clapped his hands and jumped up and down. *"Rápido!"*

As the Vega family neared their neighbor's elegant home in the cool of the evening, the festive sounds of a brass choir swelled as the entry doors parted. Servants dressed in black and white curtsied and bowed, taking scarves, hats, and gloves of the honored guests and ushering them into the great room just off the parlor.

Inside, the scene was celestial: a fire crackled in the grand fireplace as visitors were treated to fanciful concoctions displayed on fine silver platters and trays. Mounds of sweet treats—baklava, divinity, gingerbread, Turkish delight, and marzipan—lined the mahogany tables topped with doilies and sprigs of holly.

Standing at the entrance of the room arm-in-arm with her sister, Pilar held her breath for a moment. She was enthralled at the shimmering light and gilded holiday décor before her, a feast for the eyes and senses.

On the far side of the room behind the brass ensemble was a spruce tree the size of which Pilar had never seen. It was veiled in boughs of sheer gold ribbon, and candles in tiny crystal votives glowed from its branches. Her eyes scanned the room for Oliver; she spied him engaged in jovial conversation with sever-

274

al well-dressed young men in a corner. She watched as Joaquin approached and slapped him on the back. As they shook hands, the tall, blond-haired, blue-eyed Adonis caught sight of her across the room. Feigning coyness, Pilar looked away.

Elza appeared through the crowd and embraced the two young women, kissing their cheeks. Oliver's glance landed on the young woman at Pilar's side: She wasn't as tall as Pilar, but there was a family resemblance. Her hair was a lighter shade of brown, almost auburn, prolific curls pulled high atop her head with a few spilling about her delicate profile.

This must be the elusive Elena.

She was elegant in an unassuming sapphire gown from three seasons past, he would be enlightened afterwards by his mother. She held herself well but not haughtily. She seemed different than what he expected, although he wasn't sure what, in fact, he had expected. He must make her acquaintance soon, he mused. For now he would be regaled by the gentlemen in his midst swirling sherry in their small crystal glasses.

As the evening pressed on, the servants produced a never-ending supply of hors d'oeuvres, sweetmeats, and wassail. Daniella Shannon was in her element, appearing to be the ever-accommodating hostess, making the rounds among her guests and waxing poetic about her beloved London.

"Theo and I had the great fortune of being invited to Westminster Abbey for Queen Victoria's Golden Jubilee in June of '87, you know," she reminisced to the enraptured guests encircling her. "'Twas an affair I'll not soon forget."

She continued to regale them with elaborate details concerning the all-day event to celebrate the Queen's 50th year on the throne.

Though she hadn't touched the spirits, it had been a very long day for Elena, and her head was spinning. While her family and the other guests were otherwise engaged with Elza Shannon singing alongside the much-anticipated pianoforte, Elena decided to slip out of the great hall and into the respite of the empty parlor off the entry.

As she sank into the deep cushion atop a tapestried tuffet, she sighed and pulled off the heeled boots she'd borrowed from her sister, massaging her tired feet. She closed her eyes and listened to the angelic strains wafting in from the other room. It wouldn't take her long to drift off tonight, she thought. *In a comfortable bed, in my own home!*

She was startled by the sound of someone clearing their throat.

When she opened her eyes, there stood a tall, fair-haired young man smiling good-humoredly at her.

"My apologies," he said. "I didn't mean to frighten you."

She'd completely forgotten herself. Spending the

past year with her nose in books surrounded by other women at her college hardly left time for refining one's social etiquette.

She hastily replaced her boots and stood. "I'm sorry—"

"No, please, sit," Oliver insisted firmly, gesturing to the chaise longue. "'In the Bleak Midwinter' has the capacity to tire anyone. You must be Elena."

She smiled wearily and sat down again. "You must be…" straining to recall his name she'd been informed of in the letters from her mother. She shook her head helplessly. "Forgive me."

"Oliver," he said stepping toward her with an extended hand. "Oliver Shannon."

"Yes, of course. Very pleased to meet you," she shook it feeling embarrassed. "You have a wonderful home."

He nodded. "Thank you. I'm afraid my mother went slightly overboard on the decorations. My father indulged her as this is our first Christmas away from London."

She nodded and stifled a yawn.

"An arduous journey, was it?"

"I'm so sorry," she said bringing her hand to her mouth. Elena shook her head in attempt to clear the droning of the train along the tracks echoing inside her head. "A long one, to be sure. I'm very glad to be home."

"I'll bet. What is it that you're studying in college?"

"Education. With an emphasis in literature."

"Ah. A noble profession."

She nodded and glanced around the room, her eyes landing on a painting on the opposite wall. She rose and walked toward it.

"This painting…" she squinted her helplessly sleepy eyes to inspect it. Composed of greens, pinks and purples, the painting was a rendition of waterlilies sparkling in a pond.

"Yes," Oliver said joining her. "A gift from my father to my mother. A token of appreciation for her... *willingness* to leave Britain and come here."

"Oh...she didn't want to come?" She turned to him, noticing for the first time his clear blue eyes.

"I wouldn't say she was exactly excited at the prospect, no," he grinned.

"Is she warming to it?"

"The painting?"

"America."

He laughed. "Only time will tell. As for the painting, she despises it."

Pilar had wandered in behind them unnoticed. "I agree with your mother. It's a mess," she said, her head cocked to the side, eyes scrutinizing the artwork. "I mean just look at the brushstrokes, as if the artist was in a hurry. It's completely unrefined."

278

Elena turned. "The artist *was* in a hurry," she said to her sister softly. "You see, he's working *outside* instead of inside his studio, against the weather and the elements."

Pilar raised her eyebrows at her.

"Everything could change outdoors, including the lighting," Elena continued to explain.

Oliver stared at her and grinned. "That's right. Hence the short brushstrokes. The French are calling them Impressionists, since they paint outside and take a quick 'impression' of the simple shapes and colors of a landscape."

Elena briefly turned to her sister. "Do you see how the sunlight dances on the surface of the water?"

"The artist has captured it brilliantly," remarked Oliver.

"The Parisian *salon* may not be impressed with them, but I love their work. I've been studying an American female painter by the name of Mary Cassatt at school. She mostly paints mothers with their children, in the impressionist style."

Pilar blinked, looking back and forth between them, displeased that her sister dominated the conversation. Oliver had scarcely acknowledged her existence in the room. She sighed and shrugged.

"Well, perhaps it'll catch on..."

Oliver glanced at her then turned back to the painting.

"You can understand why it's symbolic of our move across the pond, can't you?" he smiled at Elena.

She nodded her head. "Because it's an entirely new approach to creating art. Which represents a new start here for your family."

He grinned broadly at her. "Well, yes. That's exactly right."

Elena strolled across to the far side of the room, drawn to a bookshelf that covered the entire wall. She traced a row of leather-bound sets absentmindedly with her fingers before turning to face Oliver, her expression one of shock.

"You have the entire published works of Shakespeare?"

"Well, not entirely," he said, walking toward her and gesturing to a stack of folded magazines. "But we do have all of the Dickens publications."

Elena gazed on them like a lovestruck puppy, thought Pilar, unimpressed.

"And over here, my sister's favorites, the works of the Bronte sisters."

He pointed just past her at the golden letters on the spines of the richly colored books. Elena brought her fingers to her lips to cover her mouth, which had fallen agape, and she looked at her new neighbor unable to contain a toothy grin. *"Do you have Jane Eyre?"* she whispered.

Oliver tapped a finger on his lips as he searched

the grouping with his gaze, then pulled out a hazelnut-colored copy and handed it to her.

"Right here," he whispered.

She stared at it with wide eyes. "I started this back at school before final exams. But I had to put it down so I could focus on my studies. I loved what I did get to read of it…"

"Take it and finish it."

Elena looked up into his pleasant face, his eyes sparkling.

"I can borrow it?"

"Of course."

She hugged the book to her chest. "Thank you so much!"

"Well, there are plenty of others waiting here for you when you're ready."

Pilar crossed the room toward them with a sigh, then laughed.

"Yes, that's practically *all* my sister does. Ever! She's always got her nose stuck in a book. Never wants to go out, or to parties, which is probably why she sneaked off to hide in here. Can you imagine, with all of the lovely things to see tonight?"

Oliver turned to face Pilar. As usual, she was the picture of perfection, he thought. Clearly, she deserved a compliment for her efforts.

"You are right. There are *many* lovely things to see tonight."

Pilar felt herself blushing and looked down, her dark, feathery lashes hovering atop her glowing complexion.

Oliver turned and gazed upon Pilar's sister, still grinning and hugging the book he'd given her. She was naturally stunning in a carefree way. Without exerting effort, Elena's inner beauty and brilliance shone through and captured his attention in a different way than did Pilar. He was struck by something deeper in Elena, not as classically beautiful as her sister, yet far more attractive to him. This college girl had him utterly intrigued. "Yes, many more lovely things…" his words trailed off quietly.

Elena was suddenly aware to whom he was referring as his gaze never left her face. She hoped Pilar hadn't seen their exchange.

"Well, come on," Pilar said sashaying toward the doorway, then turning back to face them with a smile. "Nothing exciting is going on in here."

It was clear she hadn't caught Oliver's inference toward Elena. Grateful, Elena crossed the room to join her.

"I'm sorry, Pilar," she said, touching her velvet sleeve, "but I'm no fun tonight. I'm just exhausted. Please make my excuses to Mama and Papa?"

Pilar's eyes brightened. "Oh, of course."

"Do you have to go? You just arrived—"

"I'm afraid so. Please forgive my rudeness."

282

"Well then, allow me to escort you home," Oliver offered.

"Oh no, you mustn't—"

"I *insist*."

"You can't leave your party!" Elena laughed. "I'll be fine, thank you very much. If I can just get my coat…"

Oliver stepped into the doorway and summoned one of the servants, who presently reappeared with the dowdy overcoat Elena had worn from the train station.

The sight of it made Pilar cringe. *Why did she have to wear that old thing? What must he think of us…*

Oliver helped her into it, and she turned to make her departure.

In the foyer Elena turned and thanked him again. Smiling apologetically at her sister, she waved, stepping out into the night air, her breath suddenly visible as she exhaled. "See you in the morning."

"'For unto us a child is born, unto us a son is given: and the government shall be upon his shoulder: and his name shall be called Wonderful, Counsellor, The mighty God, The everlasting Father, The Prince of Peace.' Amen."

The padre made the sign of the cross over his chest and bowed head, then gazed upon his parishioners with a cherubic expression.

"As you're aware, later this evening we shall continue our celebration of Las Posadas with the peregrinations of Mary and Joseph. Be in prayer, *familia,* especially in *novena* for the infant Jesus, as we journey together toward Misa de Gallo.

"Peace be with you."

Collectively they responded, "And also with you."

Afterwards, the men of the congregation returned with a wagonload of sand ready for anchoring the *luminarias* that would line the path tonight, lighting the way for the coming of the Christ child. The Vega family, except Mariana and Papacio who were busy in the *cocina*, would be hurrying around the plaza filling stacks of flat-bottomed paper sacks that would hold votive candles scheduled to be lit at dusk.

That evening, snow began to fall as townsfolk gathered in the San Felipe parish, where Mary and Joseph would soon make their appearances before beginning their long-anticipated journey.

From the rectory, Father Faustino appeared, followed by Ramón who, unlike the other students in the charge of the Sisters of Charity, could not be corralled into participating in the festivities at hand. Unbeknownst to the padre, as he was closing the door behind him, the tall, lanky young man had escaped him and was hastily making his way to the middle of the parish, where Mariana was seated next to her husband and family.

"*May-ana!*" he hollered joyously, crawling over parishioners packed into the pews awaiting the ceremony, his long bangs covering his eyes.

Mariana held up her arms to him as he squeezed himself directly between her and Onofre, who was visibly displeased. As she patted Ramón's back and spoke softly to him, Elena made room by picking up Nicolas and placing him on her lap.

A door off the sanctuary eventually was opened by one of the nuns, and murmuring from the crowd died down as a parade of children meandered out, dressed in biblical garb as the Magi and barnyard animals. As they made their way down the aisle toward the front of the church, they were followed by the impending parents of the baby Savior: Pilar's friend Henrietta Vargas, dressed in a too-snug peasant dress with a *rebozo* covering her head as Mary, and attentively at her side, Rico Ruiz as Joseph.

Pilar brought her hand up to her mouth as they passed by; she couldn't help but laugh at the peculiar couple. *She's certainly large enough to convince the audience she's with child...*

Rico spied Pilar smiling up at him from her place in the tightly packed pews. He winked as he passed by.

Outside, the parishioners surrounded a waiting burro where, in spite of her hefty size, Joseph hoisted his wife effortlessly onto the tethered beast.

They paraded the village square, where Florencio and other musicians played traditional *cantos,* along with which the crowd sang softly. Scattered *farolitos* lit the way for the holy couple along their route as familiar strains of "Pidiendo Posada" were being sung.

When the procession reached their destination, bands of the faithful gathered around the small bonfires seeking warmth, and consumed steaming bowls of pinto beans with green chile distributed by Mariana and several other women from the parish. There were smiles and genuine sentiments of camaraderie shared between them, hearts growing warmer as large wet flakes sputtered against the sizzling flames.

Papacio pulled his bow across the strings of his fiddle as a familiar canto emerged. Elena, her guitar slung around her shoulder, strummed along and began singing the first stanza:

> "Vamos todos a Belén con amor y gozo,
> Adoremos al Señor nuestro Redentor.
> Derrama una estrella Divino dulzor,
> Hermosa doncella nos da al Salvador."

Softly, the crowd joined in with her:

"La noche fue día; un ángel bajó,
Nadando entre luces, que así nos habló.
Felices pastores, la dicha triunfó,
El cielo se rasga, la vida nació.
 Felices suspiros mi pecho dará
Y ardiente mi lengua tu amor cantará."

Oliver watched as Elena intently sang, her eyes closed, her pure voice piercing the quiet evening punctuated by puffs of warm breath filling the freezing cold. From what he could make out in his imperfect Spanish, he understood the lyrics to say:

"Let's all go to Bethlehem with love and joy,
We will worship the Lord our Redeemer.
The star sheds a Divine sweetness
Beautiful maiden gives us the Savior.
Night was day, angels came down,
Swimming in lights, they told us this:
Happy shepherds, joy triumphed,
The sky is torn, life was born.
Happy sighs my chest will breathe
With my burning tongue, I will sing your love."

Beside him appeared Pilar, the lace shawl she'd

worn the night of *Día de los Muertos* pulled tightly around her hair and gathered beneath her chin. She sang along and looked up at him.

He never glanced at her.

She followed his gaze to her sister. Elena had captured the rapt attention of the entire crowd.

She was indeed the vision of saintliness, angelic in her cream, hand-woven *rebozo* as snowflakes began to accumulate across the curls peeking out from beneath it.

Again she turned her gaze to the seraphic creature above her, seemingly charmed by the serenade before him. *Surely not*, she thought, turning back to her sister. *The virtuous Elena?*

It couldn't be. Pilar blinked and swallowed the rising animosity she felt in her gut.

She shook her head. *Certainly not.* Surely she was imagining things.

The song ended, and the onlookers began to visit among themselves. Pilar started to speak to her neighbor standing next to her, when a pair of chilled hands covered her eyes, obscuring her vision. She impatiently grabbed them and twirled around to stare up into the smiling face of Rico.

His hands still clasped in hers, she whirled back around to see the disappearing form of Oliver heading toward the front of the crowd.

"Rico!" she glared, flinging his hands from her

288

grip. "What are you *doing*?"

Undeterred, he continued to grin at her. "I just wanted to say *Feliz Navidad*."

Again she looked to see Elena smiling as she greeted Oliver. He was taking her hand in his, bringing it up to his lips. They began to chat animatedly.

Spinning around she spat, "Well, you can't just do that to a person. You *scared* me!"

He began to apologize, but she had already disappeared into the crowd.

By the time Pilar had reached the front, the throngs of people were dispersing. Her eyes scanned the jovial bystanders. Elena and Oliver were nowhere to be seen. Her heart racing, she headed for the church courtyard.

Inside the sanctuary, Oliver helped Elena out of her snow-covered coat and wet *rebozo*. The two strolled the aisle and found themselves in the front of the sanctuary, peering up into the decorated altar, its resplendent *retablos* alongside intricately carved and painted relics and saints.

"I'm unsure of something," remarked Oliver. He gestured toward the image of a carved figure hanging high above the altar.

"*La Nuestra Señora y el Niño,*" stated Elena. "Our Lady and the Infant Jesus. She's a *lumina*."

"Hmm...she looks very old. The Virgin and baby Jesus are missing some paint," he mused, his finger absentmindedly touching his lips where on the lumina it was bare.

"Yes," Elena explained, "due to excessive acts of veneration. You see, they were placed up high there after the paint wore off as a result of a hundred years of being kissed. So, as you can see, they can no longer be reached for kissing."

"Oh...That's a shame, isn't it?" He turned to look at her, grinning.

She shook her head, understanding his insinuation. "Some things aren't meant to be touched."

She met his gaze and smiled, turning to light a candle beneath the shrine. Dozens of dim lights flickered in their tiny red glass votives. She closed her eyes momentarily, then lit one.

"A prayer for some lost soul, I assume?"

"No," she said extinguishing with a puff of air the tapered candle she had used to light the votive. "For a martyr."

They walked together slowly toward the entrance of the church as others shuffled past them wishing hushed glad tidings.

"I didn't see your mother tonight. Is she ill?"

He shook his head. "She's well. She didn't want to come. She feels the traditional practices of this quaint little villa to be a bit...primitive."

Elena nodded her head. "You don't think they're primitive, do you?"

"Of course not—"

"But you think they're *quaint.*"

"Well, yes, no—" he stammered momentarily.

Elena found this amusing. "Which is it, yes or

no?"

He laughed. "I find them *enchanting.*"

He stopped walking and turned to face her. She paused and looked back at him. His porcelain skin, taut and smooth over his chiseled features in the dim light appeared cherubic. She was momentarily distracted from her teasing.

"I apologize if I've offended you, Elena," he said, his tone light but sincere. "I wanted you to know how lovely your voice was tonight. I hope you have a joyous Christmas Day with your family tomorrow."

"Elena!" Nicolas' voice rang out, echoing within the nave.

She brought her finger to her lips as her little brother charged her and jumped into her arms. She heaved to bring him up to the curve in her hip, his long legs dangling below her knees.

"You're getting much too big for this!" she scolded him.

"You sang beautiful tonight!" he said gleefully, to which she responded by planting kisses all over his neck and cheeks as he began to squirm and squeal.

Glancing up, she saw Oliver walking away.

"I finished the book, by the way," Elena tranquilly called after him.

"Already?" he laughed, spinning on his heel. "You're welcome to anything in our library, you know."Nicolas began to tickle her as he attempted to free himself from her embrace. Giggling and trying to maintain her balance and composure, she put him down and inquired, "You wouldn't have anything by the pre-Raphaelite poets, would you?"

Oliver dramatically clutched his chest. "*Wouldn't I?* They're my favorite...much to my mother's chagrin, of course."

Elena laughed and managed to wrangle her little brother by pinning his arms down and holding his back against her as his chortling echoed throughout the cavernous space. She covered his mouth with her free hand and grinned as she had upon his lending her the copy of *Jane Eyre*. "Well how very avant-garde of you."

He tipped an absent hat to her, then turned again to leave.

Oliver was completely captivated. He managed a wave at the entrance of the parish when he could catch her fleeting attention, then stepped outside into the frigid night air.

The next day was filled with excitement through-out the Vega household, with the exception of Pilar, who was decidedly somber, especially whenever her sister entered the room.

She had pouted throughout breakfast, including Nicolas's entire painstaking retelling of his recent visit with his parents to the Alvarado Hotel for dinner.

"Elena, you wouldn't *believe* it! Mr. Fred Harvey gave us a tour of the whole place! We got to see the gardens, and walk on the ver*dana*..."

"Ver*anda*," corrected Mariana.

"Yeah, then the dining hall, and the lunchroom. And there were musicians in the lobby when you come in. And I got to try a Monte Crystal sandwich..."

Mariana winked at Elena.

"Oooo, and then I got to pick out my own dessert from behind the glass counter. I picked cherry pie, and Mama picked pecan, and Papa had lemon. Then Mr. Fred Harvey—"

"It's just *Mr. Harvey*," interrupted Mariana, amused by her small son's enthusiasm.

"*Mr. Harvey* gave me an entire can of coffee to take home!"

Before Mariana could stop him, he darted from the table and ran back from the pantry with a can in hand.

"See? It's a picture of one of the Mr. Fred Har— uh, Mr. Harvey girls on the front!"

Joaquin growled at him. "Just *Harvey Girls, estúpido*."

Elena's eyes narrowed at him. "Take it easy there, big brother."

Nicolas never slowed down. "Yeah, and I met a couple of them, too! They were real nice and pretty, those Harvey Girls."

"I'm sure they were," laughed Joaquin. A rare and fleeting smile crept over Onofre's face but vanished just as quickly as it had appeared.

After breakfast, the family went outside and watched as Nicolas familiarized himself with the hand-carved trundling hoop he'd received from Santa that morning. It took him several tries, but he finally had it rolling along for some distances at a time on flat ground. Elena cheered as Papacio ran alongside Nicolas all the way down the fence line before crashing the hoop into a fencepost. Joaquin retrieved it for him with a ruffle of his coppery hair. Onofre hollered at his daughters in Spanish to go inside and help their mother, who was preparing tamales for Christmas dinner.

Pilar rolled her eyes, and the girls walked along the fence line beside the road to their house without speaking. Before ascending the veranda steps, Elena stepped in front of her sister and folded her arms across her chest. Pilar came to an abrupt halt and gave her a fiery stare.

"What is wrong with you?" demanded Elena firmly without losing her composure. "I'm going to be leaving in a few days for school again. Meanwhile, you're acting as if you can't stand to be around me."

Pilar stood with her hands on her hips and shook her head. "You think you're just brilliant, don't you?"

At a loss, Elena tried again patiently. "What are you talking about?"

294

"You think you can just come here and everyone bows to you, and you can have everything your way," she hissed through clenched teeth.

Her sister was taken aback at her savage tone. "What on earth is it you think I've done? I haven't done anything to you!"

Enraged at her sister's apparent lapse in memory, Pilar stared off into the distance, seething.

"*What*?" asked Elena. "Tell me what it is that I have done. I promise whatever it is, I'll try and make it better."

Pillar tapped the toe of her boot, then looked at her sister. "You're telling me that you have no interest *whatsoever* in Oliver Shannon?"

Elena looked at her for a moment, not sure what to say, then her eyes grew wide at the realization. "Oh, Pilar. Of course....you have feelings for him. Look, I'm sorry you're upset with me, but I can assure you there's nothing you need trouble yourself with—I've certainly not encouraged him."

Pilar narrowed her eyes. "Don't act like you don't like him! What is all the talk about artists and novels? As if that kind of thing could really impress a man anyway, Elena!" She gave an embittered laugh. "You think you know *everything* when you're around him!"

"I never said I didn't like him. I hadn't really noticed him, I guess...." She knew this wasn't entirely

295

truthful.

Elena had indeed taken notice of her neighbor's handsome features, and his eyes that were clear as water. She couldn't help but be intrigued by his appreciation of literature and the arts; they were subjects very dear to her own heart.

"Well, he's noticed *you,*" spat Pilar.

"*No…*"

"He has hardly spoken to me since you've been around!"

"Listen," Elena rested her hands on her sister's shoulders. "I'm telling you I'm not encouraging him. He's a *boy*! I'm not interested in boys right now. I have more important things to think about. Not the least of which is my schoolwork."

Pilar pouted without reply.

Elena gently shook her shoulders. "Hey," she teased, frowning until her sister rolled her eyes and tried to stifle a smirk. "He *is* pretty, but not as pretty as you."

Mariana flung the front door open and was surprised to see them both standing there. "What are you girls doing? I need your help in the kitchen; *ándale*!"

Elena turned to follow her mother inside. Pilar caught her by the arm. "Do you promise?"

"Yes," smiled Elena. "He's *not* prettier than you."

"Come on!" Pilar whined. "Promise you're not

interested?"

Elena looked down and sighed. "Pilar, I promise I would never intentionally hurt you. You know that! You're my sister, and I love you. Now come on, let's go. *It's Christmas!"*

Before Pilar could protest, Elena grabbed her sister's hand and raced up the steps and into the house. They were met by the heavenly aroma of baked cinnamon biscochitos and posole simmering on the stove.

It was midday Christmas Day.

Elena hadn't caught up on her rest since her arrival on the train several days earlier. Mariana insisted that Elena rest after lunch, while she and Pilar took a walk around the plaza. "Some of us have our figures to think of after such a rich meal," she'd smiled.

It had always been something Elena never had to worry about. She'd inherited her lean grandfather's stature and quick metabolism, while her sister and mother cursed the Lovely Leonor for their shapely figures. In truth, the petite Mariana used it as an excuse to get out of the house for a while and enjoy the invigorating winter day. She had also detected the tension between her two daughters and thought perhaps her youngest daughter might open up to her in the absence of her eldest about whatever it was that seemed to be

297

troubling her.

Elena went up to the room she shared with Pilar and hung up the coat she had tossed on the bed after coming inside to help her mother with cooking.

Something inside the pocket that she hadn't seen earlier caught her eye.

It was a letter. She pulled it out and sat down on the bed, opening it up.

> *Join me tomorrow afternoon for a ride beside the river.*
> *Oliver*

Oliver....

Her heart leapt at seeing his name.

When had he had an opportunity to place this in here? She thought back to the church last night. *When he'd helped me take off my coat....*

She quickly folded it back up and slipped the letter back into her pocket. The last thing she needed was for Pilar to see it.

Elena sighed. While she longed for sleep—and admittedly, to see Oliver—she knew very well if she were to keep the peace with her sister she must put a stop to his advances.

She would be leaving to go back to school in just a few days, as it was. Although he was good looking and well educated, Elena knew she could not encourage him.

After all, she had promised her sister.

Having convinced herself, she got up and looked out the window toward the stately Shannon household. She took a deep breath and put her coat back on.

Then quietly, so as not to disturb her resting family, Elena hurried outside.

Oliver was in the barn with Rico, brushing the horses. Soon in the distance he caught a glimpse of what he had been keeping an eye out for over the last hour: Elena Vega riding her horse through the thick brush of the ditch bank.

"Would you help me, Frederico?" he said, gesturing toward his tack and saddle hanging on a rack nearby.

Rico retrieved the horse's reins and slipped the bit into its mouth, replacing the halter it had been connected to. Oliver lifted the saddle onto the horse's back, tightening the cinch around its girth. In a moment he was off with purpose, galloping the animal from the barn and toward the bosque beyond.

Rico's gaze trailed after him, and he could see on the horizon ahead of Oliver the figure of a girl riding a horse and disappearing around the bend of salt cedar brushes.

Elena could hear the approaching horse's hooves behind her on the ditch bank. With her heels in the stirrups she tapped her horse and gave it a click of her tongue. *"Giddy-yup,"* she ordered, and the horse obeyed, settling in to a steady gait.

From a few hundred yards away, Oliver was now in pursuit, his eyes focused on Elena's horse ahead of him. She didn't ride like the ladies in the British countryside, with both legs on one side of their saddles. Blissfully for Oliver, Elena was clearly a girl of the great American West, an accomplished rider, agile and in charge of her steed. Her curly hair was starting to loosen from its containment high on her head, with strands flying into her face as she glanced backward from time to time at him.

Suddenly, she veered from the safe, clear path of the ditch bank, maneuvering her horse smoothly through the loose thickets along the bosque, making its way blithely around twists and turns, through groves of barren cottonwoods in their hamlet along the mighty Rio Grande river.

Oliver lost sight of her momentarily as he slowed his trepidatious horse to meander down the same path Elena had taken. On the other side of a bend in the river, he slowed his horse to a trot, then stopped on the edge of the sandy riverbank where Elena stood in front of her panting horse, stroking the smooth hair of its gleaming neck.

Dismounting, he dropped the reins below his horse's head, then gathered them again, leading it toward her. She was speaking softly to the animal, with her back to Oliver.

He found himself momentarily at a loss for words, dropping his gaze to the ground in search of something clever to say.

He smirked, attempting to be witty. "Well that wasn't at all impressive—"

Elena wheeled around to face him.

"Look," she said sharply. "I don't know what's going on here."

She eyed him up and down, fluttering her hand toward him, suddenly distracted by his disarmingly mischievous smile. She crossed her arms in front of her.

He raised an eyebrow and cocked his head slightly. *"What's going on?"*

"Yes," she nodded. "Well, you know! Whatever it is...that's happening here...."

He shook his head, both brows raised now, waiting.

Her hand fluttered again toward him, and her eyes narrowed. "Between you and me."

"Ahh, I see." Oliver closed his eyes and nodded. Squinting through one of them, he watched as she folded her arms again looking relieved. "So, there *is* something going on between you and me."

Exasperated, Elena turned on her heel and reached for her saddle horn, raising a boot to the stirrup.

"Whoa, hold on a minute—" Oliver reached out and placed his fingertips on the waistline of her tattered coat.

She stopped and turned back to face him with a serious expression.

She is most definitely *a Vega,* he mused.

"What are you so angry about?" he asked quietly, his face serious now too.

Elena sighed and searched the sandy ground at her feet.

"I'm not angry with you."

"Then what? Clearly you're not happy about something."

She looked him directly in the eye. "You have to know my sister is very fond of you."

He nodded. "As I am fond of her."

She shook her head. "No. It's not like that. I mean, she *really* likes you. That's what I'm trying to tell you. Look, I'm not going to be here at home very long. I go back to school in just a few days. I can't do... *this. We* can't do this."

He stepped closer to her. "Elena, I am not interested in your sister like that. She's very beautiful, don't get me wrong. And I know how she likes me. I've been aware for a while. I'm not a complete dolt."

He looked off in the distance. "At one time, I was quite smitten with her, actually. Pilar can be quite...persuasive," he smiled, recalling her flirtations the night of her fifteenth birthday party, and in the courtyard the night of *el Día de los Muertos*. "It's just that I'm not that easily persuaded. I'm interested less in surface qualities that merely a pretty face could offer."

Now he was looking directly into her eyes again. She sucked in a breath and blinked, trying to remain composed. It wasn't going to be easy, but she remained convinced of her purpose in meeting him here...in spite of those searing aqua eyes.

"Oliver," she said looking away. "I promised my sister I would not encourage you. She knows, you know...she's noticed that you're not speaking with her like you used to before I arrived."

Oliver slowly raised his hand and felt her soft cheek with the back of his fingers. Elena squeezed her eyes shut.

"Forgive me," he whispered. "But I am utterly beguiled by you, Elena...."

She pulled his hand down but held onto it with hers.

His words became urgent. "You are an *amazing* woman. And while I would never want to hurt your sister, I simply cannot stop myself from thinking about you! From the moment I laid eyes on you that night at the party, from across the room, I knew instantly there was something about you. I had to find out *who* you were. Of course I knew you were Pilar's sister, but I

303

had a strong hunch you were...different."

She looked up, searching his face, her heartbeat pounding in her ears.

"And I was right!" Oliver continued. "You *are* different: poised, and elegant, well read. With the voice of an angel."

She blushed at this. He entwined his fingers between hers.

She is simply radiant, he observed.

"Listen," he said softly. "I respect your loyalty to your sister. If it is your adamant wish, then of course I will honor it. Just promise me you'll think it over. I have no doubt Pilar would understand if she knew your intentions were not to upset her. After all, you did not seek me out. You never encouraged me. I think the closest you got to flirting with me was mentioning you wanted to read the pre-Raphaelites."

Elena burst out laughing. "I am quite the Jezebel, aren't I?"

"Oh, yes. Quite. Speaking of which..." he squeezed her hand and turned to fetch a package from his saddlebag. He handed it to her. "Merry Christmas."

Elena tore open its brown paper wrapping, exposing a small book. Her face lit up reading the title. "*In an Artist's Studio.*"

"All right, fine." He grinned broadly. "I'll admit, I've resorted to bribery."

Elena perused the first few pages of the book and

gushed. "Christina Rossetti…"

"You'll be pleased her philosophy was that it was dangerous for the likes of us men to 'worship the female muse,'" he said.

Elena nodded and smiled up at him. "A wise woman, indeed."

Oliver took a deep breath and stared at her for a moment, replacing one of her rogue curls that had fallen into her face from behind her ear.

She took a step back toward her horse, tracing its soft, warm nose with her hand. She looked back at Oliver.

"I will think about what you said. Beyond that I can't promise you anything," she said, sliding the book into her coat pocket and pulling herself into the saddle. "Fair enough?"

"Fair enough." He smiled, mounting his horse again as well. "You're not going to leave me in the dust again, are you?"

Elena laughed and dug into the horse with her heels, clicking her tongue. It took off rapidly at a run.

Oliver shook his head and laughed heartily, soon on her heels as they cleared the bosque and headed toward home.

"Well this was nice!" sighed Mariana as she and Pilar rounded the corner at the front of their property. "The perfect way to get in a little exercise after a delicious lunch with my *familia*."

Pilar had stopped and was peering off into the distance, on the other side of the fenceline toward the ditch bank. She squinted her eyes in the midday sun and watched, as behind the Shannon household her sister trotted her horse out of the grove of salt cedar, making her way home.

It struck Pilar as odd since Mariana had told her sister to get some rest before they left for their stroll about town. She had seen Elena go upstairs for a nap....

Pilar continued toward the veranda, along with her mother, until she was once again halted in her tracks. This time her heart sank as she made out the form of another horse, not far behind Elena's; Pilar covered her brow to block the blinding sun, but she could undoubtedly distinguish its rider as it drew closer.

The second horse was carrying the figure of a man with distinctively blond hair.

TWENTY-SEVEN

Present day

The Holiday Stroll tomorrow night had every merchant in Old Town buzzing like a swarm of bees in preparation for the festive event.

This one night alone counted for 70 percent of all our holiday sales, I had reminded Cedar. He was in the storeroom, gathering supplies for our spread of usual southwestern goodies, while I was behind the counter, organizing gift bags stamped with the store's logo—the plaza gazebo surrounded by dancing music notes—into stacks on the shelves below.

Cedar emerged from the storeroom carrying a card table under one arm while cradling a crockpot in the other, when the door of Old Town Music opened and Charlize stepped inside.

He practically dropped everything next to a nearby sheet music display stand and made straight aim for her. She inspected him dubiously as he approached her with a determined twinkle in his eye.

While most men couldn't pull off his "stalker" approach with women, Cedar was an expert in the fine art of charm. Reaching for her hand, he raised it to his lips with an air kiss, inquiring, "To whom do I owe the distinct privilege of making your acquaintance this fine December afternoon, m'lady?"

Charlize threw her head back and laughed.

"Um...*oui*," she blushed. "Ms. Lewis?"

I was already making my way around the front counter. "*Bonjour*, Charlie!"

"*Bonjour*," she smiled at me, still tickled at Cedar's dramatic greeting.

His gaze volleyed between the two of us, awaiting an introduction with raised eyebrows. I simply grinned at him in amusement.

He cleared his throat. "And I'm Cedar," he said to her.

"*Bonjour*, Cedar," she smiled and turned to me. "Molly, I have some interesting news to share with you regarding your M."

"Oh? I'm surprised," I looked at her quizzically. "I wasn't expecting anything until next week maybe."

"Yes, well, we have been crazy busy, however it was easy for me to go through the church ledgers on my coffee breaks."

"Great, then!" I said, eagerly leading her back to the countertop, where she placed some paperclipped photo-copies she'd been carrying. "What did you find?"

"Well..." she said unclipping the stack. "This is a list of names of the nuns who worked with the Sisters of Charity in the orphanage and school.

"And these," she spread out several pages before us, "are all of the children under their custody within the dates of our letters."

I perused the hand-written documents etched with cursive writing and furrowed my brows.

"I thought we were looking for a man."

"So did I," said Charlize. "However, there isn't one single gentleman's name in these records that begins with

M. I'm starting with the obvious names, keeping in mind that our penman—or woman—could just as easily be using a nickname, middle or last name, or some other term of endearment that has no connection whatsoever to the real name."

"Well, that certainly doesn't narrow it down much..."

Cedar had joined us and intently listened as she continued.

"No, it doesn't. But it may tell us who it *isn't*. For example, we did find one 'M' name among the Sisters, here." She pointed to a name close to the bottom of the page.

"Sister Mary Elizabeth," I read aloud.

"Yes, she's the only one. But if you notice here," she pointed to the nun's date of birth, then to the date at the top of the roster: *1783* and *1870*.

A smile slowly spread across Cedar's face. "Wow. Sister Mary Elizabeth must've been some nun."

Charlie giggled. "Isn't that great? She was eighty-seven when the letters were written."

"Well, I'm thinking there goes Marcos's theory," I laughed.

"Yeah, I thought you'd get a kick out of that," she said. "So that's one group eliminated. Progress! I will leave these with you."

Charlie stacked the copies and handed them to me. I thanked her as she turned to leave.

"Bye," she waved to Cedar.

"*Au revoir.*" He waved back as she stepped outside. He turned to me with wide eyes. "*Oh-la-la.*"

That night at home, I poured over the list of names from the San Felipe ledgers.

"According to these records," I explained to Oscar, who was wearing readers on the end of his nose and reclining on the couch with a book, "quite a few nuns had come through the orphanage over the years. These also list the names and dates of the arrivals and departures of the Franciscan priests."

Without looking up from his book, Oscar replied. "I'm thinking by the 1880s or so they were trying to establish a new legacy from that of the so-called Roman Catholic lay priests of territorial New Mexico, thanks to Bishop Lamy."

"That's quite a legacy he left, isn't it?"

"Mm-hmm."

I put the stack of papers down on the coffee table and stretched my arms with a yawn. A glance at the clock on the fireplace mantle said 10:47 pm.

I thought about Father Faustino's relationship with the upright Lamy, and pondered if he, too, had been as convicted in his purpose to re-establish integral ties with the communities along the Rio Grande in his diocese. Was he a man of great character and purpose, as was his friend?

If so, what was the relationship that he had with the Sisters of Charity and the village in which he lived? And what of the beautiful woman in the other photo of our so-called "quinceañera girl"? The two appeared to have a closer bond than that of anyone else on that porch in the photograph. *Who was she*?

My brain swimming, I stood up and walked over to my mahogany Steinway & Sons piano, pulling out the

bench. I allowed my fingers to lightly graze the keys in
the upper register, emitting a soft tune. Sitting down, I
pressed my left foot on the damper pedal, and placing both
hands on the keys, I began softly playing a song I'd written
many years ago when I was in college. I closed my eyes and
soaked in the pristine clarity of the notes; the piano offered
my spirit instant relief, the bridge rising in crescendo,
the harmonies climbing to discord, then resolving. It was
easy to lose myself in the music, as I'd done so many times
throughout my life. It was my therapy.

As I continued to play, I opened my eyes to see
Oscar looking back at me, his glasses now along with his
hands crossed over his chest, a sleepy smile on his face.

"I'm so sorry. I didn't mean to bother you."

"Are you kidding me?" he said, rising from the
couch into a sitting position and rubbing his eyes. "I love
this."

I glanced around the room, at the glowing flames in
the fireplace, at this precious man in his plaid flannel shirt
and blue jeans, relaxing on my sofa.

I smiled at him and continued, returning to the
emotion of the music, foot off the damper pedal now,
feeling the ebb and flow of the melody. I breathed in the
release, my soul swelling with clarity and peace. Without
opening my eyes, my fingers knew by instinct and touch
what to do, something that years of practice and formal
training had afforded me.

Oscar's warm hands were now on my shoulders,
gently massaging as I played. I felt him move my hair
aside, exposing my neck to his soft lips and sending chills
down my spine. I took a deep breath and reached up,
placing my hand on the back of his head. I ran my fingers

313

through his soft hair.

"Don't stop playing on my account," he breathed quietly.

I smiled, and stood to face him.

"That's funny...I couldn't play now if I wanted to. And right now," I said, walking around the piano bench toward him, "I don't want to."

I looked intensely into his beautiful caramel eyes. There was no mistaking that he wanted me, and something was being kindled deep inside me. Without touching his body, I slowly kissed his lips. His breathing became stronger, and soon his hands grasped the fabric of my blouse at my waist, pulling me against him.

He had ignited a flame that suddenly set fire to my entire body. I pulled back the collar of his flannel shirt and began to kiss his chest. His scent made my pulse race, and I felt an urgent desire for him, pulling his mouth to mine and kissing him deeply.

With a loud release of air, Oscar stepped backward and turned around. He walked toward the front door.

We stood in breathless silence for a moment.

He shook his head and turned to face me. "I'm sorry, Molly."

I stared at him in astonishment. "I'm not..."

Again he shook his head. "I love you too much to put you in this position."

I took a step toward him. "But I want this. I want *you*."

He held up his hand. "I want you, trust me. But Molly, I also know you. And I respect you so much that I need you to know I'm the real deal."

"I know you are!" I protested, feeling a little hurt

314

and embarrassed. "Why do you think I'm so attracted to you?"

He smiled. "I want to continue to be the man you want me to be, and I want to give you everything, *everything,* eventually. I can't wait for that time. Until then, I'm going to invest in the woman I know you to be, a woman of integrity and honor. Right now you're tired, you've been working all day and trying to figure out this mystery with the letters. You have a lot on your plate right now. I promised myself I would make sure the store is in a stable position before you and I take it to the next level. I will continue to honor you until then, Molly."

Tears sprang into my eyes and I turned away from him. After a moment, I laughed. "Then you'd better get the heck outta here," I said, facing him but keeping my distance. "Because if you don't think that little speech you just gave me did anything to help my resolve, you're wrong. I will not hesitate to jump your bones right now, *viejito.*"

Oscar laughed heartily and grabbed his jacket, side-stepping toward the door.

"Damn, woman, I really love you!"

After he stepped out the front door, I flopped down on the couch and sighed heavily, my heart still racing. I just breathed for a while. My head was spinning.

I remembered a time on the back porch of the house I shared with Paul. I was feeling hopelessly between a rock and a hard place with him: I was losing him, I knew it. The man I married was completely checked out and gone. He sat complacently on the concrete, facing away from me. I was enraged with his lack of emotion and complete dismissal of me. It was the end of my marriage, and this man could not care less—about me, about the affect his walking out would have on our children. About the fifteen years we'd spent together, building a relationship, a family, a home. He wasn't merely leaving me; he was destroying a history, and in so doing, building a legacy of walking away that would have a lasting, ripple effect far beyond just Paul and me.

I recall something primal breaking loose inside my spirit and unleashing a fury of foul language on him, calling him every filthy name I could come up with. When I was done he remained obtuse except for a smirk on his face. I slapped him hard across the cheek, and except for the initial sting and surprise, he didn't respond. For a moment it felt good, but very soon I just felt pathetic and defeated. I had never touched him in any way other than lovingly, and instead of feeling satisfied by slapping his face I just felt so very deeply sad.

Tonight, as I basked in the glow of the scent of Oscar in my house after he'd gone, I felt deeply happy, and so satisfied that I finally had something in my life that was real and genuine, and someone who might have left me for the moment, but who I knew without a doubt would be coming back to me again.

TWENTY-EIGHT

1891

Elena was spending more time in the carriage house in Papacio's quarters, reading. It was the one place she knew she could be alone for a while with her thoughts and her book—the book Oliver had given her.

In spite of herself, she had thought of him almost continuously since they met in the bosque on Christmas Day.

As she reached the last page of her reading, a small sliver of paper with Oliver's handwriting on it fell out of the book:

> "Her coming was my hope each day,
> Her parting was my pain;
> The chance that did her steps delay
> Was ice in every vein."
> -Charlotte Bronte

It was a quote from *Jane Eyre.*

Elena's heart began racing. At the bottom of the note it read:

Won't you meet me again?

She wrapped the note tightly in her grasp and held it to her chest. She shook her head as tears sprang into her eyes. Part of the reason that she escaped to the carriage house was the unrelenting glare from her sister over the past several days. It seemed that after her conversation with Pilar, things had only gotten worse instead of better. When she had to be in the same room with her, Pilar's words—if any at all—were full of venom.

How can I blame her? Elena thought.

Pilar wasn't even privy to the fact that Elena had indeed begun developing feelings toward their lovely British next-door neighbor. How could she do this to her, when Elena knew exactly what attracted Pilar to him?

Yet, she was sure that what her sister didn't know was that Oliver was not simply beautiful to behold but deeply thoughtful and contemplative, finding meaning in the loftier things in life. He was genteel, yet curious. That, beneath the cultured façade stirred a wonderment and appreciation of even the most mundane details others seemingly overlooked. That night at the Shannons' party, he had remarked on the painting of the water lilies and how the artist took great care in attempting to capture the light without thought of what was considered acceptable in the art community of Paris. She remembered how it had vaguely struck her then that Oliver appreciated the artist's *process* rather than the end result.

Pilar, who seemed to resent her family's bucolic existence, hadn't a clue the evening at the Christmas party as to why this was an appealing attribute of the painting. It was not surprising to Elena; all their lives her little sister was wholly overindulged by their father. He'd lavished her with trinkets and gifts for as long as she could remember, something that had never impressed Elena very much.

While she was never envious of this exclusive treatment, she was dismayed at times by Onofre's distinct disregard of those things Elena found important and valuable. If she were to receive literature, for example, it would be from the hands of her mother or Papacio, not her father. Onofre could never understand why a filigreed necklace didn't elicit the same response in her that it did in his younger daughter.

It wasn't that Elena didn't appreciate these types of tokens from him; however, in time they would end up collecting dust in a drawer somewhere, as did the tiny jars of eau de toilette, fans made from peacock feathers, beaded handbags, and mother of pearl earrings. Onofre seemingly had no idea what gifts he could bestow on his older daughter besides costly knickknacks or cosmetic indulgences—*What else could a woman possibly want?*—nor, frankly, did he care enough to find out.

That Pilar had no patience for delving deeper in an attempt to understand artistic method was directly related to her father's dismissal of things that he, also, could not comprehend.

The small note Elena had wrapped up within her grasp served as a reminder that, while her father might not understand those things she valued as meaningful in her heart, Oliver Shannon did.

She wept as the dichotomy of emotions whirled through her head.

Elena wiped her eyes, picked up the pencil lying on Papacio's bedside table, and began to write Oliver a response.

Father Faustino's voice echoed through the morning sunlight that spilled through the windows beneath the nave of the San Felipe parish.

It was the Sunday before New Year's Eve. Elena would be leaving on New Year's Day for her return to college, a fact that hadn't escaped her as she sat next to Joaquin, with Pilar to her left in the wooden pew; Oliver sat directly on her right, with Elza next to him. Before they'd been seated, Elena handed him back the copy of *Jane Eyre* she'd borrowed from him the first time they met.

Unable to focus on the message the padre was

proclaiming, Oliver leafed through it absentmindedly. Near the end he spied the small paper Elena had left for him tucked inside.

His heartbeat surged.

Glancing about, he carefully removed the note with his finger still marking its place in the book. He inhaled her inscription:

> Yes, I will meet you again. Tomorrow. Where?
>
> Leave your response in the hollow of the old cottonwood behind the rectory.
>
> For as you are aware, trees are lofty heights such as one might hope to attain...
>
> Elena

Trying to suppress a burgeoning smile, Oliver bit his lower lip and glanced to his side.

From his peripheral vision he could see Elena brush back a curl from her forehead without acknowledging him. She turned her focus from the altar momentarily, and her eyes lingered on the book in his lap—giving a faint nod—then returned to her forward gaze.

Oliver's eyes narrowed, and he looked down again at the book. Opening it wider, he noticed there were soft pencil markings around a passage on the page he hadn't seen before.

He recognized it was a dialogue between Jane Eyre and Edward. Jane was addressing him after Edward's face had been tragically burned in an attempt to save his wife from a fire that she—insane and increasingly violent toward him—had set.

Oliver read it to himself:

> "You are no ruin, sir—no lightning-struck tree: you are green and vigorous. Plants will grow about your roots, whether you ask them or not, because they take delight in your bountiful shadow; and as they grow they will lean toward you, and wind round you, because your strength offers them so safe a prop."

Oliver closed the book and exhaled deeply. He closed his eyes and wiped his palms on his trousers. He could feel Elena's gaze on him, and he turned and looked into her eyes.

She felt bold and terrified at the same time, the blood coursing through her veins. He smiled at her with clear, electric eyes. She looked away.

Elena took a deep breath and smiled, butterflies fluttering in her stomach. She felt simultaneously nauseated and excited. He had her answer now, she thought. *There's no going back.*

Rubbing the rosary beads nervously between her fingers, she closed her eyes and prayed her sister would forgive her.

Oh Lord, what have I done?

The next day was cold and overcast in the Rio Grande valley.

In spite of the dreary atmosphere outside, Elena was full of hope as she arose from the empty bed she was sharing with her sister—who by now was completely ignoring her—and gazed out the window toward the grand house across the cottonwoods. The promise of the impending year's end brought Elena excitement about what the new one might bring her. She also hoped her rendezvous that day with the lovely Mr. Oliver Shannon would prove to be someplace warm.

She pulled on her wool robe and house shoes, and hurried down to breakfast, where her family was already seated.

Her mother passed around a large bowl of fluffy scrambled eggs, and Elena could smell the spicy sausage on a platter next to a basket of warm flour tortillas.

"Oh, my stomach is growling!" moaned Nicolas. Elena kissed him on the cheek as she slid into the empty chair next to him. He wiped his cheek with his shoulder and reached for his silverware.

"Not yet, mister," warned his mother. "We haven't thanked the Lord."

He sighed, and Papacio proceeded to recite a

prayer over the meal.

As the bowls began making their way around the table and everyone started eating, Mariana looked across at her eldest daughter and smiled. "I can't believe you just have a few more days with us, *Jita*."

Pilar mumbled something and began eating.

"Thank *God*!" laughed Joaquin. "Just teasing—I guess I'm gonna miss you. You know, when you're not putting up for the brat."

His mouth full, Nicolas narrowed his eyes at his older brother. "I am not a brat!"

Joaquin mimicked his garbled speech in a high-pitched voice.

"If he is, then he's learned from the best," remarked Elena, replacing the kiss he wiped off. This time Nicolas just rolled his eyes.

"We will *all* miss you," sighed Mariana. "Won't we Onofre?"

Her father kept eating but nodded his head.

"Look!" cried Nicolas after finally swallowing a mouthful of eggs. He was pointing out the window. "I see snowflakes!"

Like the frosty air on the other side of the windowpane, Pilar continued her icy composure, her anger toward her sister simmering just below the surface. She could not wait to be rid of the angelic Elena; she had everybody fooled by her intelligence and charm, but all she was to Pilar was a complete phony. And a liar.

After breakfast, Pilar hurried to her room and closed her door behind her. She sat down on the floor beneath her window, a perch from which she could see the snow spitting faintly from the depressing winter sky, and gazed out toward the house next door. She knew that once her sister was gone, she needn't worry herself with the horrible, gnawing ache in her chest. Things had been progressing with Oliver, and she knew it was merely a matter of time that he would once again belong entirely to her. If it hadn't been for Elena, Pilar wouldn't feel so hopeless...but as it was, she felt as if she was sinking into murky waters, being drawn under by an increasingly rapid current, against which she was powerless to fight.

She began to cry, uncontrollable, gut-wrenching sobs. She was so angry that all of the planning over the summer had practically gone to waste, thanks to her ridiculous siblings.

With all of her being she despised them.

Her sorrow began to give way to searing rage. The thought of her sister sneaking off on Christmas Day with Oliver—the only man she had ever loved— made her blood boil. She was livid at the thought.

Soon she was staring out of the window again, her breathing eventually becoming controlled and even as she sat mesmerized, gazing up into the gray clouds. She dried her face and blinked her eyes as, from the corner of her gaze, she caught a glimpse of the front door of the Shannon household opening.

It was Oliver.

Pilar gathered her skirts about her and rose, wiping her eyes so that she could get a better look at him.

He was alone and walking toward her house.

She caught her breath for a moment and watched as he made his way across their property line along the fence posts.

Oh God, what if he's coming over to see Joaquin? as he'd done many times in the past. Pilar hurried across the hallway and into her brother's empty room, where she had a vantage point now of the side of the house. She watched him as he crossed the road, away from the Vega home, heading for the church.

This was her chance, she thought. She ran back across the hall to her room and checked her appearance in the mirror before grabbing a shawl and heading downstairs.

"Where are you going?" Mariana called as Pilar raced toward the front door.

Damn her. She tried to control the rising animosity she felt toward her mother at this intrusion of her privacy.

"Just out onto the porch to get a better look at the snow, Mother!" she sang, wondering if she'd overdone it.

Opening the door she heard Mairana trail off, "Oh, that's nice. It's lovely…"

Closing it behind her, she walked to the edge of the veranda as her eyes searched the horizon, her breathing labored. At last, she spied him as he turned the corner of the church courtyard and disappeared within.

Glancing around behind her, Pilar hurried down the veranda steps and hastily made a retreat for the old church.

At the gate to the courtyard, she paused momentarily to catch her breath, then continued inside.

It was silent. Oliver was nowhere to be seen. The snow was starting to stick to the frozen ground, and she glimpsed a faint set of footprints rounding the corner of the inner patio, beneath the balcony on the far side of the fountain.

She followed the steps to the ancient cottonwood tree behind the rectory on the northeast corner. They had stopped at the base of the tree where the snow had been trodden and kicked up. Approaching it Pilar pressed herself to the trunk and peered around the other side hoping for a glimpse of her lover.

Suddenly she caught sight of him, now at a run, heading back toward his house. She pushed herself away from the tree and shook her head.

What on earth is he doing??

In an instant he was out of sight. She shrugged and cursed under her breath, turning to look around her. Out of the corner of her eye above her head, she glimpsed a white piece of paper flapping gently in an icy breeze from a hole burrowed in the tree trunk. Pilar cocked her head to one side, then reached for it.

A small rock fell out as she fetched the paper, intended to keep it weighted down until it was discovered, she supposed. Unfolding the paper she leaned against the tree and began reading it.

> "One face looks out from all his canvases,
> One selfsame figure sits or walks or leans;
> We found her hidden just behind those screens,
> That mirror gave back all her loveliness.
> A queen in opal or in ruby dress,
> A nameless girl in freshest summer greens,
> A saint, an angel; — every canvas means
> The same one meaning, neither more nor less.
> He feeds upon her face by day and night,
> And she with true kind eyes looks back on him
> Fair as the moon and joyful as the light;
> Not wan with waiting, not with sorrow dim;
> Not as she is, but was when hope shone bright;
> Not as she is, but as she fills his dream."
>   -Christina Rossetti

Where we last met, before the sun fades today.
    Yours,
    Oliver

Pilar dropped to the ground, allowing the cold to penetrate her body, crumpling the letter in her fist.

So that's it, she thought numbly. *They have both betrayed me.*

Elena went over the narrative she was to recite to Oliver whenever they met later that day: they were to keep their new relationship under wraps for the moment, at least until the next time she was to visit her family sometime in the spring or summer. For now, it would be just between the two of them. That would also give him time, Elena logically reasoned, to change his mind about her while she returned to school. She had to allow for that possibility. While it would break her heart, she knew that time could very well change things.

She tightened the shawl over her head and clasped the open neck of her coat. The snow had begun falling with big, wet flakes, and the temperature was plummeting. The late afternoon was quiet and serene around her.

When she made it to the tree, she glanced about. Seeing no one, Elena traced her hand up its rough bark surface, then finding the opening and standing on her tiptoes, reached inside in search of a letter. She felt nothing but damp, cold wood.

Her eyes narrowing, she took a step backward

and peered up into the dim tree. She couldn't see anything from there and stepped forward again in hopes of feeling it this time.

Again, she was empty-handed.

Elena stared off into the distance...*Maybe Oliver changed his mind.*

On her way home she slowed approaching the veranda. Instead of going inside she decided to head around the back.

She kept walking until she got to the barn. Entering one of the stalls she began speaking quietly to her horse, running her hand along his shanks and belly. Once he had warmed to her presence, she replaced the halter that tethered him to a post nearby with a bit, and without bothering with a saddle, led him from his enclosure.

From the front window Mariana watched fat snowflakes lazily drifting down from the heavens and growing thicker by each passing moment.

"Aw...*que bonita*," she sighed and turned to a passive Onofre attending to a fire in the massive fireplace in the great room behind her. "I wonder where the girls are?"

He grunted, and she turned back around to gaze upon the feathery white flakes as they fell to the earth and disappeared into the soft blanket of snow forming on the ground.

So peaceful, she thought to herself.

The sky was beginning to fade, and Oliver wondered when Elena would arrive.

He'd tied his horse at the bend of the river, then retrieved a woven Indian blanket he had found in the barn, rolled up and attached to the back of his saddle. It was one that Fredrico had stashed in there just for nights like this if he wasn't going home, but rather making his bed for the night in a pile of alfalfa hay amongst the horses, which he often did. He hoped Elena didn't think it presumptuous of him, but realize instead it was merely hasty protection from the elements provided to an ill-prepared Englishman during such weather.

He flung it around his shoulders and heard a rustling in the brush to his back.

Swinging around, it took him a moment to process what he saw standing before him.

It was not Elena.

He shook his head and furrowed his brow.

"*Pilar?*"

Without realizing it, the question had come out of his mouth with a laugh.

She was wearing the pale rose-colored dress she'd worn to her quinceañera, with the black lace shawl pulled tightly around her shoulders, but it clearly provided no warmth to her pallid, trembling body.

Having been expecting Elena, Pilar looked completely out of context to him as she there in her glorious summer gown, like a vision from another place in time.

The snow had ceased falling. From an opening in the sky above them she was lit by an ethereal glow.

He stepped forward, his eyes darting about them, and inquired with a grave firmness, "What are you doing here?"

The mocking tone of voice by which he had just addressed her had caused a fissure in her already fragile composure to suddenly fracture and split apart in a nauseating wave of panic. Her chest began heaving and she felt at any moment she would either hyperventilate or vomit.

She burst into torrential sobs. Oliver stared at her blankly, unsure of what to do or say. He had never seen her like this, her usually captivating face contorted into a twisted glare. He shook his head and took a step toward her.

"You're hysterical. Let me help you—"

Pilar stumbled away from him, bending forward at the waist and hissing through clenched teeth.

"I loved you!"

Her body, still wracked with gasping breaths, began bobbing hypnotically from side to side. Her voice wavered and rose in pitch.

"Don't you love *me*?"

"Pilar…" he stared at the ground, searching for something to say that would quell her rising fury. "Of course you know I find you lovely…"

She could detect the insincerity in his tone; he was merely pacifying her.

Now she screeched at him. "It's her! You love *her*!"

Oliver took another step toward her and shook his head, lowering his voice. "*No*. No, I don't know her very well. Pilar, you must stop this. It is not becoming. This is *not* the girl I know."

Her eyes were closed now, her swaying serpentine as she raised and lowered her torso, her neck swiveling about on her shoulders.

She burst out laughing.

"*Oliverrr*…" she drew out his name in a sepulchral moan. "Tell me *now* that you haven't fallen in love with her…"

He raised his hands pleadingly, trying to remain composed. "I…I can't do that, Pilar. I don't know exactly *how* I feel about Elena, and I don't know what the future holds for us. All I know is that I have recently developed strong feelings toward her, but that certainly doesn't mean that you and I can't go on being very good friends. What we *both* want is for you to be happ—"

In an instant she lurched at him, dropping the

shawl she was wearing and revealing a small hatchet in her clenched fist before raising it above her head. Before Oliver could process what was happening, Pilar had stepped backward and brought the hatchet down with vehement force, embedding it into the crook of his neck.

She heard the sickening crack of his collarbone. At once a bright crimson flow began to saturate the blanket around his shoulders.

With wide, unbelieving eyes, he stared at her before stumbling to his knees and, falling toward her, grasping her legs. His arms wrapped around her satin gown now streaked with his blood. Gasping, Pilar raised her hands, fingers splayed, and staggered backward. Oliver fell face-forward to the ground at her feet.

For a moment she stared at him lying there and tried to catch her breath. She bent forward and placed her hands on her knees. Then slowly, the magnitude of what had just transpired in front of her began to sink in.

Her breathing became shallow in the frigid stillness of the waning day. She wiped the hair that had fallen into her eyes away from her face and stood upright, peering up into the transforming sky.

Oh God...oh, God...

She looked back down at Oliver, lying motionless on the hard earth.

What...have...I done??

Dropping to the ground at his side she turned

him over, the hatchet still firmly planted in his neck. Attempting to rise, she only managed to crawl a few feet away from his lifeless body and retched into the bushes.

She returned to him and struggled to free the blanket from underneath him. Once she'd managed to, she proceeded to extricate the hatchet from within his flesh and used the blanket to sop up the gushing flood still escaping from his wound.

But it was no use; he was not coming back to her. She traced the exquisite features of his face lightly with her fingertips. His lips and skin were beginning to turn blue. Rising to her feet again she backed away from him, then turned and trampled through the dense thicket of salt cedar, heading toward the river.

The sun was beginning to fade in the western sky. Elena hastened her horse to a canter, then slowed to a walk as she approached the place along the ditch bank where she had taken the path into the bosque just a few days ago. She hoped longingly that he was waiting there for her.

Rounding the bend of cottonwood trees, she saw Oliver's horse tethered to a low-hanging branch. Relieved, her heart began beating faster in anticipation of seeing him. She dismounted and led her horse next to his, tying the reins to the same branch.

There on the ground on the other side of the tree, Elena caught a glimpse of something.

Unable to see around the brambles and low-hanging limbs of the cottonwoods, she called out.

"Oliver?"

There was no reply. Elena made her way around the trunk of the tree and stared at the ground before her.

She blinked her eyes and shook her head, her brain unable to discern the grisly scene. Little by little, it began to register to her that it was indeed Oliver lying there on the wet ground, motionless and soaked in blood.

She slowly brought her hands to her mouth. Without warning her legs gave way beneath her. She landed on all fours, choking and struggling for breath.

A primitive, guttural whisper escaped her mouth. "*Nooo…*" Rising to her feet, she scrambled toward him, tripping and falling before kneeling at his side, her hands hovering, trembling above his ashen face. Even now, it was exceptionally lovely, chiseled and handsome. She straddled his head with her arms, searching his features, listening for the sound of his breath. She began to shake uncontrollably, her voice now pleading and beginning to rise.

"No, *no, no, no, NO, NO, NO!!*"

With her fists she beat the ground on either side

of him until her body was exhausted. Elena helplessly wept, wiping the tears that fell from her eyes off his increasingly cold face. She gathered his head in her arms and attempted to warm him, rocking back and forth, kissing his hair and forehead.

"Oh, *Oliver*..." she whispered.

Gently she removed the soiled blanket from his chest and, balling it up replaced it beneath his head. She rose and slipped off her old tattered coat, the arms and front of which were smeared with Oliver's blood. Elena covered his freezing body with it, securing it under his chin.

The ground began to spin. Stumbling, she managed to untie her horse and make her way out of the bosque.

Pilar stood at the bank of the great river, her pulse ragged and searing in her lungs, the heels of her boots sinking into the sand. She was no longer aware of her surroundings: the gnarled, naked branches of the silent cottonwoods up and down the bosque, the fleeting claret brushstrokes in the sky slipping behind the western horizon. She was oblivious to the fishy odor she had always detested, as well as the blood she had managed somehow to get in her hair and smeared across her forehead.

She contemplated the black, swirling water at her feet, dropped the hatchet she had been carrying, and began to walk.

Immediately the cold seeped into her languid frame and took her breath away, the water enveloping her skin as the gauzy skirt of her ballgown ballooned and pooled on top of the water. Her body was engulfed beneath its surface. The current was strong, its frigid arms wrapping around her legs and cajoling her with its breathless swarm, beckoning her deeper, deeper still; an old, familiar friend baptizing her in its ancient dark waters.

Now she was neck deep and numb to her very heart, the only sound a deafening throb beating in her ears. She kept walking, moving with aching purpose, exhaling with each step. On tiptoe now, her feet failing to scrape the riverbed, unable to propel herself farther—until at last, succumbing, she lay back into its icy embrace. She was fully immersed now and belonged entirely to the watery grave.

Ave Maria echoed in her mind one last time, and she closed her eyes.

TWENTY-NINE

Present day

"Hola, Mamacita."

I looked up from a stack of invoices I had piled on the register countertop next to some piano songbooks I had been meaning all morning to put out on the shelves. A familiar face stood in the doorway of Old Town Music smiling at me. I smiled back absent-mindedly for a split second, until my brain registered that it was my son.

Oscar followed him inside with his camera phone recording the surprise event, with my daughter, Annalise, holding the door behind them.

"Jackson!! *WHAT HAPPENED??*" I implored, stupefied by his presence in the store.

He dropped the bag he was carrying and laughed heartily. "What do you mean, '*What happened*'? I got leave from the Navy —that's what happened!"

I burst into tears that soon became an "ugly cry." It had been a long time since I had seen my sweet Navy man, and his arrival had taken me completely off guard.

After I composed myself a bit and had released the suffocating hold I had around his neck, I kissed my daughter. "So it takes your brother visiting for me to get to see you these days?" I joked.

Ever the busy social activist on the University of New Mexico campus, where she lived, Annalise smiled. "Yes—well, a feminist's work is never done."

"I love your haircut," I said tousling the tip of her spiked hair.

"Careful," she warned, stepping backward to protect her newly cropped do. "Mom, really? I'm not seven."

"So, it looks like we got you," said Oscar proudly.

I nodded my head and wiped the wetness from my cheeks. "Yes, you sure did!"

At that moment my heart could not have been more at peace; my kids and the love of my life were standing before me, smiling back at me. I discovered Jackson was staying in town through Thanksgiving. Oscar promised to make his red chile sauce in place of gravy this year. We had some meal planning to do, and so very, very much to be grateful for.

THIRTY

1891

Within moments of seeing Pilar go under, Rico crashed through the brush and pounded down the shoreline of the river, diving beneath its dark surface. Straining against the swirling current biting his skin, he exerted all the force he could muster, his heart racing and head pounding in a rush of adrenaline. At once he felt the feathery wisp of her hair in the water, reaching fingerlike toward the heavens. Grabbing a handful of it, he propelled Pilar upward, where he could gather the fabric from her sleeve in his hand and, pulling her toward him, he wrapped his free arm around her bosom. Having been drawn down into the bleak depths in an attempt to lift her, he now felt the riverbed current angrily spiraling around his feet, causing him to be dragged lower. As he struggled to regain buoyancy, he loosened his grip on her. Panicked, he began gulping in the inky liquid and released his hold on her entirely. He started kicking furiously, taking in more river water. Rico was sure he felt a malevolent force wrapping around his ankles and dragging him down, against which he could not fight.

Determined he would not lose her, he mustered

every ounce of strength in his rugged, sinewy body to vigorously break free from the intense, monstrous presence beneath him in the water. Flailing his arms in search of any sign of her in the pitch blackness, he felt the fabric of her dress again and reached for her nearest limb. He was able to grab her wrist and pull her down enough to wrap one of his legs around her waist. Once she was securely within his strong grasp, he pushed off the bottom of the riverbed with his boot, and together they began to rise.

He gasped for breath as they buoyed to the surface. As he regained his footing, he was able to pull her to the safety of the sandy shore, her heavy dress and undergarments waterlogged and surely chilling her to the bone.

She wasn't breathing.

Straddling her, Rico lifted her torso from the ground and reached down her back, tearing open the enclosure of her dress, its small, satin-covered buttons breaking free from the hook-and-eye stitching. They scattered to the damp earth of the riverbank below. In one frenzied movement, he had the bodice removed and encircling her waist, exposing her corset. He placed his ear to her mouth, then her chest, and listened.

There was a faint beating of her heart.

Rico raised himself to his knees and balled his fists, and with restrained force pushed on her stomach.

344

Sputtering and choking, Pilar spewed forth a bellyful of river water. Rico sighed deeply as he lifted himself off of her. She rolled onto her side and vomited, then spent, fell onto her back again, blinking into the darkened sky.

Rico leaned across her and wiped the wet strands of hair off her face. She stared at him, expressionless, and said nothing.

"I'm going to take off this wet dress," he said to her, standing up.

She looked blankly at him without reply. He proceeded to pull the weighty fabric from her motionless frame and flung it over his shoulder. Then he leaned down and gathered her into his arms. He walked back into the black of the bosque, the dim moonlight the only thing to direct his path.

In the distance stood Oliver's horse, still tethered to the tree branch.

Rico carried Pilar to the waiting animal, speaking softly to it as they approached. Gingerly he hoisted Pilar on top and jumped up behind her. Freeing the reins from the tree with a jerk, he turned them in the direction of the Shannons' corrals.

Rico placed Pliar on top of a pile of loose hay in a corner of the barn. He watched as her teeth chattered, her eyelids heavy and drooping. He retrieved a few of the wool blankets on top of the tack shelf and began to cover her up but stopped.

"Pilar, we have to get these freezing things off you...can you sit up?"

Silently she stared off into the distance.

"I'm going to take them off you, *bueno*?" he said with urgency. "You're going to die of a chill if we don't!"

Again there was no response.

He placed one of the blankets over her and began to feel for the lacing of her undergarments. Glancing down to be sure he'd found it, he then averted his gaze and began to untie her corset. Once it was undone, he pulled it from her body and wrapped her securely in the blankets.

He stood over her and began shivering. He looked down at his traditional *vaquero* work clothes: the straw-colored leather vest, pants, and jacket, a small pouch somehow still secured lengthwise across his chest. Soaked to the bone and clinging to his skin, he turned around and stripped them off, then peeled off the long johns underneath. He reached for a lightweight cotton shirt and pants he had left there from the summer. Covering himself in a blanket he lay down gently beside her.

She turned her focus to him.

He stroked her hair and whispered softly, "It's going to be okay."

Silently tears began to streak down her face. She searched his kind eyes and furrowed her brow.

346

"You don't know what I've done…" she managed, her voice a sleepy croak.

"Yes, I do," Rico replied softly.

She raised herself to her elbows and frowned. "You *do*?"

He nodded. "I followed him when I saw him ride off to the river. I figured he was going there to meet—*her* again."

She blinked her drowsy eyelids at him. They felt as heavy as iron. "So…you, you saw what happened?"

He gave her a hesitant smile and nodded his head again.

"Then how can you be so kind to me?" she implored.

"*Ssshhh…*" he replied, "Lie down." She kept her skeptical gaze on him. "Because, Pilar Vega…I am in love with you."

She stared at him intensely.

"I have *always* loved you. And I know he broke your heart."

She closed her eyes now and sobbed. Rico pulled her close to him and held her tightly in his embrace. "I am here now, and I'm going to take care of you. You don't have to worry about a thing."

Before long, her breathing became shallow and drawn out. He closed his eyes, and soon they both were drifting in and out of sleep.

Within what seemed like mere moments, Rico

was startled awake by Pilar gasping for air. She bolted upright and he sat up beside her, shushing her gently and massaging her forearm.

She shuddered and looked toward him, the reality of her situation clear in her expression of horror. He began to replace the blanket that had fallen from her shoulders, but instead she pulled it off her and clung to him. Momentarily motionless, Rico continued to cover up her bare body. He could feel her heart beating through his shirt, and as if only in a dream, he wrapped his muscled arms around her, pressing her closer to him. Suddenly, as if fevered, she placed her hands on the sides of his head and pulled back his face, her fingers entwined in his thick hair. She searched his eyes ravenously, exhaling, and then kissed him deeply.

"Elena!" her mother implored. *"Please, Jita,* please just tell us what happened."

Onofre was now standing in front of the fireplace, his arms crossed at his chest, with Joaquin at the base of the staircase, Nicolas hugging the banister on the step behind him looking concerned.

Old Florencio had come in from the *cocina* and removed his soiled apron, placing it over the back of the sofa where Elena sat shaking and staring into space, Mariana kneeling at her side rubbing her arms in an attempt to warm her frozen limbs.

Her usually tawny skin was as alabaster.

"*Sweetheart,* you have to tell us what's going on," said Papacio tenderly. "You're scaring your mother."

Alarmed, he noticed the blood on his granddaughter's dress. He looked at his daughter searchingly.

Mariana's eyes were wide and starting to brim with tears. She turned and faced her husband, rising to her feet.

"Onofre, *do* something," she pleaded.

"*Elena!*" he bellowed stepping toward her and continuing in Spanish. "What the hell! *Tell us* what happened out there!"

Papacio stepped in front of him as Nicolas burst into tears on the stairway.

At this, Elena rose and looked at her little brother, her stoic façade giving way to tears.

"Take him upstairs," she whispered.

Everyone stood there motionless, straining to comprehend her words.

"*Take him upstairs*!" she screamed, causing Mariana to jump.

She turned quickly to Joaquin. "*Go,*" she nodded, and Joaquin took his brother by the arm and pulled him up the stairs.

By now Elena was sobbing. As she watched

them go, she realized Nicolas looked so small trailing behind his big brother. She called after him in a shaky voice, "I love you, *pequeño*."

Nicolas turned and wiped his face, his voice wavering, "I'll see you soon, *bueno*?"

His sister nodded and covered her mouth with her hand. She turned to face her parents and Papacio. All she could manage to do was to shake her head and weep.

"Not this, *again*..." bemoaned Onofre, his tone rising.

Mariana spun around. "*Stop!*" she screamed at him.

Turning to face her daughter, she took Elena by her shoulders. "Go ahead, we're listening."

Elena purposefully slowed her breathing. Somehow she felt that if she spoke the words out loud it would in some way make it all real, that the horrific, unspeakable scene that had unfolded before her at the river would forever be etched in their collective psyches from that moment forward. She knew that once she'd spoken the abhorrent truth, each of them would be forever changed. "He's gone," she managed before bursting into tears again.

"*Who's* gone, Jita?" said her grandfather.

Her father began pacing the wooden floor before the fireplace.

"Oliver...*by the river*," she breathed, then her

body crumpled and fell.

Before she hit the floor Onofre caught her and placed her on the sofa. By now Joaquin was standing at the base of the stairs again. His father turned to look at him, then removed the shotgun hanging from its perch over the fireplace mantle.

"*Vámonos!*"

Onofre grabbed Joaquin's overcoat from a hook by the front door and tossed it to him. Pulling on his hat and jacket, he opened the door, and they stepped out into the snowy night.

Eudora, the Shannons' housemaid, answered the pounding at the door. "May I help you?"

From the entrance of the parlor peered Daniella Shannon. She watched as Onofre Vega and his teenage son breezed past her covered in snow. She attempted a smile. "Well, what on earth-"

Onofre eyed the empty parlor and kept walking.

They haven't even the common courtesy to re-move their hats, she thought, disgusted.

"*Theo!*" he yelled.

Daniella hurried after them as they entered the great room in time to see Theophilus descending the staircase, a pair of spectacles and a book in hand.

He greeted them jovially. "Onofre!" His expression changed a bit realizing this wasn't a social call from his neighbor. "Everything all right?"

"Where's your boy?" asked Onofre.

Theo's eyes narrowed, volleying between the two of them, and he backed toward the stairway from which he'd just come. Turning, he hollered for Oliver. When there was no response, Daniella rushed past him and ascended the steps in haste.

His brow still furrowed, Theo asked, "What's the meaning of this?"

Joaquin cleared his throat. "We're not really sure. My sister returned home a while ago and she was...distraught. She is still extremely upset, so we were not able to get her to tell us what happened..."

Theo stared at him, unsettled. He shook his head. "What does this have to do with my boy?"

Daniella appeared at the top of the stairs. "Oliver isn't in his room."

On the other side of her Elza appeared. "What's the matter, Mother?"

Theo placed the book and his glasses on a small table at the base of the stairs. He made his way to the entryway, where he snatched his hat and jacket from a coat tree as the three men hurried out the front door.

From within the barn, Rico had heard the pounding at the front door of the Shannon household. Hurriedly he jumped to his feet, and with effort pulled on his stiff, frozen boots.

"They're going to be looking for me soon."

"Why?" whispered Pilar.

He sighed and nodded his head. "Because they're going to think I killed him."

He returned to Pilar and kissed her passionately. "Stay here as long as you want. They won't find you in here."

She stared after him as he leapt onto the horse, still saddled in the corral.

"*Te amaré, por siempre!*" he called back to her, then disappeared into darkness.

The Vega house was quiet.

Nicolas crept out of his bed and went to the window. He saw his sister with his mother and grandfather on either side of her making their way toward their neighbors' house through the thick snow.

He hated the feeling of being alone in the big, empty house, unsure of what was happening with his family. He opened the door, stepped out into the hallway, then walked into his brother's room. He peered out of the glass and out onto the still pasture below, covered in its frosty blanket. From this direction, Nicolas could see San Felipe parish rising from the sparkling earth to the northwest.

He remembered his brother's secret stash hiding in the flashing of the dormer, just out of reach.

Flinging the window open, he was greeted by a sobering rush of frigid air to his face that left him momentarily breathless. Sticking his head outside, he leaned up to search the roofline with his eyes.

Feeling confident he could find the hidden treasure, he reached down to pull off his socks, recalling what Joaquin had warned him about coming out onto the roof the last time; but he stopped and thought better of it.

It's too cold to go without socks, he thought, blowing warm air into his cold hands and rubbing them together.

Then, feeling brave in his pursuit of the rooftop temptation, Nicolas stepped out into the icy air.

The grandfather clock in the Shannons' parlor struck midnight. Earlier in the evening, unable to contain her hysterics, Elena had been given a glassful of cordial and laudanum, and hadn't moved from her position curled up on the chaise longue where Mariana kneeled, softly brushing her daughter's face with her fingertips. Daniella paced the distance between the front window and the parlor's leather sofa.

Florencio and the women could hear soft voices from the entryway. Eudora came into the parlor and spoke briefly with Mrs. Shannon, and she left the room swiftly as Joaquin entered, his hat in his hands.

Mariana rose and met him, imploring him with her gaze.

He took a deep breath. "We found him..."

From the entryway behind them, a shriek pierced the quiet. Mariana squeezed her eyes shut, burying her head in her son's chest as the desperate, wailing cries of Daniella Shannon filled the cavernous house.

In the early hours of dawn, Onofre and Joaquin made their back home, the women and Florencio having returned several hours earlier and by now were no doubt in bed asleep.

The men had stayed behind to make sure things were in order after giving their testimonies of the evening's events to the sheriff. They would have to wait to gather information from his eldest daughter later, Onofre had assured him; it appeared she was momentarily out of her mind, inconsolable, and not even able to stand upright.

After witnessing the same unforeseen gruesome discovery she had made in the dark bosque, Joaquin knew the disturbing image of his friend would forevermore haunt his thoughts. But he was a Vega man, and that meant he had no other choice but to stifle the raw emotions evoked from this night deep below the surface of his memory.

Along with the deputy, a posse had been dispatched to hunt down the Shannons' stable hand, Rico Ruiz, whom they surmised had left town after the murder and stealing one of the family's horses.

From the back of the property, Pilar watched as her father and brother went inside the house. An hour later, all of the lights inside had been extinguished. She waited a while longer, then crept across the backyard and up the steps of the back porch. Feeling confident she would go undetected, Pilar sneaked up the dark staircase to her room.

Her sister appeared to be passed out in her bed.

Stealthily, Pilar removed her clothing and stuffed the wadded fabric into the corner of her armoire, retrieving a fresh flannel gown and pulling it over her head. She brushed her hair before her dark mirror and slipped under the covers.

The relief she had felt being safely at home didn't last long.

The dead silence of the night was suddenly shattered when the house was filled with the terrifying screams of her older brother upon the discovery of his open bedroom window.

"Nicolas!"

The door of Joaquin's room slammed open and he raced down the stairs, his feet slipping and missing some of the steps as he flew. Without slowing, he dashed briskly through the kitchen and, flinging the back door open, leapt over the porch railing on the side of the house.

He fell to his knees a few feet from his little brother's motionless body and began rocking back and forth, his horrified cries slicing through the virgin light of day.

THIRTY-ONE

December, Present day

Garrett, Trish, and I were seated at a table at Church Street Café, where Oscar would be joining us soon for dinner. It had been a long week after Thanksgiving in preparation for the busiest shopping day of the year, Old Town's annual Holiday Stroll. We'd dropped off Jackson at the airport for his flight back to Groton, Connecticut, where he was stationed. It had been a short but wonderful visit, and in spite of our hectic schedules, my heart was full.

We were ravenous and ready to order, having already emptied two baskets of chips and salsa. It was 8:30pm, and the crowds from the Stroll had died down after the lighting of the plaza Christmas tree. The walk over was magical in a sea of dazzling paper lanterns lining the sidewalks and streets of Old Town. It was exhilarating yet dizzying; in spite of the festive excitement and acknowledgment that the holiday season was officially upon us, I sighed deeply with relief that the busy evening would be over soon.

I closed my eyes for a moment and listened to the light-hearted banter between Tricia and Garrett and the rest of the restaurant patrons intermingling with *"Feliz Navidad"* being strummed by a guitar player at the bar. I felt peaceful and centered. When I opened my eyes, I recognized a man speaking with the *maître d'*. It was Raúl,

Evelyn's husband. I hadn't seen him in a while, since the remodeling of Book It had been completed.

Huh, I wonder where his wife is...

While my brain was processing this, we made eye contact. The maître d' pointed toward our table, and he began walking in our direction.

I didn't have a chance to greet him when he took a deep breath and kneeled before me, placing his hand on my shoulder. His serious expression told me something was very wrong.

"Molly," he breathed, his eyes imploring. "I'm sorry to have to tell you this...Oscar's been taken to UNM Hospital, to the emergency room. He...he's had a heart attack."

It seemed the vast ocean of pedestrian traffic and bumper-to-bumper vehicles leaving the popular holiday event in Old Town would never cease, that a path to Oscar might not ever clear, and we would never make it to the hospital. Adrenaline coursed through my system as we had no other option but to sit and wait in traffic, surrounded by impatient drivers wanting to get home.

I wanted to crawl out of my skin, feeling trapped and claustrophobic. Sensing my unease, Trisha squeezed her grip on my hand.

I rolled down the window and inhaled the cold air outside.

"That's right, *breathe*," she whispered quietly. "Just breathe..."

When we finally made it to the hospital parking lot, I felt nauseated at the prospect of what we might discover. We hurried inside, where Raúl spoke to the attendant at the front desk, and soon we were directed to the elevator.

A member of the hospital janitorial staff slipped inside with us as the doors closed. Suddenly there was deafening silence all around us—no jovial Christmas carols, no bustling crowds, no *luminarias* or LED-lit trees. I could feel my breathing getting louder and more labored.

This can't be happening...we can't be here right now.

I didn't realize I was shaking my head.

God, please. Please *let him be okay!*

"Molly?" Garrett asked softly.

"This can't be happening," I said out loud. I could feel the tears begin to stream down my face.

Trisha grabbed my hand again and wrapped it in hers.

"We don't know what we're facing yet, Mol."

The elevator doors opened, and the janitor got off on the floor before ours.

"That's exactly what I'm afraid of," I whispered.

When the elevator stopped again, Raúl resumed the lead, and we were now headed purposefully down a hallway to the left of the elevator. He approached a nurse who was standing at the station and spoke quietly with her.

"Are all of you family?" she inquired.

"They are," Garrett nodded toward Raúl and me.

She looked at me. "I assume you're his wife?"

Tears stung my eyes as I shook my head. I was unable to speak for fear the dam would burst and I'd be rendered entirely useless.

This is not the time to lose it! Keep it together, Molly.

"She might as well be," responded Raúl firmly.

The nurse nodded. "Follow me."

Trisha nodded at me with a determined look on

her face and released my grip. In spite of her resolve, her shaky smile made me well up again. I took a deep breath.

Down another hallway, Raúl and I were greeted by Evelyn as she practically leapt into her husband's arms. She was shaking silently as she wept. His hand stroked her dark hair as she buried her face in his chest.

I covered my mouth with my hand.

Behind her in a waiting area, Evangelyn intently played on a laptop with her headphones on, seemingly unfazed. I took a deep breath and put on a brave face in case she were to look up and see me. We waited for Evelyn to speak.

She looked up after a moment and wiped her nose with a wadded tissue. Reaching over, she grabbed my shoulder and pulled me to her. In between sniffling and taking deep breaths, she finally managed, "I'm sorry. I thought I was doing better than this."

"Evelyn," I asked tentatively, "how is your father?"

She nodded and tried to smile. "He's okay, he's doing okay for right now."

I sighed heavily. She turned and looked directly at me. "But Molly, you should know he's not even remotely out of the woods. He suffered the worst kind of heart attack. Had the EMTs not already been on hand for the event, there's a chance he wouldn't have—"

She pressed the tissue to her nose and squeezed her eyes closed, as if it would stop the impending flood.

"—he might not have made it," she managed before succumbing to another wave of tears.

The nurse had disappeared, leaving the three of us huddled in the middle of the hallway amid beeping monitors and the smell of disinfectant cleaners.

"But he did," she whispered, attempting a quivering smile.

I nodded.

"They haven't let me see him yet. The doctors performed a cardiac angioplasty, put a stent in. They may have to do bypass surgery, but it seems for now they want to let his heart recover first."

I nodded but couldn't contain the tears this time.

His heart. Oscar's sweet, precious heart. I thought about what it had already endured in his lifetime. *I should've known the stress he must've been under...I should've seen it. Why hadn't I??*

Evelyn closed her eyes again and wrapped her arms around me and Raúl. "Father God, please, save my dad. We all love him so much, and we need him, Lord. Please don't take him home...not just yet."

After several hours in the waiting room, we were approached by the nurse.

"Mr. Cardenas is allowed visitors now, but only two at a time, and I'm sorry," she said gesturing apologetically at a sleeping Evangelyn, "but she won't be able to go near him for some time. Also, he must have complete quiet in the room so he can continue to rest."

We agreed Evelyn and Raúl should go in to see him first so that they could take their daughter home after what seemed a never-ending day. I waited with her until they came back and hugged me groggily. Raúl scooped up Evangelyn, and they were off with the assurance I would call them the moment anything changed.

I stood in the hallway of the ICU outside of Oscar's hospital room where he was resting, and steeled my composure before entering. Taking a deep breath, I stepped

363

inside.

There were the usual machines one would expect to see under such circumstances, the blue and green lights, the computerized blips on screens, the hum of monitors. Oscar looked completely helpless. His arms had large, blotchy bruises where they were attached to rubber tubes beneath medical tape, an intravenous drip bag perched above his head. Oscar's short cropped hair was matted to his scalp, his skin was ashen, and he appeared much older than his usual buoyant self.

My hand inadvertently rose to cover my mouth again and I stepped closer to him, dropping my purse beside a bedside chair. I desperately wanted to see those gentle, caramel eyes smiling up at me. Instead he lay motionless, entirely unaware of my presence in the room. I felt overwhelmingly alone and longed to wrap my arms around him and hold him close to me.

I ran my fingers lightly over his cheek as the tears began to fall, wiping my face before they had a chance to fall on his. Grabbing a tissue from his bedside table, I crumpled into the chair and sobbed.

I reached over and placed my hand helplessly on his shoulder as the tears continued to flow down my cheeks.

Oscar...don't go! Please don't leave me... Please, dear God, save this precious man. My beautiful Oscar, don't you dare leave me when I just found you!! Oh, God, PLEASE!

The morning sun was beginning to filter through the blinds as I blinked and sucked in air, suddenly aware of the presence of someone in the room. Evelyn smiled at me as a nurse peeked her head in the door. We both rose to our feet.

I looked at Oscar; there were the same blips and beeps of the monitors, but his skin wasn't as pale as before.

"The doctor should be making rounds here in a few minutes, around 7:30," she said. She smiled and disappeared.

I recalled speaking with a couple of other nurses throughout the night, but it was all a blur at the moment. I was surprised I'd dozed as long as I had; I rubbed my neck where I felt a crick starting.

"Think he looks a little better this morning, don't you?" Evelyn asked.

I nodded my head in agreement. "I do."

It was still a shock to see him with the discoloration on his arms and the tubes hooked up to him.

"Did you guys get any sleep?" I asked quietly.

She shook her head. "Not really."

I ran my hand over her forearm folded over her chest. "I can't imagine what you must've gone through yesterday. I'm so sorry, Evelyn."

She nodded her head and stared at him. "The old *abuelo* really scared me. I'm just thankful Evangelyn didn't see him collapse."

The door swung open, and a woman carrying a medical file entered. Her salt-and-pepper hair was braided down her back.

"Hi. Miriam Ogilvy," she spoke slowly with a southern accent, holding out a hand to Evelyn. "You're his daughter?"

"That's right," she replied.

We were both eager to hear what she had to say.

"Well, I'll tell you, your father is one tough *hombre*." She smiled and walked to Oscar, inspecting the monitors at his head. "We don't often see this kind of outcome. And by that, I mean you and I standing here in a hospital room with him. With the kind of cardiac arrest he suffered, patients just don't make it this far. They're lucky if they're able to see the inside of an ambulance.

"But he's slowly getting his coloring back, his vitals are stable at the moment, and he's out of the critical stage. I can tell he's a fighter. We're going to have to keep him here awhile, though, and he's got a *very* long recovery ahead of him."

THIRTY-TWO

1892

The first days of the new year found the families along the Rio Grande valley enshrouded in an intolerable wave of grief and torment.

In the following weeks, Elena decided that she must return to school. It was the only thing that she could imagine doing; she needed her old routine and the distraction that only books and studying afforded her. The semester was already underway, and no one except the college dean knew of the unspeakable tragedy that had taken place in the sleepy little village. Father Faustino had taken the liberty of informing him, and a return telegraph in recent days had assured Elena she was welcome to come back when she was ready. It had given her some relief knowing she had no occasion to speak about any of it to anyone again. She would lose herself in reading.

There had been few moments of clarity for Elena in the haze of everything that had happened. She had taken to spending most of her waking hours in the carriage house with her grandfather, even sleeping there at night. The hope of salvaging what remained of a relationship with her sister was less than implausible to Elena; Pilar kept her distance, and if she was to enter her room, Pilar didn't exert much energy displaying complete indifference to her presence. Her frigid composure had disappeared, and in its place loomed an inexplicable apathy toward her sister and family, the cause of which Elena wasn't able to fathom. In the wake of recent events, there appeared a remote detachment from them altogether; not that anyone else particularly noticed, each taking to their own routines and distractions, their grief unrelenting.

And there had been a moment in all of the hazy aftermath that Elena would lock away tightly in her memory, something she would question indefinitely as to whether it had even occurred between the two of them at all: as if in a moment between waking and slumber, she had ascended the staircase one of those evenings—or was it early *morning*??—when they were all so heavily shrouded in agony after the loss of two sons, two brothers in two neighboring households, when the misery seemed insurmountable...Elena was surprised at the presence of Pilar simply standing at the top of the stairs staring at her, expressionless, her fingers resting on the railing's finial. They merely looked at one another. In the darkness, Elena squinted her eyes at her sister. There was an unspoken acknowledgment in the fleeting moments that they faced each other that never occurred again after it; Elena whispered slowly to her sister, "*Where were you?*"

Pilar responded with a raised eyebrow and pursed lips without answering for what seemed an eternity in the groggy space between reality and time.

"Like I told Mama and Papa, it was snowing hard. I was in the church, praying."

Elena returned relentlessly to the nagging doubt she couldn't ever manage to rid her mind of: that she had never specifically told Pilar to *when* she was referring...

In the days that followed, she had no memory whatsoever of her mother finding her on the floor of her little brother's bedroom, having apparently removed a photo taken of her family the day of Pilar's *quinceañera* from the frame that held it, and tearing it in two. Half of it remained crumpled within her grip when her father carried her back to their room and tucked her into bed with yet another dose of sedative.

Staying here with her family in their state of paralyzing shock at what had transpired after Christmas was slowly going to drive her to insanity. Her father was to take her to the train station, where just a few days earlier Daniella Shannon and her daughter Elza had departed on the Atchison, Topeka, and Santa Fe Railway. Inside it was the body of her only son, encased in the finest mahogany coffin money could buy, headed for Chicago. They would then board the first train to the coast, where they would sail together back to their beloved Great Britain.

There had been no news on the capture of Rico Ruiz.

Mariana watched out the front window as her daughter rode into the distance with Onofre at her side.

Adjusting the shawl about her shoulders, she removed a small tapestry bag from the bottom of an oak buffet and made her way out of the kitchen. She exited from the back door and crossed the lawn to the carriage house, where her father was napping.

He stirred when she came in, watching as she gathered the stacks of letters bundled in ribbons of periwinkle she had kept inside a wicker clothes basket belonging to him in the corner. She gave him a weary smile as he held out his gnarled hand to her. With a gentle squeeze of it, she turned and went back out.

At the orphanage, Father Faustino greeted her with a warm embrace and led her to an empty classroom, where she dropped the bag she was carrying beside her on the floor, and placed some bizcochitos wrapped in a napkin on a nearby desk.

"I'm sorry for the chill in here," he said, gesturing to the adobe fireplace. "We will be getting a gas heater in here to replace that drafty old thing in a few weeks. It'll be much warmer when it's all bricked up."

He left her alone for a moment as she looked

around the room with a deep sigh.

She rose to greet him when, soon, the padre returned with a tall, lanky young man trailing him, long bangs practically concealing his eyes.

Ramón focused his gaze at her. *"May-ana!"* he squealed, rushing to her embrace.

Father Faustino leaned with his back against the closed door and folded his arms. He watched as Mariana silently clutched the young man in her grasp seemingly composed of long, thrashing limbs, tears trailing down her face.

"It *no* Tuesday," he shook his head, wriggling to free himself from her arms. She relented and reached out to push the hair away from his eyes.

"No, it's not Tuesday, is it?" she laughed, tears streaming down her face as he spied the cookies she had brought for him. He sat down and shoved one into his mouth, squinting back up at her with a devilish grin.

"He did miss you last week," said the padre.

Mariana nodded and wiped her face with her shawl. "And I miss him every single day of my life."

The tears came again and, weeping, she pulled a stack of letters from the bag.

Her trembling voice came quietly as she sat down and opened one of them. She began to read to him in the language of the Most Reverend Archbishop Lamy:

My dearest angel,

God blessed me with you the day He put us together. Despite the fact that we cannot be together every moment, I cherish your love over all others. You are my heart and soul. I cannot take a breath without knowing you are walking the face of this earth along with me, for you are the air that I breathe.

Forever yours, my sweet love.

~M

The padre rushed to her side as Mariana crumpled into a heap in his arms. Her racking sobs went unnoticed by the dark-haired young man in the corner, who was now seated on the floor, having discovered a slate board and some chalk.

After a while, she composed herself and drew a deep breath.

"Maybe this isn't the right time," offered the padre.

Mariana shook her head. "This the very best time."

"I understand...I'm just thinking maybe when things aren't so, *raw*, perhaps."

"Thank you, Julien. I can never thank you enough for what you've done for my family over the last twenty years," she said, her gaze resting on Ramón intently scribbling on the slate. Every now and again he would use his hand to erase his markings, then begin a new creation. "He reminds me so much of Nicolas."

"Yes," the padre smiled kindheartedly. "He does favor his brothers."

She nodded and wiped her face again. "The only thing that brings me any peace at all is the thought of being here, with him. This pain has been unrelenting... at least twenty years ago I could come here and visit *him*."

She raised her head resignedly. "But I will *never* be able to visit my baby again. He is nowhere! He is in the ground...."

Father Faustino softly offered condolence. "Nicolas will always be with us, Mariana, your *angelitos* watching over you. Forever."

She blinked her eyes and smiled toward her oldest son. "The nuns have been so very good to him, treating him just like the—no, *better* than the other orphans. They have loved him so, in spite of his limitations."

Father Julien nodded. "I remember when he learned how to hold a piece of chalk."

"And look at him now." She smiled through the tears. "This was the only way, the *only* way..."

He squeezed her hand as her words trailed off.

"Onofre has never forgiven me, you know. But he loves me, in his way. He just never spoke of Ramón or our arrangement again—"

"You don't have to explain to me—"

"—after he was born and came to live here with the Sisters," she continued, fervently.

"What other choice did you have?" he implored her. "You were sixteen years old! Practically Pilar's age. What better arrangement than to have you and your father, *and* your unborn child here? Onofre could provide for *all* of you that way."

"My *illegitimate* child," Mariana smiled, shaking her head.

"He is no more illegitimate than any one of the rest of us. He is a beloved child of God, Mariana. Just like Nicolas, and you, and Onofre—even in his blustery way. None of this is your fault. What happened before you came here was not of your choosing. Yet everything has worked out over the years, and this…" he paused and nodded reassuringly, "this will, as well."

"Yes, life went on then," she smiled, recalling the year after she and Onofre had married. It was the year that Elena had been born, nineteen years prior. "I suppose in time, it will again…"

THIRTY-THREE

Present day

The next several days at the hospital were absolutely exhausting. I'd gone home just once to shower and change, and feed Wolf.

Oscar had made small strides toward recovery; continuously fatigued, he was able to open his eyes for short periods of time and look around the room. He had seen me and his family, but did he recognize us? I couldn't be sure. Dr. Ogilvy explained that this was all very normal, that his body was completely worn out from the massive coronary he'd suffered. He was going to be weak, and it would take time before he could actually hold a conversation with anyone.

The next day, Trisha and Garrett convinced me to go home and get some sleep after their usual afternoon visit to the hospital. I didn't argue with them this time, knowing Evelyn or Raúl would alert me of any changes.

At home I peeled off the jacket I was wearing and collapsed in bed with my clothes on. Sometime during the night I became aware I was still wearing my boots and managed to kick them off, soon falling back into fitful sleep.

At 6:46am my cell phone rang. It was Evelyn.
She was crying.
"Molly, you need to get dressed and come to the hospital."

Somehow I managed to put a brush through my hair, grab my jacket, and be at the hospital just in time for the doors to open for visitors at 7am.

I raced to the elevator, then down the hallway to Oscar's room. I stopped in my tracks seeing Raúl, his back to me with his head in his hands, just around the corner.

My hand found the hallway railing before I stumbled. Finding my footing, I took a deep breath and went inside.

Evelyn was bent over the head of the bed, her hands enveloping her father's. She turned upon my entrance. Her face was lit up with a teary-eyed grin. Not releasing his grip, she moved aside; Oscar was sitting semi-upright with pillows supporting his back and neck. A smile spread across his face when he saw me in the entrance of his room, my palm against my forehead.

I rushed to his other side and hovered carefully before his face, not sure if I could kiss him.

I reached out and gently touched his face, frowning at the scratchy stubble he had accrued over the last week.

"What?" he croaked, smiling at me with those lovely eyes. "Do I need a breath mint?"

Evelyn burst out laughing.

"Well, you're definitely due for a shave," I managed, tears springing to my eyes.

We both giggled, and I lightly kissed his lips.

Evelyn squeezed his hands. "I'll be right outside, *Abuelo*."

I shook my head at him, and he stared at me expectantly. "You can't do that to me again," I whispered.

He chuckled and tried to clear his throat. "I don't ever *want* to do that again."

"So *don't* then. Okay?" The tears came with a flood of relief to see him in this light. It was a new day, a new start. I could not have felt more grateful to God.

Oscar reached up, still tethered to his tubes, and wiped the tears from my face. "Do you have any idea how much I love you?"

The sound of his voice, the resplendent sound of those words made the tears come faster. I reached over and grabbed some tissue, suddenly aware of how I must look—no trace of makeup with bags under my eyes—and tried to compose myself.

"I thought you were going to leave me," I managed.

"No way," Oscar smiled. "Are you kidding me? I just found you."

I smiled and shook my head, taking his hands in mine and kissing them. "Oscar Cardenas, don't you go, do you hear me? We've still got mysteries left to solve."

He lifted my head and kissed my lips. "Not the least of which is why would you want to stay with a decrepit old man like me? Especially now…"

Evelyn poked her head in the room. "I'm taking Raúl home, Dad. He's been either here or home with Evangelyn this whole time, practically without rest. I'll be back later."

Oscar nodded his head.

I smiled as she turned to go, and I said, "I'll be here."

*****

About the Author, Beverly Ann Allen

Photo credit: Gwyn Del Toro

Beverly graduated from Eastern New Mexico University with a B.A. in English and a minor in History. After teaching for seventeen years, she decided to pursue her love of writing and currently is a freelance contributor to several magazines including Prime Time and New Mexico Woman. She lives in Albuquerque with her black lab, Ophelia, and two orange cats, S-Ray and Bianca, and is currently in the process of writing her second novel, a sequel to Rio Grande Rhapsody.

Made in the USA
Monee, IL
25 July 2021

73959224R10225